W9-BXQ-917

THE GIFT OF CHRISTMAS PAST

This Large Print Book carries the
Seal of Approval of N.A.V.H.

THE GIFT OF CHRISTMAS PAST

A SOUTHERN ROMANCE

CINDY WOODSMALL
AND ERIN WOODSMALL

THORNDIKE PRESS

A part of Gale, a Cengage Company

Farmington Hills, Mich • San Francisco • New York • Waterville, Maine
Meriden, Conn • Mason, Ohio • Chicago

LIBRARY OF CONGRESS CIP DATA ON FILE.
CATALOGUING IN PUBLICATION FOR THIS BOOK
IS AVAILABLE FROM THE LIBRARY OF CONGRESS.

ISBN-13: 978-1-4328-4516-2 (hardcover)
ISBN-10: 1-4328-4516-0 (hardcover)

Published in 2017 by arrangement with Woodsmall Press

Printed in Mexico
1 2 3 4 5 6 7 21 20 19 18 17

From Erin ∼

To Silas, my "littlest"
*I rocked, held, and carried you throughout
the writing of this book,
from the first brainstorming sessions,
when you were tiny and
kicking in my womb,
to the final edits, when you were a
squirmy six-month-old in my arms.
What a special time to spend together.*

From Cindy ∼

To sweet, precious Kaden
Right from your first day's start,
You stole your Mimi's entire heart.
Days of kisses, joy, and laughter,
Toddling carefree, with
Mimi chasing after.
Eyes full of joy, your happiness light,
Your love of life was so very right.
You babbled and cooed
as little ones do,
But at the right time, your words
couldn't come through.
You wanted to speak,
and oh how you tried.
We wanted to hear you
and many times cried.
But love does not fail to give its best.
Mommy and Daddy searched for
answers without rest.

Therapies frustrated you
after they had begun,
But now the hard work you do
is often fun.
We couldn't leave our buddy with a
mouth that couldn't speak.
The battle continues, but you win
victories every week.
One day you'll be able to voice
what you think.
Your mouth and your brain
will work in sync.
You'll shout and sing and
chatter till you're done,
And you, precious Kaden,
will have won.

1

January 2003

Hadley's mind reeled with disbelief as her foster mom shoved her clothes into an old suitcase. "But . . . but I'm innocent."

"Maybe." Dianna gave a half-hearted nod. "I hope so. It'd be an awful thing to squander the opportunities we've offered you."

"I . . . I am. The investigation will prove it. I promise. You've got to believe me. Please."

"Like I said, maybe you are innocent . . . of this incident. You had seemed to be making great strides since you went to anger-management classes. I'll give you that, Hads."

"Then don't send me back. Please. My friends are here. Monroe is —"

"Decision's made. You made it when you broke curfew for the third time."

"But I was only a little late and for good

reasons. You said so —"

"I'm aware." Dianna didn't pause her movements as she packed Hadley's toothbrush.

Hadley bit back tears, hating any sign of being vulnerable. "Then why?"

"They've found two witnesses who place you in the Reeds' yard."

"What?" Hadley's knee-jerk gasp was the totally wrong response. *Stay cool. Remain calm.*

"Yeah, apparently you *were* there." Dianna released a slow sigh. "Imagine that."

Regret twisted through Hadley. She never should've set foot on the Reeds' property. "Okay, I was at their place, but I never —"

"Interesting." Dianna stood up straight, the top of her head now even with Hadley's nose. She yanked a beautiful red sweater off a hanger, a Christmas gift from Scott and her to Hadley a mere three weeks ago. "You've denied being anywhere near there until right now. They said they saw you start a fire using leaves, sticks, and what appeared to be some kind of accelerant." She shoved the sweater into the suitcase with the other clothes as if it and Hadley no longer mattered.

Should she explain her actions? The moment the question came to her she knew the answer. No matter the subject or the situation, adults couldn't be trusted. Anything Hadley said would be passed along to the authorities, distorted, and used against her.

Dianna jammed two pairs of wool socks into the suitcase. "Anyway, Scott and I think it's in everyone's best interest if you don't live here anymore."

"Please" — Hadley clasped her hands together — "don't do this. I'm controlling my temper better. Ask Monroe's parents. My few nights with them over Christmas break were good. They got to know me, and their word matters in this town and state."

None of this mess was on the horizon then. Hadley and Monroe had enjoyed the most amazing Christmas, the very best in her entire seventeen years. They'd fallen even more in love if that was possible. She'd joined the Birch family — Monroe, his parents, and his college-age big sister, Nicole — for the Christmas Eve feast and unwrapping gifts covered in gorgeous paper and adorned with bright ribbons. It was an evening straight out of a fairy tale with the large family gathering she had always longed to have. His parents had finally seemed to accept her and her wayward past, and she'd stayed a few nights in their guest room.

11

And now?

Dianna plucked two keepsakes off the dresser — a pair of hand-blown-glass hummingbirds and a glass rainbow with Monroe's and her initials inside a little heart. Monroe had it made for her, and he had given it to her for Christmas as a symbol of the covenant between the Creator and her and a symbol of the love between Monroe and her and his promise to always take care of her.

The hummingbirds were from her birth mother, given to her more than twelve years ago. Although she'd only been five years old, she remembered clearly the day. A social worker was at their house to take Hadley into foster care. Mom had packed Hadley's suitcase and had knelt in front of her. She placed the hummingbird figurines in her hand, saying one was her and one was Hadley. Hadley was to hold on to them as a reminder that she and her mom would be together again one day, that it was a temporary separation. Mom promised she would get off the bad stuff and the courts would grant her custody again.

But that never happened. Despite years of her mom sporadically coming for supervised visits and occasionally getting close to being clean, she never managed to do so long enough to satisfy the courts. She also never signed over her parental rights, which would have allowed Hadley to be adopted.

Dianna stuffed the keepsakes in the suitcase.

Hadley jolted. "Hey, those will break."

Dianna nodded, took them out, and gently placed them on top of the sweater. "We've tried to be fair, Hadley, but you're just too much for us, and we have other foster kids to think about."

"I was there, but I didn't burn down their house!" Hadley pounded a fist into her palm. "I . . . I'm not an arsonist. I was trying to do something nice for them. I . . ." Hadley grabbed fistfuls of her thick curls. "I swear it! You've got to —"

"You'll calm down." Dianna pointed at her. "Now."

Hadley released her hair, grew still, and nodded. Dianna had earned Hadley's respect. Besides, as bad as going to the state-licensed group home would be, juvenile lockup would be much worse. Tears stung. She had a fierce temper and often impulsively lashed out against the unfairness of life. Dianna and Scott had dealt with her recklessness for years, helping her learn to cope with her emotions in a less destructive way. They'd even stayed by her when she had to go before a judge on a vandalism charge. She'd been reprimanded and sent to court-ordered anger-management therapy. But because of her past behavior, they were sure she was guilty, apparently convinced before seeing any proof.

Hadley's heart seemed to weigh a hundred pounds. "But if I go there, it'll mean a new school for the rest of my senior year. I'll be separated from Monroe, and . . ."

Dianna barely glanced at her, and Dianna's lack of reaction made it clear that Hadley's boyfriend and what school she attended were not Dianna's concern. But these things were everything to Hadley. She didn't want to leave.

Dianna paused in jamming personal items into the side pockets of the suitcase just long enough to point at a framed picture on the wall. "Is that yours or Elliott's?"

In the photo white sunlight filtered through the wooden beams of a railroad trestle that stood taller than the leafy green trees surrounding it. A preschool-age Elliott stood ankle deep in a clear creek below the trestle, arm in arm with another girl, who looked to be the same age. They both had on shorts and T-shirts, and they had identical dark, straight, shoulder-length hair. Elliott had no idea who the other girl was

14

or where the picture was taken.

"Elliott's." Hadley wanted to shake Dianna. Did their foster mom care about them at all? It was Elliott's most prized possession, the only thing she had left of the family she'd once belonged to. "It's her in the photo, for Pete's sake."

Dianna looked closer, taking a moment to focus on the picture. "So it is. Speaking of her, I've told her to stay out of this room until it's time for you to go."

"Why?" Adults and institutions were so frustrating. They had rules that made little sense, and they made up restrictions at will. This was Elliott's room too, and she certainly hadn't done anything to be barred from it.

Dianna didn't answer. She laid Hadley's coat and hat on the bed. Without warning she closed the suitcase and bore down on the top while zipping it.

Stop her! But Hadley couldn't move.

Glass crunched, but Dianna didn't flinch. It was as if she'd heard nothing.

Hadley stared at the suitcase, feeling as though every dream she'd tried to protect, every hope she'd held on to was also broken.

Dianna snapped her fingers. "Hadley?"

Hadley lifted her gaze from the suitcase.

"Just take a breath." Dianna sighed, but

15

sympathy crept into her eyes for a moment. "I guess if you want to say goodbye, you could come downstairs where everyone else is having afternoon snacks."

Hadley shook her head. "I can't." It would be awkward and filled with silent judgment as her foster siblings tried to assure themselves they were too well behaved for Dianna and Scott to make them leave.

"Okay then." Dianna opened the bedroom door. "Your decision, but since I won't have my eyes on you, let me be clear. No phone calls. No leaving this room until the social worker arrives."

No leaving the room? Alarms rang in Hadley's head. Why? What was going on?

Dianna closed the door behind her and used a key to lock it. Hadley moved to the window, looking for a way to climb out. If she could get to Monroe, they could run off together. Forget graduating high school in a few months. They needed to get out of town. But the view divulged the same information it always did. There was no way to get from this second-story window to the ground below without breaking a leg or maybe her back. The only way out was through the door Dianna had just locked.

Hadley opened the suitcase. The brightly colored glass keepsakes were shattered

16

beyond repair, the emerald green and magenta of the hummingbirds mixed with the colors of the rainbow. She picked up every piece she could, feeling as fragmented as the broken glass.

Thoughts of being on the Reed property assailed her. The elderly couple's yard was a good cut through when walking to a friend's house or to town, but they looked at her as if she were a rabid dog. Scott and Dianna's other foster kids never went through their yard, but Hadley saw no reason for the Reeds to be such sticklers, and they'd had more than one run-in about it. The memory of breaking into their shed to get a rake and their five-gallon container of gas mocked her. Their attitude was infuriating her, and —

The faint sound of metal scraping caught Hadley's attention. As she turned, the lock clicked and the door eased open. Elliott, dressed in her coat and knit cap, with a backpack slung over one shoulder, glanced behind her before slipping into the room in complete silence. Hadley started to say something, but Elliott put her finger over her lips as she shut the door. She set the key on the dresser. "You okay?" Elliott whispered.

Hadley gently closed her hands around

the pieces of glass. "No."

Elliott was a year younger and a foster teen, like Hadley, but she avoided doing anything that would get her into trouble. Even so, that hadn't kept Elliott from being moved to one foster home after another. But she was whip smart, had a few good friends, and, most of all, wasn't an agitator. She was, however, fiercely loyal.

Elliott nodded at Hadley's cupped hands. Hadley slowly lifted her top hand.

"Oh, Hads, no." Elliott took off her backpack and unzipped it. She removed a stack of index cards with carefully penned notes from a sandwich-size, zippered plastic bag and held it open toward Hadley.

Hadley carefully eased the shards into the bag, scraping the big and tiny pieces from her hands. "I can't stay here, Elliott. Something's up. They're sending me to a group home and locked the door so I couldn't leave, which means I need to leave. Now."

Elliott's eyes were a strange mixture of golden brown and green. Her hair was dark brown, and her skin seemed perpetually tan. Hadley often wondered about her ethnicity, but Elliott didn't know. Her memories of her early childhood were sparse. She was clear on what life was like between kindergarten and when she was abandoned at eight, but none of those memories helped her know who the girl in the picture was or what state they'd been in when the photo was taken. The court couldn't find any of Elliott's relatives, so she eventually became a candidate for adoption, but no one had adopted her.

Hadley pressed the air from the bag and sealed it. If fragments were all she had left, that's what she'd hold on to. "Will you help me leave?" It wasn't fair to ask. If Elliott got caught helping her, she might be removed from this home too. But Hadley was desperate.

"Yeah," Elliott whispered. Hadley could hear her anxiety, but the girl held up a finger. "Wait." She eased onto the landing, disappeared, and returned with the handset to a cordless phone. After closing the door Elliott passed her the phone. With the sandwich bag of glass fragments still in her hand, Hadley pushed buttons, calling Monroe's cell. No one in this home owned a cell, but a lot of the rich kids did.

"Hey, Hads. How's it going?" His deep, reassuring voice worked its way to her toes.

Hadley moved to the far corner of the room, intending to speak softly. "Bad. I know you're busy, but . . ."

"Anything for you."

"I need to see you. *Now.*"

"Okay. I just picked up some of my mom's favorite honey at a farm in Marion."

"Where's that?"

"Oh, about forty miles northeast of Asheville, all of it narrow and winding roads. It'll take me" — he paused, apparently doing the math in his head — "about an hour and a half to get to your house."

"Don't come here. I'll explain later. I'd rather meet you at our spot." Their special place was on Blue Ridge Parkway overlooking the French Broad River, which should be about halfway between them.

"No deal if you plan on hitchhiking, Hads."

"I promise I won't hitchhike."

Elliott pulled the keys to her motor scooter from her jeans pocket. Apparently she could hear Monroe too.

"Elliott will drive me."

"Be there as soon as I can. Dress warm. It's really cold to ride a scooter."

That was Monroe, always so caring. "I will. Bye."

Elliott pointed at the bed. "I don't know what your plans are, but the suitcase has to stay. The motor scooter will barely hold the two of us."

"Sure." Hadley grabbed her coat off the

bed. She released the bag holding the shards of glass into the silky pocket, still determined to hold on to dreams that seemed to want nothing to do with her. Her mom was allowed to have two supervised visits per month with Hadley, but she hadn't come in more than two years. As far as Hadley knew, she'd never met her dad. Her parents didn't care about her, and she was weary of caring about them. But Monroe and the rainbow he'd given her were worth holding on to.

She quietly followed Elliott, who ran interference by speaking to people while Hadley lagged behind until the coast was clear. As they snaked through the house, working their way to the laundry room, Tara spotted them from the kitchen, a bowl of popcorn in hand. Elliott covered her lips with her finger, hoping Tara would be quiet. Tara nodded, looking as if she wanted to bolt toward them. She was a tenderhearted kid who wouldn't betray anyone, especially not Elliott or Hadley. From somewhere unseen Dianna spoke, and as her voice grew louder by the second, Hadley knew Dianna was heading their way. Tara dropped the bowl and yelled as though it'd scared her. It clanked hard and broke, scattering popcorn and glass and creating the perfect diversion. While Dianna rushed to clean up the glass and warned about bare feet and shards, Elliott and Hadley entered the laundry room and climbed out the window. Elliott put the motor scooter in neutral, and they walked it all the way down the long, tree-flanked driveway before Elliott started it.

"Get on." Elliott held out a helmet.

"If Dianna finds out you've helped me, she and Scott will take your motor scooter for sure." That was the least of what would happen, even though Elliott had earned the money to buy it and had been a star student for years.

"You realize this now?" Elliott rolled her eyes. "Maybe the real issue is you're worried about my driving."

Still Hadley paused.

"Are you getting on, or am I meeting Monroe without you?"

Hadley grinned. "I'm getting on." She straddled the scooter. "I have no qualms about your driving. Trus. . ." Hadley stopped short of saying "trust me." Saying those words to Elliott had been a mistake she had made only once — when she first moved into this foster home more than three years ago. When Elliott was eight, her dad had said, "You'll be fine. Trust me. Just trust me." He was inside his running car at the time, and then he drove away, leaving Elliott standing in the parking lot of an abandoned gas station.

Barren trees covered the mountains and valleys as they took the back roads to the parkway. Sunlight made the dormant trees look silvery, except for occasional spotty shadows from small clouds passing between the sun and the vast mountains. The cold air stung, but regardless of the season, the view brought tranquility . . . and lots of tourists. Elliott drove with steady caution over the miles of switchback asphalt. The river came into sight, and they continued onward until they came to the lookout spot she and Monroe had claimed as theirs. A mountain of gray rock was on their right, showing where workers once carved out part of the mountain to make way for this road.

Elliott turned left and pulled into the parking area, which was really no more than a wide asphalt shoulder just long enough for cars to park safely. She stopped at the curb.

Monroe was leaning against the side of his black BMW, a car so expensive he was embarrassed to drive it, but his parents insisted because of its safety. His fleece-lined Italian leather coat and boots probably kept him toasty warm.

The moment he spotted her, he stood up straight. He tucked his phone into his jacket pocket while walking toward her. She got off the scooter and removed her helmet.

He embraced her, holding her tight. "It'll be okay, Hads. Whatever is going on, we'll fix it."

It was easy for him to believe that the world was fair and that anything could be fixed with a little time and money. He'd been brought into the world through an upper class, educated couple — his dad was a doctor and his mom was a lawyer — who in their first ten years of marriage had built their careers and talked of one day having two children. He and his older sister were the prince and princess of their world, while Hadley was nothing in hers. He could attend a prep school, as his sister had, but he chose to go to public school. When he was thirteen, he had seen a PBS documentary on affluenza — the materialism and consumerism from extreme wealth that makes people unsatisfied with life and prone to dysfunctional relationships — and he wanted no part of it.

They had similar interests in music and nature. Hiking was a favorite of theirs, but the main thing they had in common was volunteering at a speech and occupational therapy clinic. She'd had a speech impediment as a child, and no one had made her feel more loved or powerful than her speech therapist. So when the high school offered credits to work at a local therapy center, she jumped at it and talked Monroe into it. She had dreamed of the two of them working together someday in a medical facility. But none of that mattered now.

"Let's leave," Hadley whispered. "We can marry and start with nothing to build our lives. You said that was the way to live. No rich parents securing your way."

"Sh. We can handle this, Hadley." He didn't let go.

She held tight, imagining never letting him go. He put some space between them, removed his hat, and put it on her head. He gazed into her eyes. "What's going on?"

She pulled the bag with the fragmented keepsakes out of her pocket and showed him. "Everything has gone wrong. I don't have a home with Dianna and Scott anymore."

He took the bag, studying it, looking sympathetic, and then put it in his own coat pocket. "I'll find a way to fix it for you."

Is that even possible? She couldn't imagine how, but Monroe was always true to his word.

He knew everything — from her run-ins with the Reeds, to being reprimanded by a judge, to the ongoing investigation related to the fire — so she quickly filled him in on the latest. "Please. Let's leave this town, just the two of us."

He took her by the hand, and they walked to the bluff that overlooked the French Broad River. Elliott remained on her scooter, watching and ready to do whatever Hadley and Monroe decided. Unlike Hadley, Elliott didn't trust guys — not one in the entire gender — but she would accept whatever Hadley said needed to be done.

Once in their spot overlooking the valley and river, Monroe cradled her shoulders under his arm. They watched the wide, rippling river flow onward toward places Hadley couldn't imagine. "Breathe, Hads. Let our view do its thing inside you."

She followed his instructions, taking in a deep breath and slowly releasing it. This wasn't their first time to meet here and use the serene beauty to calm their stress. The Blue Ridge Parkway was filled with endless mountains, which now were covered with thousands of leafless trees. For two years Monroe and she had come here throughout every season, but fall was the most beautiful, followed by the rare snowy winter days.

They often packed a simple picnic lunch, chose a table near the river or an overlook, and talked for hours.

He squeezed her shoulder. "If we need to leave, we will. I promise."

"I've been thinking on the ride here, trying to piece together what's going on, and it's pretty clear I'm going to be charged with arson. It's the only thing that explains what's happening. Dianna and Scott are kicking me out. From how she was behaving, I wouldn't be surprised if I was arrested within the week."

He squared her to himself, looking into her eyes. "That's not going to happen."

"You're sure?" She was confident that he knew much more than she did about this and other matters, but fear gnawed at her.

"Yep." He gazed into her eyes, love and admiration clearly reflecting back at her. "Because you're right, and I'm taking you away from all this."

"What?" Her pulse quickened. Was he saying what she thought he was?

He cupped her face in his hands. "Marry me, Hads. This wasn't the way I planned to propose, but it doesn't matter anymore. We'll drive east and not stop until we get to the coast. Then we can say our vows on the beach under the stars in front of God, and that's all that really counts. When we turn eighteen, we'll make it official in the eyes of the law."

"I . . ." Countless thoughts and emotions rushed through her, but her breath caught. It wouldn't be the mountaintop wedding she had daydreamed about, but she would be with Monroe forever, no more walls or authorities separating them. "Yes," she whispered. "Let's go tonight."

He kissed her, and the cold world melted.

He broke the kiss by smiling and pulling back enough to look into her eyes. "I think I recall enough about Virginia Beach from my visit there last summer that I can find us a cheap hotel and jobs. I have enough in my savings account to pay for food, gas, and lodging until we start getting a paycheck."

Were they really going to do this? Her mind was reeling with the details of their plan. "A few weeks ago Kyle mentioned that some states allow teens to marry as young as eighteen without parental consent. I think Virginia is one of them."

Monroe angled his head, frowning. "Can't say I'm surprised that your former boyfriend found a way to talk about marriage to you, but in this one case I hope he's right."

She chuckled. She should have known that the mention of Kyle's name would slightly annoy Monroe. Kyle was a year older than they were, had graduated from high school, and was living on his own. She and Kyle had dated for about a year when she was a freshman, before she knew Monroe. Although the romantic side of their relationship had ended, Hadley counted Kyle as one of her few friends, and Monroe didn't complain about it. But sometimes he seemed a little jealous that she'd had a boyfriend before him. For Monroe, Hadley was his one and only.

Hadley snuggled against Monroe and looked out at their view. How long would it be before they would come back here, if ever? "Wow, we're really doing this? What if they put a warrant out for me that reaches to Virginia?"

"I don't know how all that works, but we'll figure it out. I don't care if we have to leave the country. We'll be a family."

The word *family* struck hard. Monroe's family had been good to her, and she was running away with their son. It gnawed at her heart, and she knew they couldn't just leave without telling them. She'd never had a real family like that, but to save her from her fate, he was going to give up his.

"Monroe, you have to go home and say goodbye to your parents."

His eyes narrowed. "I'm not sure that's a good idea, Hads." He scratched his head. "They'd probably give me trouble about it."

"But they deserve to hear it from you, face-to-face. Not just get a phone call. They've been too good to you for us to disappear until we turn eighteen."

"You're right. Besides, now that I think about it, going home is the only way to get my stash of cash, and it'll make the next few months easier if I grab my clothes."

"And your PlayStation 2."

He laughed. "True."

She glanced at Elliott. "I'll go back with Elliott, not all the way to the house, but to the patch of woods near the park. Maybe Elliott or Tara could sneak out my suitcase and bring it to me. Meet you at the park?"

"Yeah. But it could take me a while. Worst-case scenario I'll be there after midnight."

"You think you might need to sneak out?"

"Yeah. They'll be upset and will say *no way* and eventually will go to bed. It's what parents do. They'll assure me I'm too young to know what I'm doing. But whether we marry now or five years from now, there is no one for me but you. And I say *now*. My parents will have to accept that — one way or another." He kissed her on the lips and smiled. "I'll be there by one o'clock for sure."

2

The doorbell rang, and Monroe tripped over the cat as he ran to open it. A policeman stared back at him.

"Is Hadley okay?" That question might not make sense to the officer, but it's all Monroe could say, all he could think about. Five days ago he'd told Hadley he would get things in order, tell his parents bye, and then meet her by one o'clock in the morning. He'd assumed too much.

The officer pursed his lips. "I need to speak to Mrs. Lisa Birch, please."

"About Hadley?"

"Is Mrs. Birch here?"

"Yeah."

"Monroe?" His mom entered the foyer, looking every bit the professional in her black suit and heels.

He stepped back, and she walked over to the officer. "Darren, how are you today?"

"Good. Thank you." He shifted, resting

one hand on the top of his belted nightstick. "I'm here to discuss that matter we talked about."

"Oh, yes." She grabbed her coat out of the closet. "Let's talk outside." She put on the winter jacket and carefully pulled the ends of her immaculately straightened blond hair from the coat.

As soon as the door closed, Monroe went to the home phone. Maybe Elliott had learned where Hadley was. He dialed and waited. The line was busy, which wasn't surprising since it was a Saturday, and the home had several teens. He hung up, determined to give it a few minutes and try again.

Five days ago when he'd told his parents that he and Hadley were leaving the state, they had turned into people he didn't recognize. They took his car keys, cash, and cell phone. When he tried to at least get his keys back, they threatened to call the police, preferring to see him in jail for a night while he cooled off than to let him leave town with Hadley. He'd had no choice but to settle in and rethink his plan.

He scrolled through the list of caller IDs, looking for any unknown names or numbers in case Hadley had called from wherever she was now and his parents hadn't told him. But he saw the same thing he'd seen all week, nothing new. If she'd called his house, his parents had erased the number. His cell phone was locked away in a safe in his parents' bedroom, a safe he didn't have the code for.

He lifted the phone out of the cradle and dialed Dianna's number again, hoping to get through to someone who would get Elliott or Tara to the phone. But the line was still busy. Maybe he'd learn more by eavesdropping on the conversation outside. He put on his coat and quietly went out the front door. He hung back, listening, but he couldn't make out one word.

The night he was supposed to meet Hadley, he didn't even get a chance to slip out on foot. His dad slept on the couch in Monroe's bedroom, and he drove Monroe to school the next day rather than giving him back his keys. Hadley wasn't at school. Elliott said Hadley had been caught around four that morning, and Elliott had no idea where social services had taken her. Monroe's house was stuck on the side of a mountain, looking down on Asheville, so he didn't have any close neighbors. But after school he walked to a friend's home about a mile away, and his buddy drove him to Hadley's former foster home. Dianna wouldn't tell him where she'd been taken.

Monroe tried everything to locate her, but it wasn't as if group homes were advertised on the Internet. Even if they were state-run facilities, they were people's private homes, and there was no way of reaching them without his knowing the homeowners' names.

He left the alcove of the front porch. "Mom, is this about Hadley?"

As a lawyer who offered free advice to the local police and occasionally represented them, his mom had the police come by their place from time to time, so there was a chance this visit could be unrelated to Hadley.

She glanced at the officer before nodding. "Son, this is Officer Ford. He's here because of a favor I requested last week." She took a step back.

Officer Ford walked toward Monroe. He paused, looking unsure how to begin, but once he began talking, it took only a minute to explain that the investigation was over, the evidence was solid, and Hadley would be arrested within the hour.

Monroe's heart threatened to explode. *God, please, no!* Only five days ago he'd stood with Hadley at their spot on the parkway and promised her everything would be okay.

Monroe stepped around the officer. "Mom! You can't let this happen." He gulped in cold air, trying to stay on his feet. "Please." He pointed at the estate he called home. "Look at what we have. Boats. Cars. Property galore. Surely you and Dad can use your influence. There has to be something we can do for her. I'm begging you."

His mom started to put her hand on his shoulder, but he backed away. The raging arguments between them this past week had about undone all the loyalty he felt toward them. He should've left immediately with Hadley when he had the chance.

She lowered her hand. "We've talked to you about this for days, sweetie, going round and round."

"She has no one! And I love her."

His mom flinched slightly at his proclamation of love. His parents believed he was too young to know what real love was, but seventeen was *not* too young. Sixteen hadn't been too young either.

"I know." She smiled, a forlorn upturning of her lips. "What's happening isn't fair."

"Do *not* say that to me as if you and Dad haven't done everything in your power to make this harder for her!"

"Our intent was never to hurt Hadley, but we are *your* parents, Monroe. Our goal is protecting your future. One day you'll understand the whys of what we've done, and you'll be grateful."

He wanted to tell her that one day, four months from now, he'd be an adult, and they would have to understand the whys of his walking out and never speaking to them again. But for now, as a minor he was stuck. Also, he needed their help.

"Mom, they'll take her to jail. Do you get that? The laws in this state are stupid beyond belief. You have full control of my life because the law decided I'm too young and impulsive to make adult decisions. But Hadley, who is also of the age to be impulsive, will be tried and jailed as an adult! Tell me that makes any sense!"

His mom said nothing, and he looked skyward, wishing God would answer his multitude of prayers and give Hadley a miracle. How was she going to survive jail? Juvie would be bad enough, but at least it had trained staff and safety measures in place specifically for minors. If she was convicted as a younger teen, the offense might be expunged after her time was served, but there was no guarantee of that. Unfortunately, North Carolina law tried sixteen-and seventeen-year-olds as adults.

He'd been watching documentaries online

about minors in jail and the permanent record that ruined their lives. He'd prayed constantly that the evidence stacking against her would somehow point its bony, merciless finger at someone else.

"Monroe," Mom called softly, "work with me, and I'll work with you."

He studied her. She and Dad had said this frequently over the last several days, but he'd been unable to hear anything they had to say. He was desperate at this point. "What does that mean?"

His mom turned to the policeman. "Could you give us a moment?"

The man nodded. He walked down the sidewalk to his car and leaned against it, waiting.

Mom sighed. "Look, you agree to our terms, and your dad and I will throw in however much money it takes to help Hadley. We'll pay for the best lawyer, and a good lawyer will spare no money or effort in order to win the case, even with her already having one incident on her record. If she is found guilty, a good lawyer can make sure she serves as little time as the law allows. It's possible a good lawyer can get her off with a few years of probation."

Could his mom have managed to use the term *good lawyer* a few more times just then? But that *was* her point.

"How great a lawyer does she need? She's innocent."

"She burned down a house. *You* saw her pouring the acceler—"

He clapped his hands. "Sh. Zip it!"

She glanced at Darren. He seemed unaware of what had been said, or maybe he didn't hear it. Monroe hadn't told Hadley or the authorities what he'd seen. There was no way he'd ever testify against her. He'd go to jail himself for obstruction if he had to. But in the long nights of his parents trying to reason with him about Hadley, he'd confessed that truth. Hadley hadn't told him anything about starting a fire, but his mom knew everything the police did on this matter, and she'd told Monroe about it.

"Sorry." Mom lowered her voice.

He'd been in the car with his parents on the way to a college campus tour when he saw Hadley in the Reeds' yard. It'd struck him as odd that she was pouring a liquid into the ditch beside their house. Then she tossed what had to be a match onto that area, because the air exploded with flames. But he'd thought maybe she was doing odd jobs for the elderly couple. No one had a better heart than Hadley, although her temper often got the best of her.

Mom leaned in. "Agree to end your relationship with her. You break it off in a way that makes it very clear it's over so she doesn't call you again and you two never see each other again."

"No! She's lost everyone who ever mattered, and I will not betray her. Besides, she had to be there for the right reason, maybe trying to help out or something."

"Seriously, Monroe? The Reeds gave her grief coming and going. She went to court because of an incident with them and was infuriated and humiliated by the judge's reprimand. And you want to believe she suddenly decided not just to forgive and forget but to forgive and go do yard work for them?"

"The court thing happened a year ago. She's changed since then. Why would she suddenly want to do them harm? She didn't."

"So she was there to help them in some way. And she just happened to need to pour an accelerant on dried leaves to get them to burn? And she did so by breaking into their shed instead of knocking on their door or having a conversation with them? You believe that?"

Monroe rubbed the back of his neck and walked to the fenced edge of their huge circular driveway. From this mountaintop view he looked at the valley below, realizing how peaceful it appeared.

After his parents had bent his ear for days, he wasn't entirely sure what had happened. But whatever took place — whether she set the fire out of anger or she didn't think through her plan to make things right with the Reeds — it wasn't Hadley's fault. She'd never been given a break where adults were concerned, and the Reeds were hostile toward her. All the adults seemed to understand where the Reeds were coming from in their horror story of a teen cutting through their manicured yard, yelling at them, and keying their precious car. Why couldn't those people step into Hadley's shoes?

"She's in real trouble, Monroe. We're offering to do whatever it takes to get her out of it and get her feet under her, but I want you out of her life. No calls. No secret meetings. Nothing from here on out."

Monroe blinked, trying to hide the brimming tears.

His mom put a hand on his shoulder. "I know this is hard, and I know you hate me right now. But I'm fighting to keep your life on track, and that's more important than how you feel about me."

"There has to be another way."

41

"Sure. Use a court-appointed lawyer and take a gamble. But that kind of lawyer may not have what it takes to get her case moved to juvenile court. That lawyer won't have the man-hours or resources necessary to work the case and come away with a not-guilty verdict, nor can that lawyer get her sentence reduced to probation only. We'll hire the best." She lifted the hood of her coat over her head as the wind blew. "If you'll agree to the deal, I'll put one more thing on the table: I promise to set up an anonymous college scholarship fund for her, and whether she does time or not, we'll pay her tuition. We can't buy someone off. That's not legal. But you're right. We have money. Use it to give her some real help, Son."

"That's possible? To set up an anonymous scholarship for one particular person?"

"It'll take some legal finesse, but there are ways. With a bit of research it can be figured out, but I know that when it comes to financial aid, we can flag her Social Security number. If she applies to a college, a counselor will see there's a scholarship for her. We'll set up an anonymous LLC under some name, maybe Fresh Starts, to fund her schooling. She'll never know where the money came from."

"It takes a master's degree to be a speech therapist in this state." What was he saying? No. He couldn't turn his back on her, not for any deal.

She hesitated. "Fine." She shrugged, looking annoyed. "Then we'll pay for that too, but no degree will allow her to work with children if she's convicted of first- or second-degree arson. She needs a lawyer who can, at the least, work out a plea deal."

He was caught, a deer ensnared in a gold-plated trap. Monroe fisted his hands and screamed toward the valley. This would break Hadley's heart . . . and his. He regained his composure and faced his mom. "You swear to me you'll do everything you've promised."

She held up her right hand and put her left hand on his heart. "I swear it, Monroe."

He'd lost. It was over. Either he did right by Hadley and walked away, or he stood beside her and watched as she was devoured by a system that protected property and tossed minors into adult jail.

"Okay. Write up your decree, and I'll sign it."

"Good decision. Thank you. But for now I'll take your word on it because the clock is ticking. As a favor to me, the police have devised a way to give you an opportunity to tell her goodbye before she's arrested. It'll be very hard, but you absolutely cannot let her know any part of this deal. That would give her a reason to reach out once she's free, and that's not acceptable. Do you understand?"

"I understand. I should've run off with her without returning home." Monroe walked off, going toward the policeman.

He'd made the best deal he could for Hadley and her future.

All he had to do was say goodbye and walk away . . .

3

Hadley sat in a folding chair in a circle with other foster teens. Therapy sessions inside a state-licensed group foster home were long and boring. The goal was to help the teens accept their reality without being over-whelmed with anger and hurt. How was that even possible?

Parts of the oversize house had a homey look, and other parts looked and felt like an institution — a mishmash of an original small home with several cheap additions. This group home and its round-the-clock staff seemed a perfect representation of life — welcoming, intimidating, and never short on mixed messages.

Someone knocked and then opened the door. It was Gertrude, a short, overweight redhead who could be kind and often funny. She glanced at various teens before her attention zoomed in. "Hadley." Gertrude motioned for her.

Hadley's breath caught. Was someone finally here to visit her? Five days was too long without a familiar face. She stepped into the hallway.

Gertrude closed the door, giving them a bit of privacy. "I need you to take a breath and choose to stay calm. Do you understand?"

Hadley nodded, her heart pounding.

"The police are here."

"Here where?"

For the sake of the kids living there, the police didn't come into the group home to make an arrest unless they had to because of uncooperative behavior. If the police only needed to ask questions, they would be inside, ready to sit with Hadley and an adult supervisor in a private room.

Gertrude looked sympathetic. "Outside."

The walls around Hadley began moving like rolling waves. She was going to be arrested and taken to jail. If a lawyer could convince the judge to let her return to the group home until the trial, it wouldn't happen until Monday, two nights from now. She dreaded nighttime in jail.

Hadley closed her eyes, trying to regroup. Every part of her longed to turn off the lights and hide somewhere soft and comforting, but there was nowhere like that to be found. She wasn't going to give anyone the satisfaction of seeing her fall apart.

Walk! Put one foot in front of the other. Her body obeyed the instructions her mind was giving her, and she started down the hallway. The fluorescent lights buzzing above her were loud and oppressive. She rubbed her hands up and down her goose bump–covered arms in an attempt to warm herself. But the chill of what was happening went way beyond the weather and thin clothing.

She stared at the door that opened to the outside. In another minute they would be at the end of the hall. Once they exited that door, her life belonged to an institution she feared more than any other. She wanted to cry out, *I'm not guilty. I didn't do it.*

But she'd said that a thousand times, explaining why she'd been on the Reeds' property, why she'd started the fire. No one listened. But she knew the truth, and Monroe believed her. That was enough for now. Maybe for always.

By the time Monroe and Elliott found out she was arrested, she would be locked in a world they couldn't enter. No one under the age of eighteen could visit without custodial or parental involvement, and Hadley knew her days of being in any adult's good graces were over. The proof was that not one adult — not Monroe's parents or her former foster parents or her own parents, wherever they were — had called or visited.

Gertrude stopped short, and Hadley followed suit.

"You have ten minutes." Gertrude put her hand on the doorknob to the rec room.

"I . . . I thought the police were waiting outside to arrest me."

"They are." She turned the handle and opened the door.

Monroe! He stood at the window, looking out, and with the sunlight radiating around him, he appeared to be a knight in shining armor.

Their eyes met, and he seemed to force a smile. "Hi."

She walked to him, and she felt as if she were going to a warm fireplace after being in a frigid wasteland. He wrapped his arms around her, and she fit just right in his embrace. Throughout her life she'd never had a sense of fitting in, not in any of the foster homes and certainly not in this group home. If only she and Monroe could be teleported away from here, into Monroe's life, where there was an *actual* fireplace and they could laugh at some comedy or playfully fight over who was winning at a video game.

She drew a breath and took a step back. "They've pieced together enough evidence to arrest me."

"Yeah, I know."

He gestured toward a couple of plastic chairs that were around a small table, and they moved to that spot and sat.

She forced a smile. "This is bad, but I'll be cleared. I know I will. How can they convict an innocent person?"

He nodded, not as if he were agreeing with what she'd said as much as simply acknowledging she'd said it.

Was he losing faith in her too?

She put her hands on the center of the table, hoping he'd take them into his. "Hey." She tried to echo the way she used to say that to him, especially in the school hallways before they'd gotten to know each other, back when her lower social circle should have made it impossible for them to develop a friendship, much less anything more.

He returned her small smile, but the pity was obvious. Hadley hated it. She hated the whole situation. It was so unfair.

He touched the back of her hand. "You doing okay?"

She clutched his hands. "Sure. I mean,

I'm going to keep cooperating and not lose my temper."

"Good. I can't stand the idea of your being stuck in solitary confinement." He pulled his hands free from hers and ran one through his shaggy, dark-brown hair. He seemed more nervous than she was.

"From what one guy in here said about being arrested, I'll probably see a judge tomorrow, maybe day after. *If* this goes to trial, it'll happen pretty quickly. That's the law. It won't take long to get everything sorted out since I didn't actually do anything wrong."

Monroe just nodded while staring at the table.

"No confirmation of my innocence? No hopeful words about how smooth this will go?" Was there evidence against her that she didn't know about?

"Hadley, I . . . I can't see you anymore."

"What?" She couldn't breathe, and for a moment it was as if there were a wall around her brain. His words were hitting it, but they dispersed without making sense. Just five days ago he had proposed to her, and they had made plans to run away. "What are you saying?" Hadley's voice broke and tears welled, but Monroe didn't answer. She slammed a palm against the table. "Monroe?"

He jolted. "We're over."

He was breaking up with her? How was that possible? Their bond was unbreakable, at least that's what he had told her.

Monroe's blue eyes stayed focused on the floor. "I love you, Hads. I think I always will, but —"

Her blood pounded and anger ignited. *No, no. Get it together. Don't lose control, or they'll put you in solitary your first night.*

"Why?"

Monroe pressed his palms against his eyes. "Look at the position I'm in. I can't do this."

"Position? You're in a lot better position than me!" Hadley flung her hands in the air and pointed in the direction of the waiting police. "Are you worried about your reputation? Is marrying the girl from foster care who's being sent to jail a problem for you? Love conquers all, but it can't wait until I'm proved innocent? I *am* innocent. You believe me, right?"

"I don't blame you for any of this. I don't. But I've looked for every solution, and it boils down to facts: it would be better for both of our futures if we go toward them separately."

The stark lights and walls were more crushing than ever. *No, no, no, no!* Hadley's

51

internal voice played on a loop. "Monroe . . . you can't . . . you can't just leave me. It's not like I'll be locked away forever. I'm innocent."

Monroe continued to look down. Why was he not assuring her of that?

"You . . . you think I'm guilty?"

"I think the Reeds had been spiteful to you on numerous occasions."

"I learned my lesson. I sat through umpteen court-appointed classes on anger management and participated in endless group sessions on domestic and civic awareness. I don't lose control like that anymore. Tell me you know that."

Monroe studied his folded hands, and her mind reeled back in time. After she cut through the Reeds' yard, they saw her in town later that day and made a scene. She yelled back, walked off, and keyed their car in front of them as she went. Not a smart move. They pressed charges, and she had to go before a judge for vandalism. His final judgment was called a reprimand. It'd been humiliating to be lectured in front of everyone, but he hadn't put her on probation. Instead, she'd had to attend court-ordered therapy sessions. If she'd learned one thing, it was how to control her temper, *not* let it control her.

Should she tell Monroe again that she'd been trying to make amends with the Reeds? Their usually immaculate yard was thick with leaves, and she'd raked them into a pile in the ditch. Even now she wanted to crawl in a hole from the embarrassment of believing they would appreciate her efforts, believing they could see her as a human worthy of some pittance of respect.

Of course after raking the leaves, she'd needed a way to burn them, so she broke the cheap lock on their shed and grabbed a five-gallon container of gas. She figured she could replace the lock, but right then she needed a way to start a fire. She wasn't sure which was more embarrassing — naively thinking she could win over the Reeds or not realizing her actions would be considered illegal if the Reeds turned on her instead of appreciating her efforts. Monroe would think her a fool, and she couldn't make herself tell him the full truth. "I *didn't* do this, Monroe."

"Hads, I saw you."

"What? How?" The betrayal shook Hadley to her core.

"I didn't want to tell you, and besides my parents, I won't tell anyone else. I was in the car with them, driving to the college-tour appointment at UNC, so I couldn't stop. But I saw you. They didn't."

She wanted to scream it wasn't how it looked, but she couldn't find the strength to say anything. Her safe spot with Monroe was gone. The warmth she'd felt earlier cooled to ash. He didn't love her. He'd felt sorry for her . . . all this time. What they'd had was one sided, like most every relationship in her life. She fully loved him, but he had only a light affection for her. His suspicion and judgment had obviously been just beneath the surface. She'd caught him off guard, and he'd reacted impulsively at the overlook, but it was obvious he'd rethought what he wanted — and she wasn't it.

The door to the rec room opened. "Okay, Romeo and Juliet. Time's up." A house manager thumbed toward the front door.

Panic caused Hadley's head to spin. She put her hands up in a gesture of surrender, forcing her breath to slow, the blood roaring in her head. "Just a few more minutes, please."

"It's best to end the conversation." Monroe's voice remained composed. Did he feel nothing for her? "Goodbye, Hadley. You'll end up with a better life this way, I promise."

"Maybe this promise of yours will be as good as all the others."

Pain filled his eyes before he turned and walked toward the door.

"Monroe, wait!"

As if he were deaf to her plea, he kept walking toward the outside world — his door to freedom.

She would go out that same door, be handcuffed, and be taken to jail.

Elliott and Tara stayed focused as they walked down the sidewalk toward the courthouse. It had been five long weeks since Hadley was arrested, and Elliott was aching to see her face. The heels Elliott had donned felt really odd, as if she were trying to walk on stilts. And the reading glasses she'd purchased yesterday weren't helping her stay steady. She didn't need glasses, and they made everything blurry. But she hoped both caused her to look more the age of a courthouse intern than a junior in high school. Did Buncombe County Courthouse even use college interns?

Tara tripped and looked behind her as if the sidewalk might explain why she was unskilled at wearing heels. She leaned in closer as they walked. "I can't believe we are doing this. You are crazy," she whispered in Elliott's ear.

Elliott looked at Tara over the tortoiseshell rim of the reading glasses. She put her hand on her hip, her cheap navy blazer pulling awkwardly. "Crazy prepared, you mean."

Elliott was ready to do just about anything to be through with this town. No more foster homes. No more jerk-faced, lying boys breaking her best friend's heart. Instead, a new start for both of them. And maybe in this next adventure they'd find some of Elliott's family. But she would really miss Tara. Still, she was too young to go with them. Elliott and Hadley would have enough to deal with in trying to lie low until *they* turned eighteen. Besides, Tara would fare better by staying in this crazy town and in foster care.

"Now shush, Tara. Act like we belong, and hopefully no one will ask any questions."

Elliott wouldn't be here were it not for the rumors at school yesterday that Hadley's trial had begun. It was day two, and she prayed her friend's verdict would be *not guilty.* If not, Elliott's plans would be worthless.

Yesterday, after Elliott's school day ended and Kyle finished his shift at the factory, they made their plans for today. She went shopping and purchased clothes to help Tara and her blend in at the courthouse and for Hadley to wear as they left. Very inexpensive but professional looking as long as a person didn't look too closely. Hopefully any passerby would think they were interns, not high school students cutting class.

She hoped Kyle didn't run into any trouble as he circled the courthouse, waiting to pick up two runaways — Hadley and her. Well, he might decide to park for a bit. He had already been a great help by picking up Tara and Elliott from school earlier today before they could be counted as present in their first-period class. Suitcases were packed and ready in Kyle's trunk. The plan was for them to hop into Kyle's car immediately after Hadley was released — if she was released — and before she could be placed in the care of another foster home. They would go to Gainesville, Georgia, because Elliott had recently remembered being there as a child. Of course Hadley knew nothing of this plan, not yet. But she was sure to like it . . . if she was found not guilty.

Tara was here to make a distraction so they could escape.

Elliott adjusted her large faux-leather purse and straightened her shoulders as they passed through the columns of the courthouse and entered the door. The musty smell of a historic building mixed with the odor of lemon-scented floor polish hit her. Elliott knew her friend wasn't guilty, and she'd been praying like crazy that Hadley would get the not-guilty verdict she deserved. Elliott had spent more time asking God for a miracle than she'd spent sleeping of late.

If their plan worked and Hadley changed clothes in the bathroom, could she really leave the courthouse without anyone noticing?

The guard smiled and waved them through the metal detector, barely glancing at them. *Yes!*

Elliott's and Tara's eyes met. They were in.

A sign had the word "Information." They crossed the gray-and-cream-checkered tile floor to approach a window and then asked the woman through the hole in the glass on which floor and in which courtroom Hadley's trial was being held.

The woman picked up a sheet of paper and barely glanced at it before looking up. "Fifth floor, only one courtroom per floor."

"Thank you."

They took the elevator to the fifth floor and eased into the courtroom. The large, wood-paneled room reminded Elliott of a church she once visited, complete with wooden pews as benches for the people watching the trial. But there weren't many people here, just a handful, so it was easy to spot Dianna and Scott from the back. They were on the first bench behind the bar where Hadley sat. There were also a few college-age people with pads and paper, quietly taking notes. Elliott tapped the back of Tara's hand and pointed to Dianna and Scott. Tara's brown eyes went wide. They were in big trouble if their foster parents saw them. No amount of disguise could help, so they moved behind a group of three toward the middle of the room and sat. She and Tara would need to be very careful.

Elliott could see Hadley's trademark curls, but she didn't turn around. Nothing seemed to be happening in the courtroom. It appeared that the lawyers were at the bench, at least she assumed they were the lawyers, and they were talking to the judge. Had they missed the entire trial already? It was nine thirty. Hadn't today's session just started?

Hadley, look this way. But her eyes stayed glued to the bench.

After a few moments the lawyers left the bench area and moved to either side of the barrier. The judge, a heavyset man dressed in robes as black as his slicked-back hair, called the courtroom to attention.

"In light of new evidence, the state is dismissing the case with prejudice." The judge looked down, appearing to fidget with a paper.

Elliott couldn't breathe. This had to be a good thing! Dismissing the case? Did that mean it was over?

The judge looked up and pinned Hadley with a stare. "You are clearly innocent of the crime of arson, but since you've been in front of a judge twice in your life, I encourage you to live in such a way that you are never in this position again. You are free to go." The judge struck the gavel.

Hadley's lawyer, a woman about forty with short red hair and wearing a tailored gray pantsuit, had a huge grin on her face as she turned and hugged Hadley. A ripple of talk echoed through the small room.

As the judge stepped down from his bench, Elliott noticed another woman waiting near Hadley. That had to be the social worker.

Dianna and Scott walked to Hadley and said something. Hadley was all smiles, even for them. As Hadley spoke to Dianna, she spotted Elliott and Tara. Elliott waved. Hadley's eyes met hers, and her brow rose in a familiar look of confusion, but she quickly reset her face and said something to her former foster parents.

Elliott pulled paper and a pen out of her bag and then tossed it on the floor. "Tara, when Dianna and Scott walk by, lean over and pick that up."

Tara nodded. A few minutes later their foster parents walked by. Elliott hid her face with the piece of paper, feigning to read it closely, and Tara leaned down to pick up Elliott's bag. Dianna and Scott kept moving, taking no notice of them. Tara let out an audible sigh of relief.

Elliott quickly took the bag and used it as a prop while she wrote on the paper.

Hadley and the apparent social worker were walking down the center aisle of the room. Elliott stood and eased toward the end of the pew. Hadley dropped back, letting the social worker move ahead several feet. As Hadley passed, Elliott nonchalantly held up the sign that read "bathroom." Hadley gave a small, almost imperceptible nod.

Elliott and Tara filed out of the courtroom and walked into the restroom.

A moment later they could hear Hadley's voice. "Please, I just need a few moments to center myself." Was she crying? "I've been through so much. Can I have just a little privacy while I use the *bathroom*?"

"That's fine, honey. I'll be here waiting."

The social worker sounded kind. That would work to their advantage.

Hadley walked into the women's room and threw her arms around Elliott. They hugged, and Tara put her arms around both of them. They were almost free!

Hadley pulled back and wiped her eyes. "What's the plan, Ellie?"

Elliott reached into her bag and pulled out a soft black dress. It took up very little space in her bag, but the material didn't wrinkle. "Put this on." She handed Hadley a large hair tie and some clips. "Twist your hair back in a bun. And here's a pair of glasses for you."

Hadley yanked off her clothes. "The case was dismissed. Can you believe it?"

"I've been praying until I about fainted, so, yeah, I believe it." Elliott lifted her own glasses and put them on her head. "We'll talk later. Hurry. Everything will look blurry, but maybe the glasses will help hide who we are. Tara is going to make a distraction, and Kyle is waiting in his car nearby, either parked or circling the block. Tara will catch a bus that stops near Dianna's, and Kyle is taking you and me farther south. I remembered something while you've been in here."

"I spent only two nights in jail." Hadley

slid into the long-sleeved, polyester black dress. "Once I saw a judge, he sent me to a group home with instructions not to call anyone from my former life until after the trial. I didn't dare cross that line for fear of going back to jail."

"Oh, I'm so relieved to hear that, although one would think Dianna could've told me that much." Elliott was so weary of adults she could hardly stand herself. "Anyway, circling back to my memory. The words 'chicken capital of the world' came to me while I was waking up one morning, and I looked it up on the Internet, and that place happens to be Gainesville, Georgia."

"That's great, Ellie." Hadley chucked her black slacks and white button-up shirt into the trash can near the mirror. "I'm so proud you had a breakthrough in your memory."

"I'm sure we can find work there, something under the table and below the radar until we turn eighteen. It's . . . not very glamorous, but is that okay?"

During the only phone call Hadley got during her two days in jail, she had asked one thing of Elliott: *First chance we get, we get out. Can you help me?*

Tears brimmed in Hadley's eyes. "Yes. Yes, of course."

"One caveat." Elliott took Hadley by the

shoulders. "Promise me that if we pull this off, no more boys. Other than Kyle dropping us off, who needs guys anyway? We work hard, we steer clear of the garbage that ruined our parents' lives, and we make something out of the time God gives us."

Hadley nodded and saluted before she pulled Elliott and Tara in for a hug. "Thank you both." She released them. "Let's do this." Hadley twisted her long hair into a bun and secured it with the tie and clips.

The three of them moved to the door, and Elliott peeked out. There was a man coming toward them, and she decided to wait another minute.

"You ready, Tara?" Elliott gently elbowed her friend in the ribs. "You have to accidentally knock that social worker down and really sell it while Hadley and I slip away."

"I think so. I just hope *I* don't end up needing you guys to help me escape next."

"Tara, you've done more than enough" — Hadley put a hand on the younger girl's shoulder — "but could you do me one more big favor?"

"Of course."

"When you see Monroe at school, you be *sure* to tell him that I left with Kyle."

Elliott suppressed a smile. Good for Hadley.

4

Almost ten years later

As Hadley stirred a pot of simmering enchilada sauce with a wooden spoon, the smell of the spices made her mouth water. She would use half the sauce tonight and freeze the rest. She picked up the recipe she'd printed at the school's library from the website Budget Bytes and glanced over the instructions for chorizo-and-sweet-potato enchiladas. She could put together these few inexpensive ingredients, and that would feed Elliott and her for at least four meals. But when Jason arrived for his tutoring session, he would be hungry. That was okay with Hadley, and Elliott agreed with her.

She ducked under a string tied from a cabinet to the sink. About twenty gallon-size plastic bags secured with clothespins were drying, and tomorrow morning before she left for school, Hadley would stuff them back into their cardboard container. Reuse and make do. That had been their motto since escaping from the courthouse — so for their entire adult lives.

A small radio sat on the microwave. She turned up the volume and danced to the peppy beat. She wasn't sure who sang the song, but she liked it.

Keys jingled in the front door, and a moment later Elliott opened it. "Hey." Elliott nodded at Hadley as she entered the small apartment. Her blue scrubs were spattered with dark-purple stains — most likely liquid medication — but it was the tiredness in her movements that tugged on Hadley's heart. They had goals and a set plan, but was Elliott sacrificing too much? She'd pulled extra shifts for weeks as an LPN at the hospital.

One of the perks of moving back to Asheville seven years ago was, whether they were living with Tara a few streets over or living here as they'd done for the past four years, they were within walking distance of the hospital . . . and most everything else. Elliott worked at Mission Health full-time, and Hadley worked there one day each weekend. But Elliott looked beat, and the walk home probably hadn't helped. They had a car, but Hadley used it to get back and forth to

Western Carolina University. It was fifty miles away, but none of the local colleges offered a degree in communication sciences and disorders.

Hadley reached over to the counter and tucked a small stack of overdue bills under a textbook. No need to add stress to whatever was going on with her best friend.

"Is it past seven already?" Hadley had arrived home three hours ago, but with her head stuck in books studying before she got the food out for dinner, it'd seemed as if she'd just come home.

Elliott glanced at the Timex on her wrist. "Seven twenty-one."

"Sorry, I wanted to have dinner ready when you got home from your shift. You've got to be hungry."

"I'm okay. No hurry. Thanks for cooking." Her voice was quiet. What was going on? Elliott removed her lightweight fleece jacket and went to the tiny coat closet to hang it up. Fall evenings in Asheville sometimes required sleeves. When Elliott shut the closet door, Hadley saw an envelope in her hand. A moment later she tossed it onto the counter. The words *urgent* and *time sensitive* were stamped in black and red, screaming like one of Elliott's injured patients. The return address was for their apartment complex.

Hadley didn't pick up the letter. "Is it an eviction notice?"

"Yeah."

"So soon? I . . . I knew we were behind, but I thought we'd have more time." Since the housing crash three years ago, the landlords in the area seemed to be cracking down on late rent. There were too many people in need of rentals for the landlords to have patience with those who didn't pay regularly.

"Me too." Elliott shrugged, and then a smile slowly filled her face. "I have a bit of good news, though."

This was Elliott. She preferred to get the bad news out of the way first so the good news wasn't weighed down by undisclosed information.

"Spill it, Ellie."

"Dr. Williams asked me to set up regular workshops for his lower-income patients, teaching them nutrition and health care. An RN will be present during the classes, but I'm to do the legwork, planning, and publicity. It'll be really good money — like twenty-two dollars an hour."

"That's great."

"Yeah, but unfortunately the classes won't

start until after the first of the year, and I won't get any money for my work on the project for another two months. Until then we'll figure it out, Hads. We always do." Elliott walked back to her room to change clothes and quickly wash up — her evening routine after finishing a shift at the hospital.

Hadley picked up the envelope. They'd been without a roof over their heads before, but it was a mean business and much more suited to reckless teens and war vets than educated women in their midtwenties.

Elliott reentered the room, pulling her silky dark hair into a ponytail. Her brows were knit, and Hadley knew she was deep in thought about how to avoid being evicted.

Hadley gestured at her textbooks. "Maybe I should hit Pause on my education."

"Don't be ridiculous, please." Elliott went to the kitchen and picked up the recipe page. "Half of our financial struggle is the burden of my student loans. Your scholarship is a gift from God. It has a few stipulations, and you will not break any of them."

One of the stipulations for Hadley keeping her scholarship was she couldn't drop out for even one semester. At ten thousand dollars a semester for her master's degree, it would be a long, hard climb to get out of the financial hole student loans would create if she lost the scholarship. Earning a grad degree in speech-language pathology almost meant more to Hadley than having food, lodging, or even air, but it didn't mean more to her than Elliott's mental or physical health.

Elliott put the recipe page down on the counter where they could both see it. "How about a subject change? While I was walking home, I saw a bumper sticker that you will appreciate. It had a rooster on it and said 'Chicken Capital of the World.' I think we both know which town that means."

"That's funny." Hadley and Elliott had lived in Gainesville, the self-proclaimed Chicken Capital of the World, for almost three years after escaping the courthouse together. Kyle wasn't thrilled about leaving them, but they insisted. He gave them some money for food and a motel, and when he returned to Asheville, he sold Elliott's motor scooter for two thousand dollars — or so he said — and sent them that money. Hadley was pretty sure he mailed them more than he received from selling that scooter, but the cash got them started. Although they never found any clues about Elliott's family, they didn't return to Asheville until they aged out of North Carolina's foster-care system.

"What can I do to help?" Elliott ducked under the line of drying plastic bags.

"Cut the sweet potatoes." Hadley gave the sauce another swirl before opening the pack of chorizo sausages.

When they'd left the courthouse almost ten years ago, they hoped never to return to Asheville, but coming back had been the right decision, a God decision, or so it seemed. Living in the smaller city of Gainesville was nice, but it wasn't home. They knew every corner of Asheville and soon discovered they missed that. After the first couple of months in Gainesville, they fared pretty well in the battle to keep a roof over their heads. They found work at a hotel, and for four hundred dollars a month, they could rent a room there. It had two beds, a bathroom, coffee maker, and tiny fridge but no kitchen. It worked, and it felt far safer than living inside a flimsy tent. Plus it had a thermostat to adjust the room temperature, which was *really* nice after living in a tent.

But three years later, during a conversation with Tara, they learned that Mission Health hospital was hiring orderlies for their children's wing. Tara was within weeks of aging out of the system, and she'd found a steal on subleasing a three-bedroom apartment with a fully stocked kitchen. She just needed two good roommates who would pay their share. Tara had them at the word *kitchen*. Forget whether it had any pots, pans, or utensils. They'd picked up their last check from working in housekeeping at the hotel, bought bus tickets, and returned to Asheville. That had been about seven years ago now, difficult but fruitful years.

Despite being the one who brought them back to Asheville, Tara hadn't stayed their roommate for long. She'd been out of foster care for only a few months when her life was turned upside down in order to keep her two younger half brothers out of that same system. Since then she'd been living in Sylva, North Carolina. The three of them kept in contact through texting and get-togethers. They saw her a few weeks ago, and they would see her again after Christmas, probably New Year's Eve.

Hadley turned the burner to medium high and added the sausage, chopped peppers, sweet potato, and spices. It quickly heated to a sizzle. "So what's the plan, Ellie?"

"Find somewhere to store our stuff and get it there before we come home one day to find it's been tossed out and pilfered. It's taken us too long to buy what we have. We can't lose it."

About a year after being back, they both

decided to earn a GED. Then Elliott went to remedial classes so she could learn all she needed to pass college classes. Hadley worked while Elliott got her LPN license. Once Elliott had a good job that made enough money to get by, Hadley talked to a counselor at Blue Ridge Community College about her desire to become a speech therapist. A few days later the counselor contacted Hadley, saying she'd uncovered a scholarship that would pay her tuition.

"What about church? We could ask someone there." Hadley turned off the burner for the sauce and stirred the sizzling frying pan.

"With our schedules we haven't been there much, and I'd rather not ask them for a handout." Elliott rinsed the cutting board and knife and set them out to dry on the rack next to the sink. "It would be like 'Hey, I don't have time for you, but could you give me money?' "

"Yeah, you're right." Hadley touched her finger to the sauce on the spoon and tasted it. "I hate the idea of leaving here, but at least we've done some good for our neighbors."

"Chloe," Elliott whispered. "Oh, Hads. I hadn't even thought about her or the others." Elliott looked up, and her eyes rested on their small, round dinner table. Its sole decoration was a clean jelly jar that held a small bunch of purple aster wildflowers in some water. A precious gift from a certain four-year-old's "garden," which was a small patch of mostly weeds that Chloe's mother had transplanted to a spot near their apartment and protected by a six-inch-tall plastic fence.

"Wherever we land, maybe we can work out something with Kate and Alan so I can keep working with her." Since everything in the frying pan looked done, Hadley turned off the burner and held up a bag of large flour tortillas. "Help me roll these?"

Chloe had been unable to say even one word when Hadley began to work with her two years ago, and now she had an average vocabulary for a child her age, even though many of the words were decipherable only to those close to her.

"Sure." Elliott wrinkled her nose. "Is something burning in the oven?"

Hadley sniffed the air. Smoke no longer caused her to break out in a cold sweat, but she assumed she would always hate the smell. "No, I forgot to preheat the oven. But I smell it too. Maybe it's something under the burner." She looked to make sure she had turned off the range.

"And Jason," Elliott said. "We'll have to figure out a way we can continue to keep him on the right path."

That would be tougher than helping Chloe.

"Yeah." Hadley had met Jason when he was a cute thirteen-year-old. Now he was a tall seventeen-year-old with a shaved head, who looked older than his actual age and had a knack for finding trouble. But he mattered, and Hadley and Elliott kept trying to help him see life differently.

Elliott put a scoop of filling inside a tortilla, rolled it, and set it in a glass baking dish. "I know he reminds you of yourself. But you can't fix everything in his life, especially if he makes dumb decisions like breaking into Alan's truck and stealing an iPad."

"I've yet to figure that one out. I don't think he knew it was Alan's truck, and I like to believe he was desperate to pay for his grandmother's medication. But I don't know that for sure. Still, I think I have Alan and Jason to a good, healing place."

Elliott lifted the cooling pots, looking underneath them. "I still smell it."

Someone pounded on the front door. "Fire!" It sounded like their neighbor Michael. "Elliott, Hadley, you there?"

Hadley rushed out of the kitchen and jerked open the door.

Michael's red face was tinged with soot. "Building on fire. South end is bad, and they need all the help they can get."

Elliott snatched the keys off the table. She tossed them to Hadley, who locked the door as Elliott and Michael ran down the stairs.

5

Elliott sprinted across the cracked parking lot, heading toward the green space. Smoke burned her eyes and nose as she hurried to a safe distance. Flames leaped out of windows from several floors of the old apartment building. Her stomach dropped when she saw where the fire was concentrated. Their friends lived there.

God, please let everyone be okay . . .

People were everywhere, crying and yelling for loved ones. The apartment building was L shaped and bookended on both sides by streets and parking lots. Hadley and Elliott lived at the opposite end from where the fire raged unchecked.

"Stop!" Chloe's dad screamed. "Jason!"

The desperation in Alan's voice sent chills over Elliott. She searched for Alan, and it didn't take long to spot the tall, fit man running after the younger, leaner Jason.

Why was Jason carrying Chloe? The little

girl wailed, flailing her arms.

Kate was lagging behind her husband, screaming, "He has our daughter!" She was only a few years older than Elliott, but she carried some extra weight, so she fell farther behind the men by the second.

Phillip, another neighbor, came out of nowhere and joined the pursuit. Hadley and Elliott ran in that direction. She didn't know what was going on, but Jason needed someone to intervene if three angry adults were pursuing him.

"Jason." Hadley cupped her hands around her mouth, yelling. "What's going on?"

Jason turned, panic written on his face. He did a one-eighty and then ran toward Hadley, holding out Chloe.

Hadley grabbed Chloe as Jason passed. He slowed, glanced behind him at Alan, and tore out across the parking lot. The look on Alan's face said he'd kill Jason when he got ahold of him. Chloe snuggled against Hadley, sobbing.

Elliott grabbed Alan's jacket as he ran by. "Stop!"

Alan jerked free and picked up speed with Phillip not far behind. Alan caught up to Jason and leaped for him. He landed with a thud on the asphalt, knocking Jason's feet out from under him. Alan didn't budge.

Before Jason could get up, Phillip pinned him to the ground. "Thought you'd steal a little girl this time, eh?" The man's fist connected with Jason's jaw, making a horrible *thwap* noise. "Taking electronics and money from cars no longer good enough for you?" The man pulled his arm back, ready to hit him again.

Elliott ran full force at them, knocking the man off Jason. "No more!" She knelt beside Jason. "Are you okay?"

Jason looked dazed, but he was breathing. She scurried to her feet and went to Alan and knelt beside him. "Alan?" He was out cold, but there was no blood. He'd stopped Jason, but he'd hit his head hard on the pavement in the process. He needed to get to the hospital as soon as possible for a CT scan to see if he was bleeding internally.

She stood, looking for help. She spotted a man in an EMT uniform. "Paramedic!"

The EMT turned.

"Head trauma, internal!"

He gave a thumbs-up to let her know he'd heard, and then he hurried to the ambulance. She crouched back down and checked Alan's pulse. She could see Jason wobbling from side to side, but he was sitting up now, rubbing his jaw.

She moved to Jason. "What day is it?" She

80

tilted his head skyward, looking in his eyes.

Jason shrugged, seeming unsure.

She held up two fingers. "How many fingers do you see?"

"Three."

"Yeah, that's what I figured. You need to be seen." But she knew that neither Jason nor his grandmother could pay the bill for an ambulance. She studied the parking lot and spotted Mr. Garcia. "I'll organize a vanload of nonemergency folks to get to the hospital, and when that vehicle pulls out of the lot, I want you on it. Okay?"

Jason shrugged.

Phillip walked closer and snatched something off the ground. "The only thing wrong with him is what he's been smoking." He held out a plastic bag with what looked to be several ounces of weed in it.

Elliott's heart sank. If the police were here, Jason could be on his way to jail right now.

Phillip dangled the bag in front of Jason's face. "Is this what gave you the courage to snatch Alan's little girl?"

"I didn't —"

"Yeah, save it for someone who'll believe you." Phillip walked away, yelling over his shoulder, "I'll hold this as evidence, and you can bet your life that you haven't seen the last of Alan, kid. I wouldn't want to be you when he wakes up."

"But . . ."

Elliott put her hand on Jason's shoulder. "Sh. Save your energy. Try to relax and take slow, deep breaths. All of this can be sorted out later." She wanted to know the whole story. When Hadley learned this piece of information, she would demand Jason tell her everything. How else could she be a surrogate big sister to him? But this wasn't the time or place for anyone to question Jason. "Come on. Let's get you to the curb." She helped Jason stand and steadied him until he was seated on the curb. "I'll get a cold pack for your jaw from an ambulance as soon as I can."

Chloe was in her mom's arms now with both Kate and Hadley talking to her. Kate stroked Chloe's hair and appeared to be soothing her.

Two EMTs arrived with a stretcher. They lowered it, put a neck brace on Alan, and moved him onto the stretcher. Kate spotted Alan and rushed over with Chloe in her arms. "What's wrong?" Kate asked in the middle of a coughing spasm. She grabbed Alan's hand. "Alan?"

How long had she been in the smoke-filled building?

"Head trauma." The EMT put an oxygen mask on Alan. "He needs to go to the hospital, ma'am."

"He's my husband."

"You can go but just you."

Kate pulled Chloe close. "No, we'll follow by car."

"You sure?" Elliott asked as she pointed at the number of cars blocked by fire trucks, police, and ambulances.

Kate looked distressed, but she held Chloe tighter. "I'm sure. I can't do anything for him, and he wouldn't want me to leave our girl right now."

Elliott pushed down all personal concerns for Kate, Alan, Jason, and even Hadley for having to experience another fire. She had to get into the right mental state. This wasn't personal. It was her profession, and she had to be clearheaded to help. A crowd of apartment dwellers huddled nearby, coughing, crying, and waiting for medical attention.

The EMTs were rolling the stretcher across the parking lot. Elliott strode to them. "I'm Elliott, an LPN at Mission Health. What can I do?"

"I'm Chris. We need all the help we can get. The most immediate need is triage while administering oxygen to those suffering from smoke inhalation. You any good at listening for lung distress?"

"Very." She trotted beside him as he hurried toward an ambulance.

"Tell that to the EMT near the oxygen tanks." Chris pointed at a man who was stacking several portable oxygen tanks next to the ambulance on the asphalt parking lot. "There are pockets of crowds on adjacent lawns also. Assess for smoke inhalation and carbon-monoxide poisoning." He nodded back toward Kate and Chloe and about ten other people standing nearby. "Start with them." He and his partner put Alan in an ambulance.

Elliott was surprised how many different things the man gave her to do, but she scampered to get oxygen tanks. She told the man, Carl, who she was and about her skill in detecting pulmonary issues. He passed her a stethoscope and otoscope, reiterating for her to do triage, administer oxygen, and report back.

She took an oxygen tank in each hand and moved as fast as she could, wheeling them to the lawn where Chris told her to set up. Smoke poured into the evening sky, gray plumes overshadowing the orange-and-pink sunset, but it looked as if the fire crew might be able to stop the blaze before it burned the entire building.

Had everyone gotten out? Elliott had seen no hint of a fire when she arrived home, so the fire must have spread through the old building quickly. Was that due to the size and layout of the buildings? She pulled one tank up the curb and onto the grass.

Other rescue workers were aiding people in different areas. Kate was sitting on the lawn, still coughing uncontrollably and holding Chloe against her chest. Elliott knelt beside them.

"Hey, Kate."

Kate grabbed her hand, coughing.

Elliott squeezed. "You'll be fine. Let's get oxygen in you."

Coughing, Kate only managed a nod.

Elliott put the mask on Kate's face and turned on the oxygen. Then she shifted her focus to Chloe. She stroked the girl's fine, wispy blond hair. "Don't worry, we'll get your mama fixed up."

The little girl seemed to be breathing well enough, but Elliott would check her lungs more thoroughly later. Others around them were struggling for air, and Elliott had to get to them. She pulled an otoscope from the pocket of her scrubs and flashed the small beam of light into Chloe's eyes. Her pupils responded appropriately for the panic she was feeling. Elliott ran her fingers across the girl's scalp, searching for bumps. "Chloe, can you remind me how old you are?"

Chloe held up four fingers, but her eyes revealed a level of terror that broke Elliott's heart.

"Good. You are four, aren't you?" Elliott turned to Hadley. "I'll check her out more fully later. Some people have more pressing needs, but I'll be back as soon as I can." She grasped her friend's hand. "You got this, Hadley?"

Hadley barely nodded while watching the fire. "Yeah. Go."

Elliott cradled Hadley's face in her hands, looking in her eyes. "You're a grown woman, not a powerless teen. We live in today. Educated. Capable of taking on whatever is happening." She saw in Hadley's eyes that she was coming back to herself. "*We* — you and me — Hadley, are the ones who stand ready to help others, and we don't panic, and we abandon no one." They couldn't personally rescue all who needed help, but they could assess and direct people to the right places.

Hadley took a deep breath and smiled. "Yeah, I . . . I forgot for a moment. Thanks."

Elliott gave her a quick hug and left. She

spent the next forty minutes assessing people, administering oxygen, and reporting to Carl. Jason reluctantly agreed to ride to the hospital in a van of people who needed to be seen. Ambulances left and returned for others. Additional ambulances from nearby counties arrived. Soon the panic of meeting needs slowed, and Elliott returned to check on Chloe, who was in Hadley's lap. They were sitting next to Kate, who was pale, and her adrenaline rush seemed to be crashing because she could hardly keep her eyes open.

"Hi, Chloe." Elliott knelt. "Can I listen to your breathing a little?"

She didn't reply, only burrowed further into Hadley's shirt. Hadley shook her head. "Not a word in more than forty minutes, and I've tried our favorite games and singing."

Elliott heard the concern in Hadley's voice. "It could be temporary from the panic."

Kate swiped her brown hair away from her face. "I'd like to get to the hospital and check on Alan."

Elliott glanced at the fire trucks blocking their car. "I think we can get out soon." She showed Chloe the stethoscope. "Can I listen to your breathing, sweetie?"

Chloe retreated again into Hadley's arms.

Hadley hugged her. "Ellie wants to give you a checkup, just like you gave Gray Bear a checkup. Watch, she can do me first."

Elliott moved the stethoscope to Hadley's chest and pretended to listen. She needed to get moving. There was still plenty to do, but she couldn't rush the traumatized little girl. What had Jason been doing? Rumors said Jason was headed down a bad path. Could it be gang involvement? Elliott didn't want to believe that. But she wouldn't have believed Jason had an illegal substance on him either, not after all the lectures, meals, and help with homework they'd given him since moving in four years ago.

"See?" Hadley said. "Just like you did for your bear yesterday, okay?"

Chloe didn't reply, but she also didn't shrink away when Elliott tried the stethoscope again. Unlike her mom's lungs Chloe's sounded good and clear. Elliott moved the instrument around, listening from front and back just to be sure.

She removed the earpieces of the stethoscope. "Her lungs sound great, as if she didn't breathe in any smoke."

"Why isn't she talking?" Kate asked.

Elliott tugged on Kate's shirtsleeve. "Who is this?"

Chloe loved saying *Mama* and all sorts of fun terms of endearment. Asking that question typically sparked a barrage of giggles and silly names for Mama, part of a fun game Hadley had made up more than a year ago. But Chloe didn't answer. Elliott's and Hadley's eyes met.

"I have an idea," Hadley said. "We would all feel much better if you would sing to us. How about a line from your favorite song?"

Still nothing.

"I'll sing it with you. Ready? The wheels on the bus go round and round."

Chloe covered her face, a sure sign she had no intention of cooperating.

"It's okay, Chloe. We'll sing it later." Hadley looked to Kate.

Elliott put the stethoscope around her neck. "A setback in talking is normal during and after something shocking, but she needs professionals involved, Kate."

Kate removed the oxygen mask. "But she has you and Hadley. She won't like seeing anyone else."

"I understand." Elliott put the oxygen mask back on Kate. "But this could be beyond Hadley's ability to help. If you wait, it could be days before we know whether Chloe will start talking again, and your shoddy insurance is more likely to step up and pay if she's seen today as part of this fire emergency."

When Chloe turned two and didn't have one word in her vocabulary, not even the typical two-year-old *no,* Kate did everything in her power to get help for Chloe. But the insurance company wouldn't budge. Their excuse was "It's too soon. She'll talk when it's time." Hadley stepped in, and Kate lost all confidence in ever getting a medical facility on board. She felt Hadley was the sole answer to any speech needs Chloe had. Truth was, Hadley seemed to have worked miracles with the little girl.

Later in Hadley's education process, she'd learned there was a nationwide free program for children younger than three years old with serious speech issues. Under those same government provisions, Chloe could receive help from the local school system after turning three. But Chloe's doctor never mentioned any of that, and by the time Hadley learned of those programs, she and Chloe had bonded and were making great strides. In Elliott's opinion no government program could accomplish one-fourth as much with Chloe as Hadley could.

Kate dipped her head, shaking it. "If you say so, I believe you."

"Good. If she starts talking within a few

hours, she was seen over nothing. But in case she doesn't, when we get to the hospital, I'll talk to the doctor on staff and be sure he gives a referral so your insurance will cover Chloe getting the help she needs for as long as she needs it, okay?"

Kate nodded. "Okay."

6

From a chair beside Jason's hospital bed, Hadley stared at the paper in her hand. It was filled with notes she'd written while the doctor discussed with Kate and her why Chloe wasn't talking. With Chloe's past apraxia issues and today's trauma, the doctor felt that the cause was a convergence of two speech issues. He'd used the terms *rare* and *complicated.* He highly recommended finding a good therapist and being ready to work with the therapist until Chloe could speak again. Hadn't Chloe suffered enough when it came to language?

Hadley folded the note and stuffed it into her jeans pocket. It'd taken two years of hard work to get Chloe speaking well enough to communicate adequately for her age. A child with apraxia of speech usually struggled to form words until he or she was well into elementary school, sometimes into middle school and beyond, but Chloe had made good strides in talking, and now she might be back to ground zero. Hadley sighed, unwilling to think about it anymore tonight. She leaned back in the hospital recliner and stared at the ceiling.

What time was it? The fluorescent lights made every hour look the same. Jason had been admitted, and he was lying on his side in the hospital bed beside her. Part of his back was covered in an antibiotic ointment for a first-degree burn. He had a concussion, and his jaw was fractured. His IV for replenishing his body fluids also had pain medication. But the medicine wasn't what had him staring into space. His spirit had taken a devastating blow.

"Jason." Hadley sat up and put her hand over his. "Talk to me."

He shrugged and closed his eyes, as if trying to shut out what was happening.

He was a lonely kid with no friends and no family other than a frail grandmother, who took care of him on good days and whom he tried to take care of on her bad days. To make matters worse, Jason had a processing disorder that made learning really tough. For four years Hadley and Elliott had tried to help make his school life bearable for him and to help him pass his classes. They would work with him for hours on an upcoming math or English test, and he'd finally get it, but by the next day he couldn't recall enough to pass the test.

"It doesn't matter what you did wrong. I'm here for you." The motto she and Elliott had came to mind: we don't panic, and we don't abandon those in need. "But I need to know the truth. Kate says when smoke began filling the apartment, they went to Chloe's room to get her, and she wasn't there. They stayed in the building, searching for her, and when they heard her screaming, you had her against her will and were running away. Phillip says you were using the situation to try to kidnap her so you could show Alan that you could take a lot more than his iPad if you wanted to."

"Everybody in the apartment house already hated me, and now it'll be even worse."

She couldn't argue with that, but Jason had been caught stealing from their vehicles a few times. What did he expect people to feel?

"Where's Memaw?" he asked.

"At a facility set up by the Red Cross. She's with the Browns from the complex, and they promised to take good care of her."

He nodded. "Good."

Hadley had left Jason's side numerous

times to find out what was happening with their neighbors. She had stepped out of the room to take calls so as not to disturb him and had walked around the hospital visiting a few other people. She'd like to hear from Elliott, but she knew Elliott was busy with her nursing duties somewhere. Alan had regained consciousness, and the CT indicated there wasn't any bleeding inside his skull. Hadley had been able to visit Alan and Kate in his hospital room.

Alan wanted to press charges, but Hadley pointed out that no one had proof Jason had done anything wrong. He was running from a burning building with a child. Marijuana was found on the ground next to him, but people were everywhere, carrying as many belongings as they could. That pouch could've belonged to anyone. Those were the facts. Of course that information did nothing to make Alan feel any better about Jason.

"How's Chloe?" Jason mumbled, looking embarrassed to ask.

"Good. She's asleep in the ER because the doctor wanted to monitor her overnight, but she isn't talking."

"Alan hates me even more now."

Alan managed All-in-One Auto, a car wash, oil change, and garage. Under Alan's management the business was quite successful, in part due to the lounge with great coffee and a play area for kids. Alan made enough money to live in a much better place, but they scrimped every penny, saving for their dream — Alan's own garage. Hadley felt it was God moving Alan into Jason's life, but it hadn't been easy to convince Alan of that, and Jason kept sabotaging her efforts.

Jason loved tinkering with motors, although he'd never worked in a garage. He'd brought Hadley's car back to life more than once, so working for Alan would be the perfect step into a career, maybe the only step. His high-school grades were a mess, and he intended to quit school as soon as he turned eighteen in December and could quit without parental permission. Hadley understood how he felt. Quitting was easier on the self-esteem than being a lonely misfit who'd flunked out. He needed a trade. That's where Alan came in, providing the only door Hadley could find that Jason had a chance of walking through and being a success. That job would give Jason everything he needed — self-respect, money, and the ability one day to provide for a family of his own.

Without it, she saw Jason spiraling out of

control and letting the hurt that life kept heaping on him turn into rage and recklessness. Hadley told Alan that he could take the money for the stolen iPad out of Jason's first few paychecks and that Jason would *never* do anything stupid like that again. Alan had finally agreed to give Jason a second chance after the iPad theft and said there would soon be an opening at All-in-One Auto. Alan was going to hold that spot for Jason, and he could begin the day he turned eighteen. Right now Alan only wanted to throttle Jason, and he was angry with Hadley for talking him into trying to help the kid.

Hadley squeezed Jason's hand. "There's some stuff to work through, but I'm here to try to understand your side, and we'll go from there. But when you took the iPad from Alan's truck and he brought you to my place instead of calling the police, you told him, 'If you aren't careful with your stuff, you could have something much more valuable than an iPad stolen.' I took it as you blowing off steam, but Alan feels you've now confirmed what he's thought since then — that you meant it as a threat."

Jason closed his eyes, shaking his head. "But I didn't."

"That's how he heard it, and today you

ignored the trained workers, who were there to rescue people, and took off running with his daughter."

"What does he think, that I was going to ransom Chloe for money? I'm no genius, but that'd be beyond stupid to take a kid who can identify me."

Hadley shrugged.

Jason frowned. "Your face says that's not what he was thinking. What else was I going to do with her?" The color drained from his cheeks. "I'm not like that!" Tears filled his eyes. "I've never thought like . . . that! Dear God, is that what Alan thinks?"

"He's not sure what to think. He just knows his daughter was taken from his apartment and you held on to her while she was screaming to get away. So why did you have Chloe?"

Chloe was never out of her parents' sight unless she'd been passed to another responsible adult, as when Hadley worked with her.

Jason shrugged. "I . . . I don't know."

He didn't know? "Did you sneak into their apartment?" She'd never known Jason to break into an apartment. He'd stolen some things from vehicles, but she thought she'd talked Jason out of his thieving ways.

"I've been tempted. They have more stuff

than most in the complex, and I need money for . . ."

"Go on."

He shook his head.

"Pot, right?" She'd seen it and heard about it from Phillip.

"Not for me. I swear it."

Seriously? She leaned in. "I'm here for you, Jason, but something in this mess of a story has to make sense. Understand?"

"Why? So you and Elliott have a good reason to throw in the towel and disappear?"

She remembered feeling the same way — as if no one in life was permanent, as if no one was capable of knowing the full truth and staying to help.

"Jason." Hadley fidgeted with the sheets, straightening them. "Our lives are a bit parallel, including trouble being stirred due to a fire. For four years I've believed God ordered our steps and put us at the same apartment complex. But if I don't know the truth, I can't help you navigate what's happening. I promise: I'm not leaving and I'm not giving up, but I need to know."

He hesitated. "You won't believe me."

"Maybe not, but I'm waiting for an answer."

"I buy it for Memaw."

Hadley did believe him, and her heart

turned to mush. The elderly woman was wheelchair-bound, but the hardest part of her life was the constant migraines. "You should have told —"

"Telling was a no-win deal. You would've had to stop me, which wouldn't have been fair to Memaw. She gets relief from that stuff. And you'd be in real trouble if I got caught and you knew what I was doing."

She couldn't fuss at him. He'd nailed the situation for what it was. "And medical marijuana isn't legal in North Carolina."

He rolled his eyes. "Another brilliant law, right?"

"So you've been stealing from people's vehicles in the complex in order to buy marijuana for Memaw?" Hadley rose, needing to pace. "I'd like to lecture you from here to the moon, but I'll settle for saying you should've come to me."

"It's decriminalized."

"Decriminalized . . . ," Hadley mumbled. That was a word Jason probably knew from talking with his friends at school. "That does nothing to win over Alan. Besides that, it's not legal in any state for a minor to have it. All of this — your past stealing, the incident today with Chloe, and the pot — works against you in Alan's eyes."

Jason let out a breath, his body deflating

against the hospital pillow. "Too much has happened with Alan Powell. That deal is dead, and we both know it."

"Maybe, but I'm hoping not. Why was Chloe with you?"

"I . . . I really don't remember." He rubbed his head. "It's cloudy and makes no sense."

"Tell me what you do remember."

"I was playing basketball at the rickety goal in the parking lot, and then I remember smelling smoke. When I saw thick smoke, I ran back to my apartment to get Memaw out. I put her in the wheelchair, grabbed her medicines, and hurried out of the building. Soon I heard sirens, and flames were billowing from the building, and I caught a glimpse of what looked like a kid by the side of the building. I headed that way just as the fire trucks entered the parking lot."

"The kid was Chloe?"

He nodded.

"By herself?"

"I know, but that's not the craziest part. I left Memaw in a safe spot in the parking lot and ran back for Chloe, but as I was running toward her, she ran . . . into the burning building, crying for her mommy."

"Was she running from you?"

"Maybe. I'm sure Alan's said nothing but

bad things about me to her. But isn't it instinct to run from fire?"

"It is."

"Whatever she was doing and why, that's about all I remember."

"You recall Alan chasing you?"

"Some. But it was as if I wasn't the one holding Chloe or running."

"Shock and panic had taken over." Hadley nodded. "When did you get the burns on your back?"

"I have no idea." He frowned. "Wait. I remember hearing an explosion."

"An explosion?" She'd talked to a lot of people from the complex, and no one had mentioned hearing an explosion.

"Yeah, ask Chloe. No matter how upset or confused she is, she's bound to remember that."

"It could be a while before she can answer. We can't ask leading questions if her responses are to have any validity. She'll have to agree to answer simple questions about what happened or what she remembers, and she can't right now. When we ask her anything, she's not even trying to respond." Hadley thought about all she knew of Jason and what did and didn't add up in his story. "But I believe you."

Relief washed over his face.

A nurse pushed open the curtain and walked in. She checked his vitals and left.

Jason took a deep breath and let it out in a sigh. "I'm sorry about Chloe. But even if she could talk, what could a four-year-old say to change Alan's mind?"

That was a great question, but Hadley had to try. "Yeah, but she knows the truth, and I'm going to work with her to get the full story. Helping children like her find their words is the reason I'm in school. You'll need to be patient with the process."

Hadley's cell buzzed in her pocket. She flipped it open to see a text from Elliott. She'd arrived.

"I have to go. But I promise you I won't give up until I get Chloe speaking again."

Jason smiled. "Thanks."

"We'll get this straight, hopefully *before* Alan gives your position to someone else." She walked out of the room, heading toward the front entrance. She blinked repeatedly, trying to ease the strain from the hospital's artificial lights.

She reached the front entry and saw Elliott on the phone as she approached the building. She waved at her as the hospital's automatic double doors opened and her friend stepped through. Through the open doors Hadley got a glimpse of the sky. It was barely glowing, a sign that morning was coming quickly. Hadley hadn't checked the time until she looked at Elliott's text. Hadley had spent hours consoling Kate throughout Chloe's checkup in the crowded ER. Now that things were stabilized a bit, Hadley was glad Elliott was here to take her home. Some rest would feel good, if she could sleep.

"Yeah, we're fine. I promise." Elliott mouthed the word *Tara*. "Okay. We'll talk soon. Take care. Bye." She disconnected the call. "Tara heard on the news about the fire and was concerned. She called. When you leave this building, you'll probably receive voice messages from her. She's good now."

"I should've thought . . ."

"Me too. And sorry I didn't get here sooner. Some of the tenants refused to come to the ER for help, so I went with them to the Red Cross setup, and I've been keeping a check on their vitals."

"There was nothing you could have done here. Any idea what started the fire?"

"Yeah, when things calmed down, I got a chance to speak to the fire chief. He said it was a grease fire in 1G. Rumor has it that Gale Johnston had been frying chicken, and when she packed it up to take it to her husband at work, she forgot to turn off the burner under the skillet. How much of that is true I don't know, but the chief has already ruled out arson."

Hadley took a cleansing breath, grateful the incident was as simple as a grease fire. "Did you get any sleep?"

"Some."

"You need more rest before you do your shift. Let's get you home."

Elliott nodded. "Yeah, about that . . ."

"What's wrong?"

"We have to find another place to stay for a while."

"The damage was that bad on our end of the building too?"

"There was structural damage on the far end. Our wing has only water and smoke damage, but management is temporarily evacuating the entire building while they repair it. On the up side, we can go in once to get what we need."

Why had they declined the renters' insurance? Oh, yeah, because they had more important things to spend those few bucks on each month.

"So where should we stay?"

"Red Cross has set up a place for —"

"No." Hadley shook her head. "Something less communal, please. Besides, we would just have to move again in a week. Red

Cross help is very temporary."

"You up for camping?" Elliott gestured to the world outside the hospital doors. "It's September and beautiful outside. Not too cold or hot. It'll give us a month or so to find other housing before the nights get too chilly."

Hadley knew that tone. "You're just trying to sound upbeat."

"I am. Camping isn't my favorite thing, but since we can shower at the hospital and get an employee discount for meals, it'll be the most inexpensive way to live while looking for an affordable place. Besides, we live in Asheville. People come here this time of year and pay to get a few days to do what we're going to do. As hospital employees, we can occasionally crash in the on-call rooms."

Elliott's determination to be upbeat spilled onto Hadley, and she nodded. "Yeah, it'll be an adventure, but hopefully campers in tents aren't the soft tacos of the bear world."

Elliott chuckled. "Nah. More like hot pockets, but only if we can get the tent set up and don't end up sleeping on top of it."

With a smile on and her attitude adjusted, Hadley gave Elliott a quick hug. "We can make this work. If anyone asks, we'll say we're trying to be closer to nature."

"Absolutely," Elliott said. "We'll find a good, pretty spot and do what we do best — make do with what we have." Elliott stretched her back. "What's the latest on Chloe?"

"Her official diagnosis, the one the doctor wrote down, is regressive apraxia due to trauma and stress, possibly selective mutism." She shrugged. "The doctor isn't sure what's going on, but he's covering all the bases so the insurance company is less likely to balk at covering the therapy she needs. The tests show no sign of head trauma, so that's not the cause. But the bottom line is she still isn't speaking. So we have to deal with it as a speech issue to the best of our ability. She'll get a referral, and the staff is looking for a clinic that will accept their insurance. It can't be just Chloe and me anymore. She has to be checked out, and we have to follow the doctor's guidelines."

"You're okay with this plan?"

"Sure. Even though Alan is angry with me for pushing Jason his way, he and Kate asked if I could go with Chloe to the clinic and work with her as a volunteer."

"If my work schedule allows it, I'll come too, as moral support for you, and maybe we can use that time to talk some sense into Alan."

7

Monroe stared at the list in his hand, disbelief sandblasting his emotions. The paper shook. Were his hands trembling, or was his head swimming? He didn't know, but one or the other was happening. Maybe both.

"Something wrong?" Trent's somewhat monotonous voice broke Monroe's concentration. The tall medical researcher was leaning against the doorframe of Monroe's spacious office.

When had Hadley returned to North Carolina? Monroe released the breath he'd been holding since he saw her name. Hadley. Coming to his clinic? What were the odds? This clinic, Children's Therapy, was in Weaverville, a small town ten miles north of Asheville. For the past two years, he'd lived on the outskirts of the city limits, not too far from work. Was she living in Asheville again and he'd just not seen her? His apartment was near the clinic, and he spent all his time at work, so perhaps it was possible. He set the paper on his desk so Trent couldn't see his hands shaking.

Could her visit be canceled at this point? He always checked the list of volunteers several days before they were scheduled to arrive. Every single time. So why hadn't he done so this time? Hadley's expressive brown eyes and beautiful face flashed in his mind. She usually had a smile despite her circumstances, and her gorgeous curly-brown hair ran the length of her back. Of course, Monroe had no idea if she still looked like that, because he hadn't seen her in almost ten years.

His parents had told him the charges were dismissed, and he'd thanked God for good lawyers. The last he'd heard about Hadley, she'd disappeared with her former boy-friend, Kyle, and she'd taken Elliott with her. The incident was scandalous — two underage teens fleeing the courthouse after dismissal of a case and under the nose of social services.

He'd known Hadley would find someone else. It was inevitable the moment he broke up with her and walked away, but he hadn't expected it to happen within weeks.

"Monroe?" Trent called.

"Oh." He jolted out of the past. "Did you already approve the volunteer coming in for today's session with Chloe Powell? H-Hadley Granger?" Monroe's heart rate increased as he stumbled over Hadley's name.

"Yep. Approving her seemed like a no-brainer. She works for Mission Health in Asheville, and the hospital provided her background check and vouched for her as a good worker."

"The background check was fine?"

"Of course. I wouldn't have approved it otherwise."

Monroe nodded, trying to wrap his head around the facts. If the background check on Hadley was clean, she hadn't been arrested since her case was dismissed. That was good.

Trent flipped through a file. "Hadley is working on her master's in communication sciences and disorders."

After all that happened during her senior year of high school and her escape afterward, if she had this much schooling under her belt at twenty-seven, she'd clearly settled down at some point, and his parents had apparently kept their side of the bargain. But if she worked here, even for a day, he'd be breaking his side of it. They could stop paying for Hadley's schooling, and he would be in breach of his junior partnership agreement. Even though he hadn't heard from Hadley since she left with Kyle, his parents had included in the junior partnership agreement that he could not hire her or have her in this clinic in any capacity. He'd signed it two years ago, and it hadn't been hard to do. She'd been gone from his life too long for him to hesitate. Fortunately no one but his parents and he would have a reason to read that mortifying part of the legal document.

"You're frowning, but free help is free help, right?" Trent gave a thumbs-up.

Monroe smothered the urge to whack his coworker and friend with the heavy scheduling notebook. Not that it would likely hurt, since the man was built like a large brick wall.

"Well, she isn't going to work as a volunteer here. Please give her a call and cancel."

"I've already put her on the schedule. For like thirty minutes from now."

"You what?"

"Remember when we met to discuss the workload and talked about the situation with the Powell family?"

"Of course. What's that case got to do with this volunteer?"

"The parents specifically requested Hadley. And I get the feeling you're not going to like this next piece of news, but all of them — the family and Hadley — are already here, waiting in the lobby. Someone involved with the Powells found a facility that would accept them and their insurance, and that place is your place." Trent chuckled. "You agreed to all of this, remember?"

The urge to smack Trent with the binder returned. Monroe typically liked Trent but not so much right now. Monroe rubbed his temples, but that would do nothing to avert the massive headache that would soon crawl up the back of his neck like a snake. "I remember. You read the info, and I listened and approved, but Hadley's name didn't come up. You clearly said 'Haley Powell.' "

Trent blinked. "Did I?"

"Yes."

"Sorry." Trent walked to the desk and flipped through the thick stack of papers that had come through with this case. "I'd logged too many hours on research and became name blind, I guess. The mom is Kate Powell. The speech therapist volunteer is Hadley Granger, not Haley Powell."

"Uh, yeah, I'm clear on that now. Thanks."

"Look, it was an innocent mistake. But whatever her name, we can't deny that her

grades, volunteer work, and recommenda-
tions are worthy of her being here."

Monroe sighed. "I'll adjust."

"Good." Trent left the small office and
headed toward the front entryway, no doubt
to greet the new patient, family, and volunteer that were apparently a package deal.

Trent usually knew what he was doing.
Monroe had met him the first Sunday Trent
stepped into Vista Springs Church. Single,
mid- to late-twenties guys in church were
sort of odd men out, so Monroe struck up
a conversation, hoping to make him feel
welcome. As it turned out, they hit it off.

As a doctor focusing on research, Trent
had a grant to study the field of childhood
apraxia. When Monroe told him about
Children's Therapy and the kind of work
they did, Trent's eyes grew wide, and he said
that Monroe's clinic was on his need-to-
contact list. A lot of clinics didn't want to
participate in the research because it meant
they had to open all records to Trent, and
many were poor record keepers who'd
rather not be scrutinized.

Trent asked if he could log some hours at
the clinic, accessing the clinic's records and
helping out a day or two a week to get
hands-on experience. Monroe pushed the
paperwork through, and here Trent was

until his yearlong study was finished in seven months. It was rare for a doctor to work at a therapy clinic, and rather than griping at the man, Monroe should be grateful to him. Having someone with Trent's education on site had given Monroe new insights into how seemingly unrelated medical issues can influence speech problems.

Monroe took a deep breath, stood up from his office chair, and followed him. Perhaps after touring the facility, the patient's parents could be convinced to do therapy without Hadley as a volunteer. Children's Therapy had several exceptional speech therapists. But how could he even suggest that idea with Hadley touring with the Powells? He shoved his hands into his pockets. A small part of him wanted to run to the lobby to catch a glimpse of Hadley. It was good news to know she'd pulled her life together and was getting her master's. That'd been her dream for as long as he'd known her. As it turned out, he'd been influenced by their time as volunteers in this field, and he'd gotten his degrees in communication sciences and disorders also, plus he had a master's in business.

More important for the issue at hand, could they remain professional around each other? Would she yell? From her perspective he was the jerk who broke up with her minutes before she was handcuffed and taken to jail. She could've been over him completely inside of a few months and still feel the need to rip him apart for leaving her as he had. What could he say in response? *It just looked that way, Hads. Actually I'm the reason you're now educated.* Yeah, that would go over well. Besides, it would break his agreements with his parents while it made him sound like a self-righteous moron.

He caught up to Trent, and they passed through the double doors separating the lobby and the therapy rooms, and there she was. He saw her, and for a moment nothing else seemed to matter. She was in the center of the lobby, crouched to the level of the small child she was talking to. The sunlight coming through the all-glass front of the building framed Hadley's now shoulder-length curly hair in light, making natural highlights stand out from the dark-brown ringlets. Her skin seemed to glow in the morning light as she made a silly face, trying to get the child to laugh. She looked more stunning than he'd imagined her, which was often, despite his great efforts to forget her over the years.

She looked up. Her fun-loving, goofy face and smile disappeared instantly. Color drained from her cheeks as she stood, her honey-brown eyes meeting his.

What could he say? *I'm sorry. Can we talk privately? Can we just pretend we don't know each other?*

Trent moved forward. "Welcome. I'm Trent, a medical researcher and part-time staffer. How is everybody this morning?"

Monroe heard the child's parents greet Trent. But Monroe couldn't budge, couldn't remove his focus from Hadley.

"This is my boss, Monroe Birch. He runs the facility and is going to help Chloe get all set up. Coming from the city, you probably were in a hospital setting. You'll find that Children's Therapy feels a lot more like a family practice."

Having Trent introduce him forced Monroe to look past Hadley. It was then that he truly saw his newest young client with her family. And Elliott. It was bad enough to have to face Hadley, but Elliott too? Evidently they were still thick as thieves because there was no other reason for her to be here. She wasn't on the volunteer roster.

He stepped forward and smiled. Chloe was now clinging to her father's leg, and Monroe waved and smiled, knowing better than to try to immediately engage the scared preschooler. "Good to meet you." He shook Kate's and Alan's hands. "I'm glad you're here." And he was. The information regarding what had happened to the family had tugged at his heart. "I think you'll love our place. We have fun, but we also get things done." He gestured to the hall where the therapy rooms were located. "I'll actually let Trent start the tour while I talk to our volunteer and her friend. Then we'll meet up and get started with your therapist. Sound good?"

The parents nodded in agreement, and Trent gave an after-you gesture toward the double doors. "This exciting tour starts with an important place — the restroom. We have a room outfitted for small children . . ." Trent's dry speech faded as the family walked with him into the hallway.

"Monroe." Elliott's voice was flat and yet somehow accusatory as her green eyes pierced him.

Hadley studied the floor, her features set with a hardness he'd seen before.

"I'm sorry," Monroe spoke softly. "Believe me, I didn't know that you were the volunteer today. This shouldn't have happened."

"So you would have denied Hadley the opportunity to help?" Elliott raised an eyebrow, and before Monroe could respond, she continued. "We checked the website for this place, and if the link to the page that listed you as a therapist had actually worked, we wouldn't be here. I'd rather have driven the seven hours to the Hyde County facility that also takes the Powells' insurance."

He ignored Elliott's anger. She believed he'd fainted from the heat of what was happening to Hadley and had left.

"I'll look into getting that link fixed. Thanks for letting me know." Did he sound as professional as he hoped? "But clearly you agree it would be best if you weren't here."

Surely Hadley was as uncomfortable with this situation as he was.

"But we're both here and not leaving," Elliott said. "I simply needed to run some errands, so I drove, and I only came inside to be sure everyone was situated before I left . . . but I've decided to stay." She held up her hand. "No invitation necessary."

He didn't recall Elliott being sassy and difficult. She'd been mostly a silent observer ten years ago. Clearly not anymore.

"No." Hadley's quiet response sent chills down his spine. She looked up, meeting Monroe's eyes again. The anger of her youth seemed less intense, but it wasn't gone.

"Chloe needs me. We're medical professionals. We can be impartial for her sake."

Monroe didn't respond immediately. Could they really? Could he ever think of Hadley, much less look at her, without imagining what their lives would have been like had she not stepped foot on the Reeds' property — whether she'd set the fire to help or to hurt? Would he own Children's Therapy if they had remained together? Certainly not by age twenty-seven. As the years went by after the incident, he had justified in his mind the deal he'd made with his parents by telling himself Hadley and he wouldn't likely have made it as a couple anyway. They'd been in high school, for Pete's sake! Also, by taking the deal his parents offered, he was able to help so many more low-income children like Chloe.

"I agree." Did Monroe sound as stilted and uncomfortable to them as he did to himself? "Or at the least we need to give it a try, but I make no guarantees."

Elliott opened her mouth to say something, but she closed it, folded her arms, and barely shook her head. A moment later she smiled, looking in control like a well-trained professional. "Thank you."

She'd never liked him, but she'd been reserved and respectful in the past. Apparently that was a challenge this morning. It seemed to him she would love to speak her mind, even if it meant being confrontational. His guess was if they weren't in this professional setting, she would gladly tell him all of what she thought.

He gestured down the hallway. "I'm going to join our new clients. You need to check in with HR and fill out some paperwork."

He quickly turned and strode away from Hadley.

Just like before.

8

Elliott stood behind Hadley, watching her in the mirror above the sink. The sound of Hadley's sobs tore at Elliott's heart. Hadley's bag, filled with toys and puppets for working with Chloe, sat on the floor, looking as droopy and dejected as Hadley felt.

How deep this old wound was for her dear friend. Monroe had just treated them as if they were second-class citizens, unworthy of coming into his precious clinic despite their education and skills. Truth was, to people like Monroe, she and Hadley *were* second class, and that was true of them even if Hadley hadn't been arrested.

She rubbed Hadley's shoulders. "Sh, Hads. Get a grip. Don't give him the satisfaction of hearing you cry."

Hadley turned on the water, filled her hands, and splashed it on her face. "I don't know what's wrong with me." Her usually confident voice shook. "I *know* I didn't do anything wrong. But I still feel like the unworthy interloper. How on earth did we end up coming to a therapy center that *he* owns?"

"I'm not sure, but temptation is giving me a dozen ideas per minute to make this connection worth my time." Elliott grinned. "However, my resulting court case would not be dismissed because of evidence that I was innocent."

Hadley laughed, her tears flowing harder.

"Kidding aside, Hads, the man hasn't had an original idea in his entire life. You were the one with this dream, and he simply got Mommy and Daddy to buy it for him." Elliott pulled two paper towels from the holder and held them toward Hadley. "*You* aren't unworthy at all. You have worked hard for your bachelor's degree, and you are talented at what you do. As for Monroe, it was inevitable that you would run into him somewhere, especially since you both ended up going into the same field."

Hadley wiped her face and dabbed her eyes with a paper towel. "If Tara hadn't had an apartment with two extra rooms, and if the hospital hadn't been hiring entry-level workers, I never would have returned to Asheville."

Elliott rubbed Hadley's back. "If we'd

stayed in Georgia, you wouldn't have gotten the scholarship. And if we were living there, what would have happened to Chloe and Jason?"

"True." Hadley straightened herself and brushed off her clothes, staring at their reflections in the mirror. "We can do this, right?" Hadley's eyes filled with tears again.

"Of course we can. He's all smoke and mirrors, Hads. He owns nothing other than opinions. Wrong ones."

"That's not all he owns." Hadley gestured at the room.

Elliott looked around the immaculately clean restroom decorated with framed art by children, somehow looking both professionally styled and child friendly. In the spacious room there was a smaller toilet for toddlers in addition to the standard-size one, a changing table equipped for an older child with special needs, and both a hand dryer and paper towels, to accommodate sensory-processing disorders.

Owning something like this was Hadley's dream, and she could've built it into a place that made a huge difference for the under-privileged. But that was a pipe dream.

Elliott was weary of this mood. She reached into her purse and pulled out her tiny pink iPod nano that one of her coworkers had given to her after upgrading to a smartphone. Elliott scrolled down the playlist until she found the song she had in mind. She plugged in the earbuds and stuck one in her ear and one in Hadley's. "Not only *can* we do it, but we'll teach Mr. Know It All how very little he knows."

Kelly Clarkson belted out the words to "Mr. Know It All," and soon Hadley was singing softly with Elliott, "But I ain't laying down, baby, I ain't going down."

They danced a few soft steps, singing with Kelly.

When the song ended, Hadley grinned. "Let's do this." She tossed the paper towels into the trash and opened the door.

Elliott picked up Hadley's bag full of items for working with Chloe. "Maybe when Chloe's better and you've graduated, we could move to the coast." Elliott followed her out the door. "I want sand, sun, and the sound of waves."

"Road trip to the beach?" Trent asked. His monotone voice didn't match his lighthearted expression. "Think they'd notice if we all cut out early?" Trent leaned in as if he were attempting to keep a secret.

Elliott chafed when men invited themselves to be a part of something. "I think they'd notice but nice try."

Trent had to be the tallest man she'd seen in a month, and as she studied him, something about him seemed vaguely familiar.

He smiled. "Hadley needs to stop by HR now, because that has to be done before she can engage with Chloe."

"Lead the way." Elliott gestured.

When Hadley slipped into the HR office, Trent turned to Elliott. "Do I look familiar to you?"

"No." She shrugged. "Maybe?"

He pursed his lips sideways, looking a bit amused. "We should have a cup of coffee sometime and discuss it."

"No thanks, and to save time you can make that an across-the-board answer."

"Direct much?"

"Very." She started walking back to the lobby to wait for Hadley and the Powells. Maybe he would get the hint and go back to whatever he should be doing.

He fell into step with her. "We could brainstorm ideas."

"About?"

"Ways to help Monroe and Hadley deal with whatever past they have so Chloe benefits."

She stopped abruptly.

He smiled. "Ah, I have your attention."

"Open much?"

"With my thoughts and feelings? Very. With conversations spoken in private? Not at all."

She liked the idea of coming up with ways to lift some of the emotional baggage off Hadley's shoulders, but no amount of brainstorming would fix much. Still . . .

"One coffee." She held up her index finger. Why was she agreeing to this? Men were trouble. All of them. Not that she'd experienced it personally since her dad abandoned her, but she'd seen the fallout of their being in women's lives. Men said all the right things until the moment they disappeared.

He held up one finger, smiling and nodding as if in full agreement. "French Broad Chocolate tomorrow afternoon at one?"

"Sure." She shrugged, resigned to what she'd agreed to. "Why not?"

Hadley straightened herself as she walked down the hall toward the therapy rooms. Elliott was right: she was qualified to be here. She had stepped into the HR office and filled out her paperwork. The HR director had been positive enough when she had completed her paperwork for volunteer work. She was certain Monroe wouldn't mention why he didn't want her here.

Just focus on Chloe. She had been responding well to Hadley over the past two years. Any therapists worth their salt would respect that. Hadley just needed to ignore Monroe's presence and do her job. She shifted her "Mary Poppins" carpetbag on her shoulder. Elliott had gifted it to her last Christmas. It was a thrift-store find that resembled the magic bag the character used in the movie, and her friend thought it would be perfect for Hadley to carry her therapy toys and supplies.

She turned the corner and there *he* was, standing in front of the room she was supposed to go to. His blue eyes caught hers, and for a moment she thought they softened before he refocused and glanced down at paperwork attached to a clipboard.

"Looks like it's almost time to begin. We are going to try this, but I still feel it might be best if you let us take this from here. You get Chloe comfortable and then let her work with our therapists. We'll take good care of her." He glanced up, and she saw a tiny echo of the smile he used to give her, a smile she still saw sometimes when she closed her eyes at night.

Dozens of emotions rushed through her. Embarrassment at seeing Monroe somewhere unexpected. Frustration at herself for still being affected enough to cry over him. Relief that she would get to work with Chloe despite his owning the center. And anger that he had the power in this setting where she longed to be an equal.

She pushed down the conflicting thoughts and nodded. *Professional.* "Just let me do my job." She walked past Monroe and into the therapy room. It was a typical speech therapy room — small with minimal decorations to avoid distractions and a video camera in an upper corner. A wall had an insert of one-way glass, probably so other therapists and perhaps parents could watch the sessions. Chloe wasn't here yet, but the therapist was.

"Hi, I'm Rebecca." The woman in her midforties with bobbed brown hair extended her hand to shake Hadley's. "I'll be Chloe's speech therapist." She glanced at the information in her three-ring binder. "You're Hadley, correct?"

"Yes, ma'am." Hadley tried to focus only on the moment and not the fact that most likely Monroe was watching her, either with the camera or through the one-way glass.

"How exciting to have one of Chloe's friends join in and a fellow professional no less."

"I've been working with Chloe for a

couple of years, and I appreciate being allowed to be here with her now."

"Well, I think it could be really beneficial for her. With selective mutism, which might be one of the issues Chloe is facing, the root of the problem is anxiety."

Hadley nodded. "Will we approach the issue differently since Chloe's had speech issues in the past?"

"As you know, this case is very unusual. There's no way to know what the root cause is: regression with apraxia or trauma due to the fire or a mixture of both. But just as we would do with any other speech therapy patient, we'll hone our methods based on how well she responds. Our goal for this first session will be simply to play games with Chloe. We won't ask her to speak. We'll do nothing that will remind her of the fire. She needs to be completely at ease."

"I brought something Chloe and I have played with before." Hadley shifted her carpetbag forward.

Rebecca raised her eyebrows. "Ooh, therapy toys always pique my interest."

"I sewed these guys, mostly out of repurposed toys from Goodwill. Meet Patch Mishmash and Merri Go-round." Hadley lifted out two puppets.

Rebecca pretended to peek inside the

carpetbag. "Do you also have a lamp, a mirror, and a coatrack in there?"

"What?" Hadley tried to think what purpose those items would serve in this session.

"I just need to know if you actually took Mary Poppins's bag."

Hadley laughed, and it felt really good. Rebecca did too, and Hadley noticed the door opening and Chloe's shy blue eyes peeking inside, most likely to see what was going on that made two grown women laugh.

9

The sidewalk under Elliott's feet seemed as hard as the suspicion that raged in her head. Still, hope kept nudging her onward. The afternoon sun warmed her shoulders. Her navy-blue-and-red-plaid dress absorbed the late-afternoon September heat, maybe a bit too much. But it was better than showing up for something in scrubs. She wore them way too much, whether grocery shopping or taking a stroll around the block. This change felt good. The tops of her cowboy boots touched the bottom of the dress. Perhaps she should have opted for tennis shoes. It wasn't a date, after all. Just a chat over coffee.

After ten days of camping, she thought it was a miracle she didn't look like a vagabond. But she and Hadley were skilled at making do and looking as if all was fine, and it was. Camping out wasn't a hardship. They had places to eat and shower and a

Laundromat nearby, and the weather was gorgeous in the fall.

She maneuvered around people. Why was this part of Asheville always so crowded? The thrum of a slightly out-of-tune guitar came from somewhere, perhaps a desperate musician playing for spare change. If so, he should consider spending a few bucks on new strings. The aroma of caramel apples rode on the air as she squeezed by a group of young women, probably tourists, clogging up the sidewalk in front of the candy shop. She smiled to herself at their giggles and arms full of shopping bags. Elliott hurried by and turned the corner, finally seeing the sign for her destination: French Broad Chocolate Lounge.

Trent was standing by the door, impossible to miss. Was he more than six and a half feet tall? At five eight she wasn't a short woman, but Trent towered over her.

"Hi, Elliott. Glad you could make it." If he was glad, it wasn't apparent in his voice, which Elliott was beginning to suspect was monotone by default.

"Thanks. I've often walked by here, but I have to be the only local never to have been inside. The name always sounded intriguing." And expensive, but she wouldn't tell him that part.

Trent chuckled. "Chocolate plus coffee does equal awesome." He opened the door to the building and held it for Elliott.

She ducked inside. The fragrance of chocolate and fresh-roasted coffee beans hit her like a wave. "Whoa, that smells amazing." She took a deep breath of the exquisite aroma as she walked into the crowded space. "The line, however, looks less appetizing." People were snaked throughout the small space, some checking their phones, some talking among themselves, and others looking at the lengthy menu.

"Yeah, crowds are pretty much the routine downtown on weekends, especially in the fall but year-round really."

Trent's voice kept the same uniform tone. Did anything faze him? Could be a useful trait for a doctor, but it probably didn't matter much since his chosen field was research.

"I personally think it's okay. More time to talk up this pretty nurse I met."

Elliott narrowed her eyes, her pulse quickening. He was a charmer. She didn't usually appreciate that trait, but somehow he pulled it off, looking more endearing than conceited. "Where are you from, Trent?"

They scooted forward as the line advanced.

"Maryland, originally. But I've been in

North Carolina for a lot of years. You're from here, right? Lived in Georgia for a while and then returned?"

"Did Monroe tell you that?" Did Monroe even know what state they'd fled to ten years ago?

"No. Monroe's said nothing other than being caught off guard that Hadley was at the clinic yesterday."

"And so?" Elliott held both hands palms up.

"We met before when I was an intern at Mission Health. I think I even asked you out." The line moved, and they both stepped forward.

"You think?" She relaxed a bit, chuckling. "You ask out so many nurses that you're unsure if I was one of them?"

"Okay, fine. I know I did. But since you don't remember me, I was trying to keep some of my ego intact."

"Yes, I've noticed that ego is in short supply for interns, even more so for specialists and surgeons."

He laughed. "I bet you've experienced that."

Elliott had been asked out often enough over the years. With her shield in place, she'd stopped paying attention to who asked . . . or why. She and Hadley continued to keep their agreement of *no guys* until they finished their education and training. She studied him, trying to recall the voice. She should remember that voice and his height.

He shoved a hand into his jeans pocket. "So apparently my doctor friends with those inflated egos are as wrong as I figured. Nurses don't chase doctors, and they don't necessarily care that we ask them out."

Elliott pressed her lips together, attempting also to press down the irritation she felt at that particular stereotype. "I opted out of all that drama and nonsense before it began."

"I can respect that. Care to share why you feel that way?"

"I probably shouldn't, but I think too many women let too many men knock them off course, and I can't afford to be one of them."

"So you're a practical, licensed practical nurse."

"Yeah, I suppose I am. So how did you know I lived in Georgia for a while?"

"A group of employees in scrubs were on lunch together, sharing the same table."

She recalled that. It'd been really enjoyable. "Christmas Day, last year."

"Yeah, and we were talking about the various places we've visited."

"You're Gledhill. You were the only one at the table who had been to as few places as I had."

"That's me. World traveler extraordinaire."

She laughed. "Or not."

"Or not." He nodded. "My childhood didn't go as my parents had hoped. Serious illness. Loads of medical bills. Job losses. You know how it is. Or maybe you don't. Anyway, when I'm making some money, I hope to take my folks and my sister on the trips they didn't get to do for us." He shrugged. "If their health is where they can go."

"Yes." She nodded.

"Yes?" He seemed confused.

"I'll go out for coffee with you, today actually."

He chuckled. "Sorry. I'm no longer interested."

"And your schedule is entirely too tight for you to step in line at a good coffee place."

"Exactly." He shook his finger, chuckling. "I knew when I first saw you that you were a smart —"

"If you say *cookie,* I'll buy one when we get to the counter and hit you with it."

"Can I eat it afterward?"

"Sure. Eat it. Choke on it. Either will be fine."

He'd yet to stop chuckling. "I was going to say *woman.*"

She believed him. "Sure you were."

He held up both hands. "I've never called any woman a cookie, and I wouldn't dare start with one that Monroe is leery of."

"Is he wary of me?"

"Yeah."

"He may be smarter than I give him credit for."

"You don't like him."

"Fellow Christians frown on not liking people, so let's stick to I don't have a fond appreciation of his type."

"His type?"

"Persuasive. Rich. Powerful. Full of promises he's willing to break whenever it suits him."

"Monroe?" Trent's monotone voice clearly held disbelief. "I'm not sure you have the right guy. He seems like a good guy to me. He works long hours, and when he says he'll do something, he does it."

They were next in line. A moment later Trent stepped forward. After ordering a pot of French press coffee to split and two slices of different types of chocolate cake, they sat down at an empty table near the window.

She watched people walking on the sidewalk. Was Trent's viewpoint right, or was hers? Her disgust with Monroe ran pretty deep, and she couldn't hold a conversation with Trent as if it didn't.

"You know, I don't think I can offer any ideas or solutions where it concerns Monroe. This was a waste of your time." She rose. "Sorry."

"Elliott, come on. It's not a waste of time." He gestured toward her chair. "Please."

She stood there, wavering, feeling as if she were in that parking lot again, the one where her dad told her she would be fine and to trust him — right before he drove off and left her. Why was that nagging at her now?

Trent looked up. "We don't have to talk about Monroe and Hadley. We could talk about anything. Like the other day, when my three-year-old nephew was told to pee in a cup at the doctor's office. He unexpectedly got nervous. With a shaking voice he asked, 'Do I have to drink it?' "

She wasn't sure she even smiled at his joke, but she sat. Neither said anything, and Elliott felt she owed him some kind of explanation. "I'm not good at this, Trent. I'm guarded and opinionated."

"And loyal, smart, and gifted with an amazing rapport with patients."

"What?"

"I saw you in motion at Mission Health."

"That's a little creepy."

"Nah. I just caught glimpses of you. No stalker stuff involved."

She could feel herself staring at him, but who was this guy?

A coffee shop worker put their food and coffee on the table and took the metal marker. Trent thanked him and then pushed the plunger of the French press a little too fast, spilling some of the hot, dark liquid on the table.

"I'm hitting this not-date out of the park." He blinked. "That was sarcasm."

Elliott grabbed some napkins to mop up the mess. "I know."

He poured a cup and passed it to her.

She stared into the dark liquid. "I was a foster kid." She made herself look up. How else was she to know his reaction?

Trent poured himself a cup of coffee. "I'm not sure what to say to that."

"Thank you."

He looked at her.

"That was the best possible answer," Elliott said. "No pity. No horror. No assumption you owe me an apology." She breathed a sigh of relief. "I've never told anyone that before."

His dark-brown eyes seemed to reflect pleasure in the conversation. "I like that you told me and that I gave an appropriate answer. That may not happen again, but I'd like to hear more if you're comfortable with it."

"We were both foster kids, Hadley and I. We shared the same foster home and room for about three and a half years. We've been together since. She's as much my sister as if we were blood related. Tara, another former foster girl, is like a sister to us too, just one who lives about an hour from us. Anyway, the three of us went to high school with Monroe, and he and Hadley were an item. It didn't end well." She needed to change the subject while she was still ahead because she was tempted to say negative things about Monroe. "Did you know that only ten percent of foster children graduate from college?"

"I didn't, but I knew it was lower than average."

"Hadley and I made an agreement: no boyfriends until after graduation."

"Well, lucky for me you have now graduated, right?"

"No, actually. My goal is to be an RN.

Maybe even a nurse practitioner. But I had to settle for an LPN for now because I needed to go to work full-time."

"*That* I understand — the need to work. But with one college graduation under your belt, you could consider yourself graduated, and then we could relax about it and date."

She opened her mouth to argue.

He put his hands up in surrender. "I'm just kidding. My voice doesn't have a lot of emotional range, as you can tell."

"I find your voice calming and soothing." Elliott also found him amusing. He was entirely too confident with women, and that was scary, but he seemed genuine, and he was entertaining. "But you were only half joking."

He dipped his head, scratching a brow with his thumbnail, looking a bit resigned at being called out. "Actually . . . less than half."

She chuckled. "Another good answer."

"I'm stopping while I'm ahead. I'm not saying another word. Can't make me. I'm fantastic at shutting up when I'm ahead. Yes sirree. That's me. Mr. Silence. I was just telling myself the other day how great I was at being quiet."

"Trent?" She ate a bite of her truffle-like cake, which was delicious.

"Yeah?"

"Could you shut up shuttin' up?"

"Bugs Bunny!" He dug his fork into the cake in front of him. "Do you know how few people our age even recognize that reference?"

"Uh, is this you when you've shut up?"

He laughed and took a bite of cake. "Oh, wow, try this cake." He held a forkful out for her and moved it around, gesturing for her to eat it.

"You have no issue with being annoying, do you?"

"Sometimes I do." He pushed the plate toward her. "Now take a bite."

She used her fork to scoop some cake from an untouched corner. "Mm. That is pretty amazing." She chewed the fluffy cake, which was also chocolate, though very different from her slice. "Can't beat mine though."

"Oh, really? You're going to share?"

"I'm considering it." Her cheeks ached a little from smiling. She passed her small plate to him.

"Really good."

She relaxed, and the conversation veered.

They swapped funny stories about working at the hospital, and they talked about their struggles and victories in anatomy and biology classes.

When they were finished, they left the café, never pausing in conversation as they walked. The day was warm, but the air was light and filled with the aroma of fall. The buildings that lined the streets of the village were artistic and charming, regardless of whether they were old or more recent. All were part of the appeal of Asheville. They entered Pritchard Park and sat down on a bench surrounded by trees that were hinting at their future fall beauty. Their conversation skipped and jumped, but it didn't ever turn dull. When the air grew cooler, she realized the afternoon was slipping into evening.

She pulled her phone from her pocket. "It's going on six. Oh, my goodness." She stood. "I need to go. I'm sure you do too."

He stood. "So . . . I know this is not a date and all, and I wouldn't dream of suggesting we go on one, but do you think you'd like to share some coffee and food again next Friday? Maybe walk around downtown? They have a music festival after five on the third Friday of each month, which just happens to be next Friday. It could be fun. We can take a walk downtown, maybe taste a few types of local brews . . . coffee brews."

Elliott suppressed a smile at his coffee af-finity. "Maybe, although we've talked so much that I'm not sure there's anything else to say."

"Good, because the point is to listen to music. Could I . . . pick you up after I fin-ish at the therapy center on Friday?"

"We're getting awfully close to date terri-tory."

Trent made a halo circle over his head with his hands, and she broke into a chuckle despite herself.

"Fine." Elliott shrugged.

"Yes!" Trent beamed. "You won't regret it. You'll be fine with the outing. Trust me."

The words jerked her back through time, and she was suddenly a gullible eight-year-old kid, staring into her dad's face as he told her the same thing — "You'll be fine. Trust me." — right before he disappeared, shattering her life. It wasn't a good sign that Trent reminded her of that shiftless man, who hadn't been responsible enough even to take her to a safe place before abandon-ing her.

"I . . . I'm sorry." Tears stung her eyes. "I can't do this." She clutched his arm. "It's not you. But . . . I can't."

Without waiting for him to reply, she walked off.

■ ■ ■ ■

Monroe blinked, exhaustion burning his eyes as he, yet again, looked at the therapists' schedules. It was stupid of him to have tossed and turned last night, especially after a fairly relaxing weekend. Why couldn't his subconscious be as logical as his waking mind?

Monroe saw Trent pass the office door. "Trent?" he called.

He tried to quell some of the annoyance in his voice. Maybe Trent had forgotten to adjust the schedules. After all, the discussion they had regarding this was on Friday afternoon. Perhaps he just hadn't gotten to it yet.

"Yeah, boss?"

"I'm looking at the schedule for the week, and I still see Hadley for Tuesday and Friday. I thought I was pretty clear when we talked after the session on Friday that continuing to use her as a volunteer wasn't going to work."

"Yeah, about that . . ." Trent walked into the office and tapped on the paper with the printed schedules, his finger hitting Hadley's name. "You can't let your personal baggage keep Chloe from getting help."

Irritation flared. Monroe recalled seeing Trent talking with Elliott in the hall of the center. "Did you have a conversation with Elliott about it?"

"I did, in fact, have *a* conversation with Elliott. She said that the three of you went to the same high school. That you and Hadley were an item and that it didn't end well. That's all I know, but it's enough to deduce you have to let this go, man."

"We will give Chloe more than adequate care without Hadley being a helicopter over her. Do you doubt our facility?" Monroe shook the roster. They were doing just fine before Hadley arrived. Surely Trent could see that.

"Of course not. I just know from reading Chloe's file that the poor girl needs every bit of help we can give her to start talking again. If Hadley's bond with her can speed that along, can't you give up whatever is bothering you about that past fling?"

"It wasn't a fling." Why had he said that out loud? He shook himself before his mind led him down the path of painful memories. "It's a good thing that Hadley has been successful so far in school and in her career. You'd never understand how happy I am about that. But she can't be here at this facility."

"Why?"

Monroe sighed. What could he say to quickly put this conversation in the past and get Trent to drop it? "What's said here stays here."

Trent nodded. "Okay." He closed the office door.

"At seventeen Hadley was in a really bad legal situation. I made a deal with my parents concerning several things Hadley needed, a very skilled lawyer for one. The trade-off was I agreed not to see Hadley again. And I signed contracts that are tied to this clinic. Her being here compromises the agreement."

"Monroe." Trent looked sympathetic. "That's hard, man."

"I'm not looking for sympathy. My point is she can't be here."

"Maybe you should tell her that straight up."

"No. She can't know anything about the whys or what fors."

"That's in the agreement too?"

Monroe nodded. But even if it weren't, there was nothing he could say to her that she would remotely believe.

"I've been around your parents a little, and I just don't think they would be so unreasonable that they couldn't understand this situation with Hadley is temporary. It's only so you can help Chloe in her progress."

Someone knocked on the door, and Trent opened it.

Rebecca stuck her head inside. "Do you still have the binder for Chloe?"

Monroe picked it up off his desk and held it out to her. Surely this professional he'd assigned to the case would have a more reasonable view on Hadley's volunteer work. "About Chloe . . ."

"Isn't she sweet?" Rebecca asked. "I just love her already."

"I was discussing with Trent that I don't think we need a volunteer for Chloe's sessions."

"That's ironic because I was about to tell you the exact opposite."

What? Monroe was outnumbered.

"Chloe is the first case our clinic has had of an absence of speech caused by a traumatic event. I feel it needs a name, even if only for our record-keeping purposes. It makes sense to call it ARI — Apraxia Regression Issue. Although she has an obvious history of apraxia, I believe this current issue is anxiety related, similar to selective mutism. All the diagnosis issues aside, it's an ideal situation for Hadley to be in the sessions with Chloe since she has such a great bond with Chloe and a history of working with her. Problem?"

"Not for me," Trent chimed in. "I think it's a brilliant plan, Rebecca."

It made sense to use anyone Chloe was comfortable with, but did it *have* to be Hadley? "Couldn't we use the parents instead as comfort people for her?"

Concern flickered across Rebecca's face as she shook her head. "There's something odd going on there. Chloe seemed more relaxed and at ease when it was just Hadley and me. We tried bringing in Mom and Dad, but Chloe shut down a little and just went back and forth between cuddling in her mama's and her dad's arms instead of continuing the games. I think we got lucky with this setup. If I were you, I'd consider offering Hadley a job when she graduates, before another clinic snatches her up."

Be polite. She doesn't know. Monroe forced a smile. "I'll keep that in mind."

10

Hadley pulled into a parking spot at Children's Therapy.

"Okay, sweet girl" — she looked at Chloe in the rearview mirror — "you ready to go play and work with Rebecca and me?"

Chloe, of course, didn't respond, but she was smiling.

Hadley removed the keys and sniffed the sleeve of her green flannel shirt. It didn't smell like a campfire. At least she didn't think it did. She and Elliott had tried to keep their clothes looking professional, despite the past two weeks of camping. *Clean clothes* didn't mean the same thing when one was camping. The aroma of musty woods and smoke tended to seep into fabric. What would Monroe think if he knew she and Elliott had been camping out since the fire? At least the fire gave them an excuse for being homeless. The apartment building was being repaired, but would she and Elliott be allowed to move back in, or would they be evicted?

This much she did know: she and Elliott had it better than a lot of people. Health strengthened them. Hope sustained them. And God guided them. Add the ability to get an education and to be flexible and patient in every circumstance, and it was a recipe for appreciating life for what it was — a beautiful, tough challenge.

She got out, walked around the car, opened the passenger side, and then leaned the seat down to reach Chloe's car seat so she could unbuckle her.

It didn't matter what Monroe thought. All she had to do was focus on helping Chloe, and when Chloe was done with Children's Therapy, she hoped she wouldn't have to see Monroe again for another decade. Or maybe ever if she was lucky. She'd managed to avoid running into him on Tuesday.

She lifted Chloe out and locked the vehicle. Thankfully Elliott didn't need the car, and Hadley would be free to enjoy an outing with Chloe after the session was over. She shifted her carpetbag onto her shoulder.

Chloe held Hadley's hand and skipped across the parking lot. Hadley smiled. It was a good sign that Chloe looked so relaxed. Perhaps today she could bring up a new game and bounce different consonant sounds off Rebecca. Hopefully Chloe would repeat the sounds, as she used to do for Hadley when they first worked together.

Her phone buzzed. She pulled it out of her pocket and flipped it open. Kate had texted her:

I appreciate your agreeing to keep Chloe for us after the session. We really need to look at apartments, and I'm so glad Chloe will be somewhere she is relaxed and having fun. Thanks!

Hadley hoped they'd find an apartment soon. The Red Cross had provided a place to stay for about a week, and after that several local churches had host members who'd given displaced families a place to live, but that was temporary too.

They walked inside the double doors. "Hold up just a sec, Chloe."

The girl skipped in place instead of going forward. Hadley smiled as she quickly sent back a text to Kate.

SOUNDS GOOD. GIVE ME A CALL WHEN YOU FINISH APARTMENT HUNTING, AND I'LL DROP CHLOE OFF.

153

THX. IT'LL BE A FEW HOURS. RECEPTION IS
IFFY WHERE WE ARE. I TEXTED YOU THE
SAME MESSAGE SEVERAL TIMES AND
RECEIVED "NOT DELIVERED" BEFORE THE
TEXT GOT THROUGH.

NO PROB.

Apparently Kate's reception around Asheville was as spotty as Hadley's. Hadley had always purchased the least expensive phone and plan possible, because the mountains tended to make good cell reception difficult no matter what cell carrier a person had. It shouldn't be an issue for a few hours though. She had packed Chloe's favorite snacks and planned a great day.

Hadley slid her phone back into her pocket and put her hand on Chloe's head. "We're gonna have fun at the zoo after our session with Miss Rebecca. I wonder what Chloe's favorite animal will be?" Using "I wonder" questions was a great technique for giving children with speech issues a chance to answer without creating stress by addressing them directly. Hadley had hoped to use other tips for gently coaxing Chloe to make sounds, maybe say a word or two, while at the Western North Carolina Nature Center, termed "the zoo" by Chloe after their first trip there eighteen months ago. "Let's go find Miss Rebecca's room." When Hadley turned, she was face-to-face with the man she would rather have avoided.

Monroe studied her, making Hadley feel as if she were under a microscope. "Can we talk for a moment?"

What now?

He leaned down to look at Chloe, and his face immediately glowed with warmth. "Hello." He smiled. "Rebecca is so looking forward to seeing you. She brought a new toy to play with. You ready?"

Chloe nodded. Still holding Chloe's hand, Hadley led her to the therapy room. She went inside and helped Chloe engage with Rebecca and the new toy keyboard shaped like a cat. "Chloe, I need to talk to Mr. Monroe, but I'll be back in a few minutes."

Chloe waved with one hand and pressed a few keys with the other, causing different meow sounds. When Hadley stepped into the hallway, Monroe was at the doorway of the viewing room that looked into the area where Rebecca and Chloe were. She measured her breathing and silently counted, trying to pull together her frazzled nerves. It annoyed her to feel this way before Monroe said anything, so she hoped he walked lightly.

They went inside the room and closed the door.

He smiled, but it looked strained and fake. "I really wish I didn't have to ask about this. But I was at the front desk when you entered the building, and please tell me I misheard about Chloe going with you somewhere after her session. Also I need you to say that Kate or Alan will be here to pick up Chloe after her session."

So that's what this was about. "The Powells and I are friends. You know that. I drove Chloe here today, and afterward I'm taking her to the nature center."

"But HR went over the rules with you that first day. Anyone can drop off or bring a child, but without written permission from the legal guardian, no one can leave with a child. I'm sorry, but I can't let you take any minor patient from this facility."

She laughed. "You're kidding, right?"

"I'm not."

She couldn't believe this. "But you know the circumstances. I've worked with Chloe for years. I was with them during their first visit."

He shifted. "I know I sound like a jerk, but Kate didn't give permission on the affidavit for you to leave with her. It's probably an oversight, and —"

156

"*Probably* an oversight? You think everyone distrusts me as much as you do?" Why had they ever been a couple? If he thought so little of her, what had drawn him to her to begin with?

He ducked his head and pursed his lips for a moment before regaining his professional stance. "No amount of trust would change the protocol that was established by lawyers, medical personnel, and insurance companies."

"Fine. Let's call her right now." Hadley flipped open her phone and dialed Kate's number. It rang twice and went to voice mail. She dialed the number again, and again it went straight to voice mail.

Monroe pulled out his phone from his pocket and scrolled the touch screen. The process took a while, and Hadley wondered how many contacts he had. He touched the screen and held the phone up to his ear.

"Voice mail," he mouthed to Hadley. "Hello, Kate. This is Monroe Birch at Children's Therapy. Chloe is fine. No problems at all. But I need you to verify who has permission to leave the clinic with her. Give me a call back when you get this." He moved the phone away from his ear, touched the screen to end the call, and slid it back in his pocket. He shrugged at Hadley. "I'll try again after Chloe's session is over."

"How about you look the other way today, and then Kate can verify with you at *her* convenience?"

"You signed papers in HR that state you'll follow all rules that govern this clinic. If I bent the rules and went against the protocols and then something happened — you got in a fender bender, Chloe fell and was injured, or Kate later objected to her leaving with you —"

"Martians invaded the planet."

"Please, Hadley. I'm telling you how it is, and your sarcasm is off the point. You like to think the rules don't apply to you, but they do."

Hard, unyielding, and obstinate. Those were words she never would have used to describe Monroe ten years ago, yet they sprang to mind now. Was this who he'd been the entire time?

"I shouldn't be surprised that's how you view me, but if you had a brain, you'd know how many ways I've experienced 'the rules' and the power of how they apply to me. And . . ." Hadley was ready to unload on him, but she made herself pause. She silently counted to three, calming herself. This wasn't about her or how Monroe viewed her. She was here for Chloe, Kate, and Alan. It's what friends did for each other, and she was strong enough to cope with Monroe in order to follow through for her friends.

She paused in her silent counting. "Do you know how difficult it is for parents like Kate and Alan to find time together so they can search for an apartment? Of course you don't." She gestured at his expensive clothes. "Alan works six days a week most weeks, sometimes seven. Kate stays home with Chloe but doesn't have a car. Alan's arranged to get today off so he and his wife can find a place to live before they have to move out of their temporary housing. Chloe isn't speaking because of an apartment fire, and the last thing they want to do is drag her from apartment to apartment as they search. Can you find an ounce of understanding for them?"

He took a deep breath, and Hadley readied herself for more arguments. "Well, there is one way."

Was this some sort of trick?

"You drive her to the nature center, and I will ride with you."

"And how does that solve the problem of unsigned forms? The rules don't apply to you too?"

He looked rather sheepish. "Kate filled

out the necessary forms."

Hadley raised both hands in the air. What on earth was his problem then?

He glanced at the floor and let out a sigh. "Uh, well, see, she put my name in the blank, and I'm well aware that she probably meant to put yours, but my hands are tied until we can reach her."

Hadley rolled her eyes. He had to make everything ridiculously impossible. "Next time how about you start with the info that doesn't add to my list of reasons you grate on my nerves? But okay. Maybe we'll get lucky and hear from Kate before the session is over."

He nodded.

She walked out and went toward Chloe's therapy room. She willed her heart rate to calm down, but her body wasn't listening to her. The last thing she wanted to do was spend the day with Monroe. The only silver lining would be that if he was part of the outing, he might recognize she could be trusted with Chloe.

But could he ever trust her when he obviously felt she was unworthy?

From inside his office Monroe watched the monitor that fed from Chloe's therapy room. Hadley and Rebecca were talking back and forth in a series of funny noises. Earlier in the session Hadley had defined a few syllables as part of "fairy language."

"Sa sa!" Hadley was holding a doll with wings, making the toy wave excitedly.

"Ooh, that means 'how are you?' in fairy." Rebecca was holding another doll. "I'm going to respond with a *pa pa,* and that means 'having fun.' Pa pa, pa pa."

"Pa."

Was that Chloe? Monroe turned up the volume. If it was, that was the first sound Monroe had heard her make. According to her records it was the first sound she'd spoken since the fire.

"Pa pa pa pa!" Hadley and Rebecca made their dolls say, pretending they were flying around.

Chloe lifted her doll too. "Pa pa!"

Chills covered him, and he smiled. Finally a victory. Approximately ten out of every one thousand children had apraxia, so it wasn't rare, but selective mutism due to trauma — if that was Chloe's issue — was almost unheard of. That meant the therapists had no data to rely on, no set protocols to follow, and no expectation of what normal progress would be.

Would Chloe be this far along without her bond to Hadley, who had continued to work with her? He doubted it. He checked the time. The session should have been over five minutes ago. He touched the contact on his phone and tried to reach Kate again. Voice mail. He stood, realizing that he better be waiting outside the therapy room when they finished, or Hadley might try to leave without him.

He hurried out of his office and down the hallway. It would be awkward to go along, but he couldn't risk ignoring the protocols established by the board. He had gone to college with a guy who ignored a rule once. Just once. A freak accident happened, and he lost his license.

He reached the room just in time apparently. Hadley and Chloe were already on their way out to the lobby. He followed them, feeling sillier by the step. This was his center, and somehow this student had invited herself in and overridden his authority.

But he really shouldn't expect any less of her. Her tenacity was one of the big things that had attracted him all those years ago. As irritating as the situation was, his heart was glad that this part of her personality had remained intact.

Finally she turned, giving him a small glance over her shoulder. "I take it you tried

Kate again and didn't reach her?"

"You can try calling if you want."

Without looking at him again, Hadley knelt on one knee next to the little girl. "Chloe, Mr. Monroe told me that he really wants to come to the zoo with us. Think that would be okay?"

Chloe's little blond brows knit together as she regarded Monroe. She shook her head as if to say *no.*

"I think a trip to the zoo would make him feel happier. He looks like someone who's never been to the zoo." Hadley looked him up and down, shrugging at Chloe.

Monroe glanced down at himself. Dark-gray dress pants, a blue dress shirt, and a gray-checkered tie were way too overdressed for working with children, but he'd had a board meeting earlier today and had arrived back at Children's Therapy a little before Chloe's appointment.

Hadley leaned in closer to the small child as if she were telling a secret. "I bet we could make him touch and feed the goats in the petting zoo, and then when he goes to eat whatever fancy dinner he's planning later, he will get hay on the floor."

"You don't know my plans, Hadley. I could be having a fancy dinner *with* goats."

Chloe seemed to be sizing him up to see

whether he would be fun or not.

"Mehhhhh." He made a goat noise for good measure.

She nodded at Hadley. Apparently he got a pass. For now at least.

11

Hadley slid the gearshift into Park mode, turned off the ignition, and quickly got out of the car. It took some self-control not to slam the door. No one in the vehicle had said a word on the twenty-five minute drive from Children's Therapy to the Western North Carolina Nature Center. Hadley couldn't bring herself to talk to the man who'd forced himself into their outing. Monroe probably thought himself above small talk, and Chloe was, of course, quiet.

Hadley had brought a CD of Chloe's favorite songs: the soundtrack from the movie *Tangled.* She'd intended to pop in the CD and encourage the little girl to dance in her car seat while Hadley sang along animatedly, the way they used to. But that was not going to happen with the ghost from her past sitting in the front seat of her Civic. Rapunzel had sung cheerily by herself from the car's speakers.

Hadley walked around the car to the passenger side so she could get Chloe out. Monroe was looking at his phone, but she needed to fold his seat down to get to Chloe in the back of the two-door vehicle. "Move, please."

He got out and dusted himself off, as if whatever was in her car had contaminated his nice clothes. She couldn't believe she had to spend several more hours with him. It was enough of a nightmare to have to enter his facility in order to work with Chloe.

She pulled the lever that released the front passenger seat and helped Chloe out.

"Mmm!" Chloe made an excited noise while pointing to the entrance of the nature center. She knew where they were.

"Zzzz." Hadley crouched in front of her. "Zzzooo."

Chloe nodded. "Shhh."

"Good try!" Hadley grinned, but it hurt to be back to ground zero with Chloe. They'd both worked so hard to make these simple sounds in the beginning. Hadley held Chloe's hand as she hit the lock inside the car door, put the keys in her pocket, and walked toward the entrance.

Monroe followed, but she wished she could ask him to wait outside. Wasn't it enough that he'd escorted them to the zoo? Did he have to encroach on their entire outing?

When they got to the entrance, he stepped in front of her and paid all three entry fees, the way a parent would for a child.

As Chloe entered the first building containing animals, Hadley turned around, making sure she was out of earshot of the little girl. "You know, I was prepared to get that."

"I'm aware. But I wanted to get it."

They walked through the different animal habitats, and Hadley pointed out features she thought Chloe would enjoy, even though they had been to the center in the past. They walked back outside to where the otters were housed. The otters had an outdoor rocky play area that was meant to look like the rocks in the streams that went all through the nearby mountains. Children of different ages cluttered the viewing areas, one located above the water and two that let children look through glass to see underwater. Chloe pulled Hadley and Monroe toward the glass to look at one of the underwater areas.

As they arrived at the viewing area, an otter jumped from his rock, swam through the almost-clear water, and slapped his little paws against the glass near their faces. Chloe gasped in surprise. The animal quickly repeated the trick, and Monroe acted as if the animal had scared him, holding his chest in mock terror. "He got me again! Chloe, you have to warn me before he comes back."

The otter repeated his action, and Monroe looked shocked. "Ah, not again!"

After a few minutes Chloe was giggling at this grown man being "startled" by an otter. A few older children nearby were looking at him as if he had lost his mind.

"Mmm." Chloe pointed to a red barn down the hill from them. Like many places in Asheville, the outdoor portions of the nature center were cut into the side of a steep hill, with paved walkways and boardwalks to the various animal exhibits. The light breeze blew Chloe's silky blond hair into her eyes, and Hadley brushed it away, tucking it behind the little girl's ears. Whatever his motivation, Monroe seemed to be trying to get Chloe to have fun, and her giggles were encouraging to Hadley. Maybe she should try to get the two to play longer.

"I think Chloe wants Mr. Monroe to have that fancy dinner with the goats now. Meh?" Hadley did her own version of a goat noise.

She glanced up at Monroe. Was he having a good time with Chloe or faking it?

Chloe nodded and took off toward the stairs to the lower terrace, where the petting area was located. Hadley hurried after her.

"Oh, you speak goat now as well as fairy?" Monroe kept in step with her.

"Not up to your standards, I'm sure." Who exactly was he?

"Maybe I can teach both of you to be fluent in goat, and in return I can learn fairy next time Chloe comes to play at the center. Deal?"

He, of course, was allowed to enter into any of the sessions at his center that he wanted, and Hadley didn't have much choice in the matter. Was he saying he didn't trust her in that area either, even with a licensed and well-experienced therapist like Rebecca in the room?

Before she could answer her own question, Chloe reached up and grabbed Hadley's hand and Monroe's hand so she could bounce down the steps and they could swing her in the air. Once they reached the bottom of the stairs, they had to pull the little girl back to prevent her from running into a woman walking by.

"Sorry, ma'am." Hadley smiled at the gray-haired woman, who was most likely on her way to walk the paved path for some exercise.

"No trouble. You're a cute family. Enjoy these years. They go by too fast." She waved and continued her brisk pace.

Hadley felt her cheeks burn at being mistaken for Monroe's wife. Her brain flitted to a thought she would have rather avoided: If they had married all those years ago, would they now have a child about Chloe's age? She tried to mentally bleach the thought from her awareness. Why would her mind even go there?

"Thank you," Monroe said to the woman's already-retreating figure. He turned and shrugged at Hadley. "Not worth correcting." Clearly he didn't ponder these sorts of what-ifs, so why should she? But she wouldn't have wanted to raise a child with someone like him, so in a way he had done her a favor. She had dodged a bullet before they were more entwined.

"Meeh." Chloe pointed at the goats.

Another sound! Chloe was really into animals, and Hadley hadn't realized how much until they were at the "zoo" today. Maybe she should try to get a goat toy or puppet for the next session.

After touching goats and sheep, they ended up at the top terrace to see the mountain lion, bobcat, and wolves. Chloe grabbed Hadley's hand and pointed at a rope play structure in the shape of a human-size spider's web.

"Yes, sweetie, you can go play." The last time Hadley was at the nature center with Chloe, the four-year-old had spent more than an hour on that play structure. They didn't have an hour today, but Chloe certainly could climb several minutes before Hadley needed to get her in the car and take her home. She wondered how much success Alan and Kate were having in their apartment hunting.

"Do I need to stand under her?" Monroe looked skeptical of Chloe climbing up the tall rope web with several children about the same age.

"She's fine. She's been a climber since she was tiny. Can scale any apparatus without falling."

"If you say so."

Hadley sat down at a nearby picnic table. Monroe didn't sit, but he didn't hover around Chloe either, although perhaps he wanted to. He had his arms crossed and a slight frown on his face. He was probably counting the minutes until they could take Chloe back to her family and he could return to whatever he originally had planned.

"You know what this playground reminds me of?" Monroe didn't remove his eyes from Chloe, who was now almost at the very top of the spider's web.

"What?"

"That rope obstacle course at the weekend youth retreat we attended the summer before our junior year. The one I fell off of. Man, that was embarrassing. You crouched beside me, asking questions, afraid I was concussed, and wouldn't let me get up." He chuckled. "I remember thinking, *These are the best and worst few minutes of my life.* Then sleeping on that awful mattress in the boys' cabin that night didn't help my poor back. I think I was trying to impress you with the climb."

She flinched at the memory. She used to treasure thinking back to the ill-fated outdoor trip where she got to know Monroe better, but now it was just uncomfortable. Why would he bring up something like that?

He walked to the picnic table and sat across from her. "Look, I know you're furious I'm here. And I get it, Hadley. I really do. But if I break any of the rules and regulations, it could cause issues for the clinic." He pointed at Chloe. "And for those who need us."

Her first thought was, *I'm not sure furious covers it.* But she admitted, "I know I've been a little difficult."

He smiled, holding his index finger and thumb as far apart as they could go. "Just a little?"

"Yes, absolutely just a little. I'd liked to have caused more trouble." She thought back to the facility with its therapists, like Rebecca, and all the care that had gone into the entire setup. Holding on to frustration wasn't helping anyone. "But it's a great clinic. I can tell you're doing a lot of good for those who come through your doors."

"Thank you. It's harder than I'd banked on, and getting everything up and running involved a lot of sleepless nights . . . and signing of contracts. All I can do is hope I'm handling things well enough to make the kind of difference people need."

"Can I ask you a question?" She heard the words tumble out before she was sure she wanted to voice them. Would she regret this? Maybe she should just continue to speak to him as little as possible.

"Yes?" He looked and sounded unsure.

"You have areas where you're doing good, and clearly progress matters as you provide services to people like us, but do you actually *like* people like us?"

He tilted his head, seeming interested and confused. "Who is 'us' exactly?"

"Working-class folks and below. Myself. Chloe and her parents. Observation says, many of your patients."

"I'm not sure you'll believe me, but, yeah, I actually do. I'm just not good with people like you are. I know the facts and rules. I often know exactly what needs to be purchased or done to accomplish a needed goal, but I come across as stiff and uncaring, especially to adults. I know that. But I spend endless hours chasing down government grants and jumping through hoops with insurance companies so the clinic can provide affordable care to families who need it. I do so through strict adherence to every regulation, because patients can't afford for us to close down, and if we violate regulations, the board could replace me with someone who doesn't care about the working class and poor."

Monroe hadn't changed from being a rule keeper. And she hadn't stopped pushing back against rules as much as she probably should have. She needed to let go of the aggravation of his intrusion.

"Sorry for asking you a question like that. It's just that I don't trust you, and you don't trust me, but that can't get in the way of what needs to happen for Chloe. I love that little girl. I've known her since she was a baby and . . ." She trailed off, her mind spinning on the best way to convey her thought.

"You want to make sure I'm doing what I am for the right reasons so I don't pull the rug out from under her and walk away."

She nodded. That pretty much said it all.

"That won't happen, and I know the whole situation is awkward. But it's clear that neither one of us is shaking free of the other until Chloe is where she needs to be, so could we call a truce?"

They both watched Chloe as she climbed back down and began following another girl, who was maybe a year older than she was. The older girl was asking Chloe questions, and Chloe made sounds, much like a crow cawing, but the intensity on Chloe's face said she wanted to answer the girl.

Hadley's heart ached. They had to get her speaking again, and soon, because the thought of her never getting to say what she was thinking, never getting to add her own voice to the pretend games of childhood was heartbreaking.

But the words wouldn't leave her mouth. How could she call a truce with someone who thought she was a felon that had been released only because of a lawyer or some technicality? She wasn't defending herself. He could think what he wanted to.

Monroe checked his phone, probably glancing at e-mail. "You know what else I remember about that weekend? Some of the guys and I were returning to our cabin late one night after a snack run or pulling a prank on a counselor or something. Anyway, we heard a whispery voice coming from a cabin on the girls' side of the camp. She seemed to be saying a name over and over, and then we heard this thump, and a group of girls burst into laughter, as did the guys."

"I remember it well."

"Were you in that cabin?"

"Yeah. The girl was in a top bunk and fell out, leaning toward the screen of an open window to get the attention of one of the guys."

"That was funny."

"Yeah, I thought so too . . . even though . . ." What was she saying and why?

Monroe's eyes grew big. "You were the girl."

"Maybe."

Their eyes met, and they broke into laughter.

Monroe put his phone away. "We were kids, Hadley." He shrugged, looking grieved.

"Just two high school kids who faced a no-win situation . . . and no one won."

She nodded. They'd been young, and regardless of how wrong he'd treated her, they weren't kids anymore, and she needed to set aside the past and work with him to meet an important goal. "A truce sounds good. For Chloe."

And once Chloe was better, they could return to existing separately, and Hadley would no longer have to deal with the ache that crept into the deepest recesses of her whenever she was reminded of what could have been.

12

Elliott sat on a log and watched the French Broad River sluice ripple along. The faded tent was behind her. Above the old buildings across the street, majestic hills were covered in trees that continued to deepen in color, but she was fatigued of camping. The nights were dropping into the fifties, and it was impossible to get warm when the coldness of the ground seeped through the tent and thin sleeping bag.

Living arrangements aside, she couldn't get Trent off her mind. She looked at her prepaid phone and for the umpteenth time read his two texts telling her he didn't know what had happened but they should talk about it.

Why hadn't he given up on her? They'd had one outing for coffee, and by the end she'd freaked out. Any man in his right mind never would've called or texted again. He'd done both, twice.

The voice inside her screamed at her to delete his contact info, but instead she pressed the call icon. It rang several times.

"Hey. I was hoping you'd call."

"You really want to talk?"

"Talk. Eat. Drink coffee. Listen to music. Yeah, why not?"

"Because I acted a few bricks shy of a load."

"Happen often? That shy brick thing?"

She laughed. "It's not a shy brick. It's bricks shy of . . . Oh, never mind, and no." Most of the time God's peace and her few good friends kept her stable, even when chaos was happening around her. When she didn't feel particularly tranquil, she usually wrestled her emotions to keep them hidden from others.

"We had a really nice time last week, Elliott, or at least I did. At the end, before you left, you said it wasn't me, so I didn't take it personally . . . unless I should. Should I?"

"No."

"Then we're good."

"I'm starting to think you're a few bricks shy of a load too."

"Maybe so, but friends loan bricks when needed."

"I'm not that person I became right in

179

front you the last time . . . not usually, anyway."

"Two things. First, I know that. Second, your reaction was only a bit out of sorts. You're making a mountain out of a mole-hill."

"Am I?" She liked the idea that she was overthinking her reaction and making it out to be more than it was.

"Definitely."

As a kid she'd felt that even asking for a sandwich or for soap to wash with was a huge imposition. She was criticized and chastised as if she were a pain for just being human. Then she was left like an unwanted dog. Her parents were drug addicts, and her home had been a contentious one. Logically she could blame their continual bad moods and neglect on the drugs, but emotionally, Elliott often felt like that little girl who seemed to be a huge pain in the neck to those around her, except for Hadley and Tara, of course. And maybe she shouldn't.

"I told you I wasn't good at this guy-girl thing."

"Me neither, not really. But we click, Elliott. Don't we?"

"It seems so, but that scares me for me and for you and for us."

"Yeah, I can see that. Where are you? I'm

in my car on Biltmore Avenue, near Doc Chey's. I could pick you up. Do soup, noodles, coffee, and a conversation sound good?"

He was about two miles from her, but she wasn't telling him that.

"I'm twenty-six, and I may never be ready to really date."

"I hate to sound like a clichéd romance movie, but . . . let's not date. Let's enjoy friendship. We have more in common than you know, Elliott."

Letting him in — any guy in — sounded dangerous. She didn't want her heart broken like Hadley's had been. She didn't want to feel the anguish of being left again. It'd been all she could do to survive intact when her mom left, and then a year later her dad abandoned her. And her fears concerning Trent were particularly huge, probably because she liked him.

"You're asking for a lot, Trent. What do you want? I mean, really want."

"To enjoy a beautiful autumn with someone who has no idea how rare and interesting she is. Someone to share coffee, conversations, and an occasional music festival with."

His words moved her, and she felt as if she could breathe again. "Just autumn?"

"Could you do me a favor?"

"Maybe."

"Could you not ask questions you don't want the answer to?"

"Yeah, that's probably a good idea. I'll work on it."

"I was invisible to you during my internship at the hospital, but in the glimpses I caught of you, I saw *you,* Elliott. I saw you engage and care. I saw a hundred things, including ER nurses pull you off your floor to help with emergencies. That doesn't happen for an LPN unless you're the whole package. Whatever they needed, you were up for it. I imagine that wherever you are in the course of a day, now or in twenty years, whatever your pay grade, your strength and skill and courage are way above it."

She didn't know whether to believe him or call him on his purple-prose nonsense. "That was nice." It was. She just wasn't sure if she trusted it to be real. They hardly knew each other.

"Elliott, all I need is for you to relax about the dating thing, and let's be friends and see where it takes us."

"Maybe."

" 'Maybe is good. If you'd like to share a meal between now and when you decide, call or text."

He'd asked where she was, and she was ready to tell him. "Riverside Drive. Campsite across and down from the old cotton mill."

"Yeah?" Even with his monotone voice, he sounded excited. "I'll make a left turn ahead and be there in five. Have you pitched a tent for this gorgeous fall weekend?"

"For the last three weeks, actually."

"*Camping?* Like, since the same apartment fire that Chloe was in?"

"It's just temporary. We've been without a house before. When I mentioned living in Georgia, what I didn't say is we were homeless the first two months we were there." Why would she tell him that?

"It takes strength to go through something like that. There are lots of ways to be poor in this life, but I'd choose no money and real love over any other path."

"I'm not sure I would've chosen this path, but I'm used to it. Some people, like Monroe, seem to have it all."

A gold Honda Accord pulled off the main road, and Elliott walked toward it.

Trent hopped out. "It's a nice spot. Flat. Close to town."

"I agree."

He gestured at the car door. "May I?"

"Sure, be noble."

After she got in and he closed her door, he hurried around to his side.

He pulled onto the main road, shifting gears. "Could I talk you into dinner? I'm starved."

"Sure."

"Doc Chey's?"

"I love that place."

"Good." He pushed the clutch and came to a stop at a red light. "What did I say that bothered you? So I can avoid it."

She debated whether to tell that vulnerable, embarrassing story, but she decided she might as well. If he thought he liked her enough to want to date, she needed to be honest. Maybe he'd change his mind about her. Maybe she'd change her mind and be willing to date. Who knew? But she was so weary of being guarded against everyone except Hadley and Tara. Besides, Trent was cute.

She told him the story of her parents being drug addicts and her dad abandoning her and what he said before he drove off.

"I can't imagine what that must've felt like."

"I get that what he did wasn't about me. It was about what was going on inside him, but it's hard to shake the anger that phrase causes, you know?"

"I think so." Trent shifted gears, driving cautiously as crowds milled around them. "My mom had stage-four breast cancer when I was about eight. I was sent from pillar to post — relatives who wanted to want me but didn't want me, and neighbors who wanted me even less. It was hard but nothing like that. Still, I think that experience makes what you're saying grab something familiar inside me. She beat the odds, and she's still a survivor."

"Experiences like that make me determined to pay attention to the good times and pray I'm ready for the bad." She found talking to him easy, and that felt really odd.

It scared her a bit. If this was who he was, why was he single?

The area was busy with tourists, but within a few minutes Trent was pulling into the Biltmore Avenue Parking Garage. They hopped out, wove their way out of the building, and walked toward Doc Chey's.

They paced themselves with the flow of the crowd. In the midst of the wall-to-wall buildings, there was an empty spot. Rather than a shop, the space was filled with a large chalkboard covered in writings. She knew the wall well. She and Hadley had walked past it on multiple occasions. It was called the Before I Die wall.

Trent stopped walking and examined some of the drawings that people had left. She did the same. She'd never written on it.

A man lifted a young girl, presumably his daughter, up on his shoulders to write on the wall in a space where no one else had written. The girl giggled as she wrote, "Own a tiger" on the very top, and then he whisked her back down, and they walked away.

"That was sweet." Trent gestured to the pair.

"Maybe. You never can tell, though, so save that smile until you know the situation."

"Whatever the real situation, that was a sweet moment."

Once again he was right. "True."

"You mentioned Monroe having it all." Trent appeared to be reading the wall as he talked. "But I see it differently. I think he borders on being miserable. I hope I'm wrong." He shrugged. "I didn't become a doctor for the income, which is good, because my goals changed a few years ago. I decided to forego becoming a developmental pediatrician and chose instead to focus on researching apraxia. It's on the rise in the United States, and no one has a clue why."

"I know what it is and some things related

to addressing it, but I don't understand what causes it."

"No one does for sure. Certain research indicates that at least some children with apraxia have a disrupted brain structure, but even then we don't know what caused it. I won't be rich, but I pray we find answers. It's so hard on a hearing child to be unable to speak the words they can hear. You've witnessed Chloe. Children like her seem to know what they want to say, but they can't get the words to release through their mouths. It's heartbreaking, really, and I want to be a part of the team of researchers who unearth why it's on the rise and what can be done to drastically reduce that number. I don't mind living in a tiny house for the rest of my life, but I want my place filled with love." He picked up a piece of chalk from a plastic container attached to the wall.

After the words Before I Die, he wrote "live fully and love intentionally." He tapped the board with his chalk. "That's the dream."

She once again wondered why he was still single. There had to be a story or two there, but she wouldn't ask, because she wasn't sure she wanted to know. What if he got bored with women once he won them over?

Or maybe he was still in love with an ex-girlfriend.

He shrugged and held the chalk out to Elliott. "You write something."

Elliott twirled the stub of pink chalk between her fingers. The chalkboard asked a question she wasn't sure she knew how to answer. She and Hadley had spent so many years surviving. Finally she wrote "have my own home" in the blank space.

Trent smiled at her.

Her cheeks felt warm, and she looked away. This was silly — them sharing long-term hopes and dreams.

Why was she being so open with a man she hardly knew?

13

Monroe looked out the passenger-side window of Hadley's red Civic. It was so weird to be in a vehicle with her again. Not bad. Just not something he imagined he'd ever do again. She stopped at a red light and glanced at him out of the corner of her eye. Chloe was in the back, strapped in her car seat, listening to Disney songs panned to the back speakers.

A xylophone sound let him know his phone was ringing. He slid the bar to accept the call and held the device up to his ear. "Hello."

"Monroe?"

"Yes."

"This is Kate Powell. I just got your message. Hadley does have my permission to take Chloe after her session."

"Okay, sounds good. Thank you." What else could he say? He felt more than a little silly. He knew that Kate trusted Hadley and intended to put her name on the form instead of his, but because of the technicality, he had to insist on going too.

"So we're good? They were able to go to the zoo?" Kate asked.

"Yes, everything worked out. Thank you."

"Oh, I'm so glad. Are you with Hadley and Chloe?"

"Yes."

"Could you tell her for me that we are headed back to our temporary place? We'll be there in . . . five or so minutes."

"Will do. Bye." Monroe disconnected the call.

"Was that Kate?"

"Yes."

Was Hadley holding back a smile? Her lips were oddly pursed together as she kept her eyes on the road. The light turned green, and she gently accelerated. "Get the verification you needed?"

"Yes."

Hadley looked quite amused, but she simply nodded.

He ran a hand through his short hair. "Go ahead. I probably deserve a good 'told ya so.' It's okay."

"Well, since you admitted you were wrong, I don't have to say it." She was grinning now, eyes still on the road.

"Kate said you could head back to their place. They'll be home soon."

Why had he insisted on going? Maybe it was because of the technicality of the wrong name on the signed form. Or maybe he'd been so curious about the person Hadley had grown into that he needled his way into having an afternoon with her. Based on the questions she had asked him while they were watching Chloe climb, Hadley was also curious, although her interest was about his intentions regarding the clinic. It was good to relax a bit with their truce in place. If only they had been able to come to a truce before departing from each other's lives all those years ago.

Hadley stomped on the brake as a dog yanked away from its owner and stepped into their lane. The pedestrian recovered the pet and waved an apology at them.

"Sorry, Chloe." Hadley looked at the girl in the rearview mirror.

Monroe turned and looked into the back seat. Chloe seemed fine, as if the stop hadn't fazed her. But she appeared tired, probably from all the excitement, walking around, and climbing.

He faced forward. "How much trouble will we be in if we let her fall asleep at five thirty in the afternoon?"

Hadley resumed driving and shrugged a shoulder. "Instructions were no nap."

"I made the mistake once of allowing a late-afternoon nap while watching my then-five-year-old nephew, Ian. As payback Nicole let him FaceTime me that evening . . . at eleven o'clock, when he was still awake and bouncing off the walls."

"Your sister always did seem quite spunky." Hadley chuckled as she carefully turned left through the green light. "But that doesn't seem like nearly the payback you deserved."

"You know, you're a lot better driver than you used to be." Since they were under a truce, he couldn't resist trying to get a small rise out of her.

She bristled. "Excuse me?"

"Probably was the fault of your unpaid teacher." Even though they were only months apart in age, Monroe had been the one to teach her how to drive, on these very streets. He had his license before she did. Dianna, her foster mother, had attempted to teach Hadley, but the two got into such heated arguments whenever they went out that they both gave up. Monroe had to coax Hadley into the driver's seat of his then brand-new black BMW because she was terrified of wrecking it.

She relaxed her posture a bit. "You know, it occurs to me that you really aren't *that* much of a rule keeper after all, because teaching me to drive was technically illegal. A learner's permit only allows someone to learn from a parent or guardian or an adult who has been driving for five years."

I only break rules when it comes to you, Hads. But he couldn't say that out loud. "Psh, rule keeper? Me?"

She removed one hand from the steering wheel and shook a finger as if she were lecturing someone in front of her. She feigned a low voice. "You can't take this child with you to some unknown place. Aliens may abduct her."

He laughed. "I do *not* sound like that. And the aliens part was all you."

She rolled her eyes but wore a smile on her face. She turned right into a neighborhood. "Alan and Kate are staying with a family from their church. Did she say if they found a good apartment?"

"She didn't." Would it offend her if he offered to get Chloe's family, and perhaps Elliott and her, a good deal on a condo in the same complex as his? Of course that would accomplish the exact opposite of what he should be doing — keeping his contact with Hadley to a minimum and then parting ways for good after Chloe's treatment was done.

Junior partnership agreement aside, and that was impossible to set aside, there was too much baggage between them to have anything except a truce and professionalism. She thought he'd abandoned her when she needed him most, and when she escaped from the courthouse, she'd run off with Kyle. They each had ten years of anger and ten years of living with the finality of the breakup.

Hadley pulled into the driveway of a moderately large brick house. The home had a beautiful front porch, painted white, and a separate basement entrance around the right side of the house. That was probably where the displaced young family was staying. Hadley parked the car, and Monroe turned around to look at Chloe. The preschooler was out like a light.

"Hadley." Monroe pointed to Chloe.

Hadley turned around and chuckled, possibly at Chloe's soft snores. "She's adorable. That'll be trouble for her parents for sure when she wakes up at five in the morning. Luckily, we are giving her back."

Monroe opened his door and let down the front seat. He reached in and gently unbuckled Chloe and then lifted her out of the seat.

She stirred enough to reposition herself and lay her head on his shoulder. Hadley unbuckled the car seat and pulled it out of the small vehicle.

"I can get that too." Monroe shifted Chloe to his right arm and offered his left to get the seat.

"I've got strong arms, Birch."

"Clearly, though not as strong as your attitude."

She narrowed her eyes at him and continued carrying the car seat. "They are staying in the basement. Come on."

He followed her, Chloe continuing to snooze on his shoulder.

Before Hadley could knock on the basement door, it opened.

Kate smiled at them, though her smile fell a little when she noticed Chloe was asleep.

"Sorry." Hadley set the car seat down and rubbed Chloe's back. "She wore herself out."

Kate chuckled. "I was expecting this. Come 'ere."

Monroe passed the sleeping little girl to her mother. Chloe snuggled her face into her mom's neck, and Kate carried her into the basement apartment.

"Come on in." Alan waved at them, getting up from a faded blue couch.

Monroe picked up the car seat and set it just inside the door. Hadley eyed him as he did it but didn't say anything. He followed her into the living area. It smelled a little musty but was otherwise outfitted to be a decent apartment. It even had a small kitchen and dining area.

"She had a lot of fun." Hadley smiled at Alan.

"Thank you both so much. I have to say, I'm impressed with Children's Therapy. The owner going above and beyond and all." Alan offered a hand to Monroe.

Hadley's eyes met Monroe's, and she bit her bottom lip, no doubt holding back some additional comments.

He shook Alan's hand. "It was no trouble, Mr. Powell. It was good to get to know Chloe better. Hadley and I even came up with some good ideas for future therapy sessions."

"That's wonderful. I have some good news too."

"Yeah?" Hadley pinned loose hair behind one ear.

"Kate and I signed a contract on an apartment that's owned by the parent company of All-in-One Auto. We got a great deal."

"I bet that's a relief."

"It's a three bedroom. And the third

bedroom is yours and Elliott's."

Hadley blinked. "Ours? But why?"

Alan chuckled. "Because you and Elliott are living in a tent. And we like you and don't want you to be cold."

Living in a tent? Could that be true? Or was Alan teasing? He figured Hadley was in temporary housing like the Powells were.

Hadley looked at the floor. "We are *camping* by choice." Was she blushing? "Sort of by choice at least."

Alan glanced at Monroe, probably realizing he may have said too much. "I know, I know. You guys are doing just fine, and this will only be for a few months at the most until the other apartments are repaired from the fire and open again. But we want to offer you something." He rubbed the back of his neck. "You've done so much for Chloe. Please consider it."

Hadley looked up and nodded. "Yes. That would be nice. Thank you, Alan. But you probably know what I want even more than a roof over my head, right?"

Alan sighed. "Yeah. I know you want me to reconsider about Jason. I can't say I understand why this means so much to you."

"Because I was a kid similar to Jason. I did dumb things despite wanting to do the right things. And life is too hard for high school dropouts. He won't get into a trade school, but he's good with cars. *You* have the power to make a difference for him."

Alan walked into the small kitchen and got a glass from a shelf. He held it up. "Either of you care for a drink?"

They shook their heads.

He turned on the tap to get some water and then tilted his head back as he swallowed it. "That's a tough one, Hadley. Until I hear from Chloe exactly what happened, I just can't offer Jason a job."

Ah, so that's who Jason was. The kid who was running with Chloe after the fire. His name hadn't been in her file, but a detailed account of the incident was included on the chance it was pertinent as they tried to help Chloe.

"But you'll hold the spot for now, right?"

"I can probably hold it to the end of the year but not any longer."

"Thank you. Jason has trouble communicating what's going on in his life and emotions, but he's a good kid. He loves his Memaw. I went by and saw them both yesterday in their temporary housing. He just needs a good job to make their finances work."

Alan set his water glass down on the worn

white-laminate countertop. "You have a good heart, Hadley."

"Thanks. So do you."

She'd always had a good heart in Monroe's opinion, even if all her past decisions weren't the best. How common was it for neighbors to help each other out like this? Monroe didn't even know the people who lived in the condos beside and below him.

She caught him smiling at her, and she quickly looked away.

When Kate came back into the room, Hadley wished her and Alan a good evening, and Monroe did the same. Then they walked back out to Hadley's car.

"You don't have to drive me all the way back to the clinic to get my car. I can call a cab." He had to offer, but he hoped she would say no.

"That's tempting. But get in. It'll only take a few minutes."

As Hadley pulled out of the neighborhood, Monroe broke the silence. "So . . . will you tell me why Jason is so important?"

"Excuse me?"

He shrugged. "You told Alan that a job opportunity for Jason was more important than having a roof over your own head. That's a lot of affection for a neighbor kid, Hads." Although considering what she was doing for Chloe, maybe it wasn't uncommon behavior for Hadley. Perhaps the relationships and friendships with her neighbors were like the missing family she used to long for.

"You wouldn't get it."

"Humor me. I know what you said to Alan, but . . . could you tell me more about Jason?"

She pulled to a stop sign and looked at him as if she was weighing whether to let him in or not. "An impulsive teen who does impulsive, stupid stuff. Remind you of anyone?"

"He's been that way since you've known him?"

She shook her head. "No. Four years ago on the day we moved into our now-charred apartment, Jason showed up near our car. He didn't ask if we needed help. He just started unloading stuff and carrying it up the steps to our place." She laughed. "Talking the whole time about PlayStation games and wanting a cell phone and the ridiculous things various politicians had said. He was in eighth grade although he could've passed for a sixth grader, and he said he was failing and would have to repeat that grade, which was all I needed to know to take him under my wing. Then I learned he had deadbeat parents and his grandmother was raising him." She pulled forward, eyes on the road. "He struggles in school. I mean, really struggles. But we started studying together, and he passed eighth grade and ninth and tenth and eleventh." She shrugged. "His grandmother, Mary Lou, aka Memaw, loves him, and he loves her. Now he's seventeen, almost an adult, and they've made it without getting separated — though if the state had known he has basically been taking care of her for years instead of the other way around, they might have been."

Monroe felt a pang in his heart as the truth hit like an arrow. Hadley wanted — *needed* — to save this family in a way she couldn't save her own. He nodded.

Hadley touched a hand to her heart. "I'm rooting for Jason, like my lawyer pulled for me. But he's not cut out to succeed in college. He *needs* a good trade, but that's hard to come by when a person has a double whammy against them: poor grades *and* no money. If I can get him this job with Alan, then not only can he and Memaw make it as a family, but he'll feel good about who he is. He'll stop his petty thievery and become a productive citizen who enjoys his life. He'll build a skill that will keep his head above water for the rest of his life. How could I not care?"

He wanted to reach out and grab her hand and then perhaps say a prayer with her for victory for Jason. But he didn't dare. Instead he looked out the window and prayed silently.

They rode in silence for a few minutes. Maybe he should let the ride continue in quiet, but he couldn't help but bring up something he'd been curious about. He wasn't likely to get another chance to have this kind of conversation with her.

"I was caught off guard by a lot when you showed up at the clinic, but one thing that stood out was you've yet to finish school."

She kept her face straight, but he could tell he had slightly upset her. "Sorry. No offense intended. That was too personal, wasn't it?"

"Some of us have to work before we can afford school, you know."

"But . . . didn't I hear you had a scholarship?" As soon as the question escaped him, he hoped she didn't ask how he knew that.

"Yeah, and it's a godsend for sure. But I still had to worry about the cost of living. Food. Vehicle. Roof over my head — tent fabric or otherwise." One side of her mouth turned up a little. Good, she wasn't mad. He rather liked their truce. "Elliott and I struggled for a while after leaving Asheville."

Elliott and her? Then things must not have lasted long with Kyle after they left town together.

She kept her eyes on the road as she continued. "It got a little easier after we turned eighteen and no longer had to hide from the authorities. We came back to Asheville when Tara found a good apartment. I got my GED when I was twenty, and then Elliott and I worked at Mission Health and saved for a car. For years I didn't even know I qualified for a scholarship. Anyway, a little more than four years ago, I began at WCU. I'll have my master's in less than two years."

"That makes a lot of sense. It sounds as though you have worked hard to get where you are."

"Thanks." She frowned, turning the car onto the highway that led to Weaverville. "Monroe, don't take this the wrong way, but I'm getting a little uncomfortable here."

"Oh, sure. I get it."

Hadley shook her head and shrugged, looking a bit apologetic and a bit defensive. "I *have* worked hard to get where I am. But getting close to you again seems like it could wreck some of that progress. I know today was a favor to Chloe, but maybe we shouldn't talk about our lives or anything other than what's relevant to her. Don't you think that's best?"

He looked out the window at the blur of trees in the fading light. Yes, her idea sounded like what he should be doing. His parents probably had been right; it was best for Hadley and him to live out their separate lives. But talking with her just felt so . . . right. Clearly she didn't agree though. And once she was no longer in his clinic, he could put her out of his mind.

Yeah. Like that would work.

Hadley scrolled through job listings on the library computer. Sunlight from the large windows reflected off the computers, making it a little hard to see. Elliott and Jason were in chairs beside her, both looking at their own computer screens.

After Jason and Hadley had finished with their school day, they met here, and Elliott walked here after work to join them. They should've done this sooner, but with her schooling, Elliott's and her work at the hospital, and volunteer sessions with Chloe, they were just too busy.

Her mind flashed back to yesterday's therapy session with Chloe at the clinic with Rebecca. It'd been a really good one. To-morrow Chloe would have her Friday appointment, and Hadley had all sorts of ideas to try.

"Oh, what about this?" Elliott clicked on a link. "Ice cream delivery driver. Oh, wait. The job requires having a high school diploma. Sorry."

Jason leaned back in the springy library chair. "I could always take this warehouse job."

Hadley glanced over. "That's a late-shift job, so it's not legal for someone your age."

"I can take it as soon as I turn eighteen in a few weeks."

"Only if you drop out of high school." Hadley drummed her fingers on the library computer table. "We've talked about that two dozen times. When are you going to believe us that your plan is a *really* bad idea?"

"So you keep saying, but I don't see it."

Hadley gave the teen a raised eyebrow. "Just trust us on this. It'll be easier on you in the long run if you finish now. You are so close."

"But some things are more important. Like Memaw."

Hadley nodded. "We agree that she's more important, Jason. But let's keep looking. Maybe the right job is listed here and we just need to think outside the Alan box."

"That box is sealed tight," Jason said. "And I'm on the outside of it."

"Maybe not. He said he just needs to hear from Chloe what happened."

"Great. A choice job is sitting there, but I'm waiting on a preschooler's testimony. Come on, Hadley. Even I'm smart enough to figure this one out. He's being nice, stringing you along because he owes you favors, but he *will* give the job to someone else." Jason bounced slightly in the chair. "But in the last few days, I've been remembering more and more of that day until it all came together."

"Really? Why didn't you say so sooner?"

"Will it make a difference?"

"It will to us, and we'd like to understand what happened."

"Okay, well, I'm skipping all the stuff I told you at the hospital. But when I saw Chloe outside, I looked at her second-story apartment and saw an open window. I guess she climbed out and down the fire escape by herself."

Hadley knew Chloe was a confident climber, but to go down a wobbly set of stairs by herself? "How would a four-year-old open a window?"

Elliott shook her head. "She didn't have to open it. Kate opens the windows during the day when the weather's nice, remember? Maybe she opened it a little too far. Chloe's a wiry girl."

Hadley nodded. "What happened next, Jason?"

"Like I said at the hospital, I ran to get her, and she was running into the complex. I went in after her, snatched her up, and hightailed it out of the building. As I was running, an explosion pushed me forward, making me run faster."

"That's how your back was burned."

He reached over his shoulder to touch his back. "Yep. Like you said in the hospital, panic had set in. I kept running with Chloe, trying to find a safe place away from the fire. We went through the patch of woods, and the smoke cleared, but when I came to a road, a police car was buzzing by, sirens blasting, and it startled me, and I ran the other way. It made no sense. I promise it was as if I was outside my body, looking down, but I kept screaming at myself to find her parents."

"Then you returned to the apartment parking lot." It was starting to click a little better for Hadley now.

He nodded. "Alan spotted me running like crazy with Chloe screaming, and I thought the building was going to explode, so I took off with Chloe, going in the opposite direction. When I realized Alan and Phillip were after me, I was acting like a squirrel in the middle of the road, just too confused to know what to do until I saw you, Hadley, and shoved Chloe at you and kept running."

"I'm so sorry this happened."

"Me too, especially for Chloe. I never intended to scare her. Or her parents."

Hadley took a deep breath and sat back in her chair. Jason's story finally made sense. But could they convince Alan of that quickly enough to get Jason the trade opportunity he desperately needed to better his and his Memaw's lives?

14

Monroe's fingers flew across the keyboard, taking notes while Rebecca talked. The oversize conference room with its floor-to-ceiling windows on one side wasn't enough to keep the walls from closing in. The sweet scent that clung to Hadley as she entered the room and walked by him had far more of his attention than it should.

Focus, Birch.

But she was mere feet away, and he wanted to discard his professional demeanor and talk to her.

It was Friday afternoon, and all the patients were gone. Monroe, nine therapists, and Trent, were having their end-of-the-week patient-review meeting, discussing met goals and new goals and brainstorming possible solutions for any roadblocks the children or their families were dealing with.

He'd saved Chloe for last so that Hadley needed to come only for the final twenty minutes of the meeting. She had quietly slipped into the meeting and taken a chair toward the back corner a good thirty minutes before time to review Chloe's case.

The two weeks since Hadley, Chloe, and he had gone to the nature center had dragged by, except when Hadley was at the clinic. His pulse raced on the days he knew she'd be here. Watching her work with Chloe confirmed to him why he'd entered this profession. Hadley's passion for speech therapy was contagious. Highly contagious.

Occasionally something akin to magic happened between speech therapists and their young clients — moments when tiny victories were won, and the two hearts celebrated with as much wonder and joy as if it were Christmas. But victories didn't come quickly for most children. It could take months, even a year, to get a child to speak a few odd-sounding syllables. But no matter how skilled adults were with words, they couldn't explain the beauty and power of a child trapped inside apraxia who began to communicate, however poorly at first.

"Her receptive ability is excellent for a child her age," Rebecca said. "My guess is that's from her two years of having structured one-on-one sessions with Hadley. From simple to complicated instructions, she hears, even in the middle of play, and does as asked. Her expressive skills are rock solid too, as long as it doesn't include speech. Without a word or tantrums, she lets us know how she feels, what she likes, when she's angry. But there's an unusual issue that's overwhelming her." Rebecca turned to Hadley and nodded.

"She won't have anything to do with flowers," Hadley began. "She used to love the card-matching game with only flowers, but she refuses to play it now. When I pull it out, she gets angry, jerks it from my hand, and throws it. But early on the afternoon of the fire, she'd picked flowers for me, and she and her mom brought them over. I've tried numerous times — here at the clinic and at the grocery store — to get her to respond to fresh flowers, but she shuts down."

Monroe continued taking notes, but he paused and looked at Rebecca. "So you're wondering if somehow in her mind the fire and flowers are connected."

"As illogical as that sounds, we have to trust her reaction and read into it."

"Okay." He gestured to the group. "Ideas of where to go from here?"

Rebecca tapped the table in front of her. "I'd like permission to break protocol and ask Kate and Alan *not* to enter the therapy room for a few weeks."

Monroe typed that in the notes, unsure how to respond. He trusted his therapists, but parents were the golden key to unlocking a child's motivation and continuing the hard work into the child's home life. He'd never seen a case where the parents didn't play an instrumental role in their child's success.

"Look," Rebecca said, "I know how this sounds. In all my years of doing this, I've pulled reluctant or busy parents into the room. But we've brought Kate into Chloe's session twice, and Chloe shut down both times. I gave Chloe time to pull out of it, but when she didn't, I asked Kate to return to the lobby."

Monroe refused to glance up. "What's your take, Hadley?"

"I know Kate. There's no chance of abuse, and Kate isn't pressuring Chloe in or out of sessions. Chloe seems fine with her mom and dad outside of sessions, but inside the sessions, I agree with Rebecca's observations."

He continued to type. As hard as he tried to focus on work, his mind kept drifting to their relationship, even in his dreams. In his dreams they argued, they laughed, they played games, they climbed mountains to rescue others, they went through war-torn countries, trying to find ammunition for broken guns.

But they never just talked.

They never trusted each other . . . not even in his dreams.

Going to the nature center had unleashed a decade of questions for him. But since then, Chloe seemed to be responding better to the sessions — except, apparently, when Kate entered the room. He had participated in half of the past three sessions. They used puppet animals and made animal noises. Monroe had supplied a number of farm puppets to supplement the play, and his presence gave an additional character for Chloe to interact with. It was working. She had given them several additional consonant sounds.

"Okay." Monroe skimmed over the notes concerning Chloe. "I'll speak with Kate on Monday and let her know we feel it's best that she not come into the room during sessions until further notice."

"Monroe, honey?" The singsong soprano voice of his mother echoed down the hallway.

He sat bolt upright. His mom's voice reminded him that he had a date tonight.

Was Vickie here with his mom? And why was his mom at the clinic? He was supposed to meet her, his dad, and Vickie at his flat in Asheville in a few hours. He glanced at the clock on his computer. The meeting had run over by an hour.

The next few minutes could be awkward, but his main concern was that his parents would know he was in breach of his junior partnership agreement. If only there were another exit from the room so Hadley could leave quickly. Not that she would likely go easily if he tried to shove her out.

Rebecca went to the doorway and looked down the hallway. "Lisa, Greg, we're in here." She stepped into the hall. "Good to see you. It's been a while." Rebecca's voice faded as she made small talk.

Monroe stood. "That's it for the week. Great job. I know all of you have things you'd like to do on a Friday evening that aren't work related, and I apologize that we ran so late."

As people gathered their personal belongings, Hadley moved toward the group, probably hoping to escape unnoticed as she filed out with the others. But his parents knew all the therapists. They were majority owners of the medical group that owned Children's Therapy, and his mom was chairman of the board.

Before anyone reached the door, his parents entered and stopped just inside the room. A tall blonde in a professional-looking maroon dress and carrying a large leather purse was right behind them. That had to be Vickie, another blind date set up by his parents. She was the daughter of some friends of his mother's, and they'd invited her to come to town.

"Mom, Dad." Monroe closed his laptop. "Hi." He smiled at his date. "You must be Vickie."

She returned his smile. "Yes. I've heard a lot about you."

Of that he had no doubt. His parents were doing their best to lead him into the perfect marriage. "Come on in." He motioned for them, hoping they'd move and unblock the doorway. They walked a few feet forward, but that wasn't enough. Hadley eased toward the door, clearly uninterested in speaking to his parents, although she knew nothing about the contract he was under. What had it been like for her to be welcomed by him and his folks into their home and then dropped like burning coals?

"I hope we aren't interrupting. I knew you had to finish up at the clinic, but Vickie's plane landed early, so we thought we'd show her around town before we all go out to dinner." His mom smiled. "I thought you could give her a tour of this beautiful building tonight, although you did pick a plot of land that's a bit in the boonies." She laughed as if telling a tale about an independent-minded child. "With the tour handled tonight, tomorrow is free for something more fun."

"Lisa and Greg." Marissa nodded. "Good to see you."

Monroe glanced at Hadley. She had no idea how much trouble her presence would cause.

Marissa made a bit of small talk with his parents and Vickie, who were still standing in front of the door, and then excused herself with "It's good to see you, but I need to go. I have to pick up the kids from daycare."

"Oh, certainly." His dad ushered Mom and Vickie to the side, and people spoke as they left. Hadley was almost out the door.

"Hadley?" His dad blinked as if the very real girl mere feet from him were some sort of apparition.

Hadley nodded. "Mr. and Mrs. Birch. I hope you're doing well."

"Hadley, . . . *you're* working here?" His mom was smiling, but she was obviously

216

stunned.

"No, ma'am. I'm just volunteering to help out a neighbor."

"Hadley is close with a little girl being treated at the clinic," Monroe quickly added.

"Oh, I see." His mom looked her up and down.

"So, Hadley," his dad said, "how is school going? I know one of your professors at Western Carolina University quite well, and he speaks highly of you."

Hadley looked at Monroe, clearly a bit confused. His parents didn't know she was volunteering at the clinic, but they knew she was in school and where she went to school. How could that compute in her mind? To her credit she simply smiled.

"We're glad you've made it so far in your education," his mom said.

They probably felt quite good about paying for Hadley's degree, but Monroe knew it was a drop in the bucket of all the money they had.

"Oh, where are my manners?" His mom gestured to the sharply dressed young woman standing beside her. "This is Victoria George, or Vickie, as she likes to go by. She's the daughter of one of my colleagues and is considering a move to Asheville to join my law firm. She's staying in the same condo complex as Monroe for the next few weeks. She's a smart girl. She went into the same field as her mother. Monroe's known her since they were in diapers."

That was news to him.

Hadley nodded and smiled. "Nice to meet you, Vickie." She looked at Monroe. "I need to go."

"Yes, of course." He turned to Vickie. "Excuse me just a second. Let me walk Hadley out, and then we can go to dinner."

Hadley didn't wait for him outside the door but was quickly walking down the hallway.

He hurried to catch up. "Hey, I'm sorry about that." Even though they were out of earshot of anyone, he spoke quietly. "I didn't know they were coming here."

"I figured. It's okay." She didn't look at him and continued to walk toward the front entrance.

"They keep bringing people they want me to date. It's pretty embarrassing. I'm sorry."

She stopped. "Why are you apologizing to me?"

Why was he? Monroe wasn't completely sure himself.

"You think another woman's presence bothers me? Why would I care about losing a relationship with someone who still thinks I committed a felony? I come to this clinic and attend meetings for Chloe. *Only* for Chloe. I'll see you at her next session." She turned and briskly walked out the front door and to her car.

He watched her drive off. What had just happened? Whatever it was, she was clearly angry that he believed she'd committed a felony. Had she truly been innocent of arson when her case was dismissed? When he saw Hadley pour the accelerant and start the fire, he'd been sure she was trying to help the Reeds with yard work. But that was before his lawyer mom pointed out all the reasons that couldn't be true. What did it say about him that he still wavered on what to believe?

"Monroe?" His mom's voice was a hiss, reminding him of when he was in trouble as a teen. "Why is Hadley here?"

Monroe looked past her. Vickie was nowhere in sight, but Dad was walking this way with Monroe's laptop in hand. "She told you why. She's here helping out one of her neighbors."

Dad held up the computer. "I looked up the file."

"That is confidential patient information."

"Then it's a good thing I'm a doctor and

majority owner of this establishment. The report said the young patient has a prior diagnosis of apraxia and is dealing with regressed speech issues and possibly selective mutism due to the trauma of watching her home burn."

Mom gasped. "Monroe, this is just too weird. Why is Hadley involved in another fire?"

"Hadley is *not* involved," Monroe snapped and then lowered his voice. "Where is Vickie?"

"Bathroom."

"It's just a coincidence. Hadley's apartment caught fire. She's here to help a neighbor. You showed up."

"Anyone suspected of arson?"

"No. It was a kitchen fire."

"And you don't suspect —"

"Yeah, Mom, I suspect Hadley. That's why she's here at the clinic, because I'm convinced it's all a setup. Maybe Chloe doesn't have any speech issues either."

"You have no cause to talk to me like that."

Maybe he didn't, but it sure felt as if he did. "I'll apologize, and you change the subject."

Dad tapped the laptop. "Look, we're glad Hadley is doing well in school and finally getting her life on track. But I'm not comfortable with her being in our clinic, and you agreed to these terms when you went into business with us."

Mom nodded, looking sad. Was it a real emotion, or was it something she was just supposed to express? "As much as we hope for the best for her — and we're backing that with action — she shouldn't be here. Your dad is right. We made a deal."

Monroe pushed down his desire to say more on the topic, because it wouldn't do any good. He understood their being cautious. They firmly believed she was guilty of intentionally setting the Reeds' home on fire, and now she was here, and in their minds she was connected to another fire that'd destroyed a building. But she had been a positive influence on Chloe, and to imply, just because of her past, that Hadley might have been involved in the apartment fire was wrong.

"She'll be finished here soon, but you put me in charge of this clinic, and that means letting me judge what's best for the patients. Chloe needs Hadley here, but as soon as that changes, Hadley will not be working at the clinic in any capacity. Okay?"

Dad looked as if he had a further objection, but before he could speak, Vickie walked into the lobby. Dad handed Monroe his laptop. "All right, who's up for some dinner?"

Monroe wondered what Hadley's plans were for the weekend. He assumed Trent was seeing Elliott tonight.

And what am I doing tonight? The answer was obvious. Catering to his parents during what was certain to be a long and awkward evening.

15

Elliott lifted the lid off the stockpot, and the aroma of homemade chicken noodle soup wafted all around her. She slid a wooden spoon in and stirred the pot, causing slow-cooked chicken, fresh-cut veggies, and homemade noodles to swirl about.

She dipped out a spoonful and gently blew on it. It felt so incredible to have a kitchen again, even one shared with another family.

Hadley stood nearby, slicing a warm loaf of bread. Kate was setting the table, and Alan cut apple wedges and peeled oranges and put them on small plates in lieu of a salad. Chloe was somewhere in the house playing quietly.

Trent set a stack of bowls beside her. "I've never had homemade chicken soup before."

Elliott pulled a clean spoon out of the drawer, dipped up some soup, and held the spoon toward him.

He leaned in and took a sip of the broth

and noodles. "Wow." His eyes lit up. "There should be a name other than soup for something that delicious."

She couldn't help but smile. He saw value in the simple pleasures, just as she did. "Glad you approve. I imagine you had doubts when I invited you to join us for soup."

"I had no doubt that I wanted to be here but a little doubt about enjoying the food this evening, which was fine with me. Every meal doesn't have to taste wonderful for me to appreciate having it, but I'm not a soup eater . . . or apparently I'm not a canned-soup eater."

"Even without the extra step of homemade noodles, soup from scratch is delicious in ways canned soup can't compete with, and it is actually less expensive when comparing ounce for ounce of food." She set the wooden spoon aside and picked up a ladle and began filling a bowl while he waited.

In the past three weeks since Trent had picked her up at the campsite and they had eaten at Doc Chey's, they had gone on a couple of dates. Each outing had been equal parts deeply satisfying and somewhat terrifying. She didn't understand why she continued seeing him when the concept of being in a relationship troubled her, and yet she couldn't imagine throwing in the towel just yet.

Her phone chimed, and a moment later Hadley's did too with the same tune.

"I know that sound," Trent said. "It means you've heard from Tara."

"Hadley and I both texted her earlier today, so she's probably just now off work and can respond." She passed him a full bowl, and he took it to the table while she filled another one.

There were evenings she and Trent could've gone on dates but didn't. On those free evenings they'd texted and shared pictures of what they were doing. That was nice too. Maybe it was his way of letting her know he wasn't dating anyone else even though he hadn't asked for them to be exclusive. He seemed comfortable with and respectful of her need to take things slow. But he'd yet even to hint at why he wasn't with someone else, and she had lingering concerns that he bored easily with women.

Sometimes she caught herself looking for red flags with Trent so she could justify not seeing him again. What was wrong with her? Maybe nothing. Maybe the mistake wasn't wanting to step back despite how much she liked him but continuing to date him despite feeling so leery.

Soon there were six bowls of soup on the table. She put three ice cubes in Chloe's so it would be a comfortable temperature for the little one's tender mouth.

"Chloe, come to dinner, sweetie," Kate called.

Chloe bounded into the room, carrying a familiar picture, and Elliott knew where the little girl had been playing.

"What do you have?" Kate put a hand on her hip. "I told you to stay out of Hadley and Elliott's room. That's not yours."

Chloe approached Elliott and offered her the framed picture. Elliott took it and ruffled the little girl's hair. "It's okay. I was a little older than you in this photo . . . I think."

Trent leaned his chin over Elliott's shoulder, looking. "Cute. That's an interesting train trestle. Where are you?"

"Wish I knew. I call the girl a relative, but I'm not sure she is. Still, I look happy, and it feels like a good memory." She set the picture on the kitchen pass-through.

The room was too quiet, and Elliott wanted to ease the discomfort. "Let's celebrate today for what it is. Now get busy." She snapped her fingers.

Everyone bustled to place food on the table, and then they sat.

Alan gave thanks and said *amen.*

Kate immediately held up her hands, signaling everyone to halt. She looked at Elliott. "Would you say the quote I love so much?"

Elliott nodded. "When you rise in the morning, give thanks for the light, for your life, for your strength. Give thanks for your food and for the joy of living. If you see no reason to give thanks, the fault lies in yourself."

Kate grinned. "That's the one. It's beautiful."

"I don't recall who said it originally, but I found it on the Net years ago, and it has a piece of my heart."

Kate lifted her spoon and looked at Trent. "I was so happy when Hadley and Elliott agreed to move in with us. They've been good to us for a lot of years, and the friendship means more with each passing year, but I had no idea how pleasant it would be for them to be here. I thought of tight quarters with shared bathrooms, kitchen, and laundry room. But it never dawned on me that I'd have two chefs who also wash dishes. I'll be spoiled beyond repair before they find a place of their own."

Alan raised his brows. "Hopefully not beyond repair. My cooking skills are limited to grilled cheese, scrambled eggs, and hot dogs."

"Yum!" Hadley's face said the opposite of her word, and Chloe laughed.

Alan nodded toward Chloe. "I don't know how we could ever thank you for all you've done."

"Sure you do." Hadley wiped her mouth with the napkin.

"Don't start *that* again," Alan said.

Hadley lifted a brow. "Even if he is guilty of all you believe, he deserves a second chance."

They didn't use Jason's name around Chloe. No one needed to say his name to know the person they were talking about.

Alan picked up a piece of homemade bread. "For the sake of argument, let's assume I wanted to help him, which I don't. He's bad news, and I'm sorry you can't see it. But if I wanted to help, how could I? The All-in-One Auto is filled with equipment he could steal, some of which is very expensive."

"But you were willing to overlook his past thievery before the . . . incident."

"That was before I realized he was willing to snatch more than inanimate objects and was so opportunistic he'd use the chaos to do so."

"He remembers everything now, and it didn't happen the way it looked."

Elliott knew Hadley was being careful not to say too much. Chloe was playing with the noodles in her soup, picking them up with her fingers and carefully putting them on the spoon so she could eat them. She seemed in her own world, and if she overheard anything, she didn't know they were talking about Jason. But Hadley couldn't tell Alan right now all that Jason remembered, because that could alter Chloe's view of what happened and would taint her account when she did talk.

Alan rose, went to the stove, and ladled more soup. "He's had weeks to work out a good, solid story that justifies his actions, and you've bought into it, but I won't."

Hadley nodded, but Elliott saw the disappointment in her eyes. Alan hadn't budged an inch in his stance against Jason.

Alan returned to his seat. "I know you care about him and believe in him. I'm sorry, but I don't share your viewpoint, and I can't afford to give him the benefit of the doubt and hire him."

Elliott was ready for a change of subject. "Trent and I will drop off soup and bread for them, and then we may catch a late movie. While it's still in theaters, we want to see *The Impossible,* the movie based on a true story about a family on holiday in Thailand when a tsunami hits."

"I've heard it's really good," Kate said.

The conversation continued, and when the meal was finished, Elliott packed up food, and Trent carried the box to his car. They were soon on their way to Jason and Memaw's.

"Good food. Interesting conversation." He eased into Asheville's Friday evening, mid-October tourist traffic. It would take them at least ten minutes to go the few miles through the heart of the city. "Hadley can be very direct, can't she?"

"And determined, yes. Does it bother you?"

"I'm far more comfortable with directness and stubbornness than superpolite people who never say what they actually think."

"Which may explain why we're together on another Friday night."

"It's not the reason, but it helps. Super-sweet and polite people tend to be two-faced and sneaky, and I've had all I can take of that kind for one lifetime."

She laughed. "I was insulted by that confession. You know that, right?"

"No, you weren't. You're real and honest. Plenty polite, but too honest not to say what you're thinking, even if it's as simple as 'I'm not ready to date' without any other explanation."

"I'm glad you feel that way, but I think it's unfair to label all extremely polite people as two-faced and sneaky."

He hesitated, seemingly in deep thought. "Yeah, true. *Some* are that way."

She detected clear animosity. "Perhaps too many in your life?"

"Only one too many. I've wanted to talk about this for weeks, but I'll look like an idiot, and I'm not sure you can deal with that and still want to go out . . . as friends, just friends."

He was too adorable, and Elliott had to resist putting her hand over his on the gearshift. "You are the perfect amount of savvy and normal. So why on earth are you single?" She covered her mouth, unable to believe she'd asked that. "I'm sorry. Forget I asked."

"No, it's okay. That's the story where I look really stupid. Several years back I was with someone, engaged actually. She was perfection — outwardly — and always unbelievably agreeable and kind. After a few months of dating, we started attending church together." He nervously fiddled with the knob on the gearshift. "You can see where this is going."

Elliott nodded. "I think so."

"We made a commitment not to sleep together until we were married, or maybe I made the pledge and she just nodded her head. I don't know. But three years down the road, I discovered she'd had several affairs. She was in the middle of one with a classmate when I walked in on them."

"I'm sorry."

"It was tough. I thought what I went through with my mom was almost unbearable, but she couldn't help being sick, and she was fighting to get healthy, fighting to be on this planet with her family." He pulled onto the driveway of the host home where Jason and Memaw were staying. "Ansley's betrayal was the opposite. My anger against her was equal to the hurt, and both were inexplicable. But . . ." He put the gearshift in reverse, pulled the emergency brake, and turned off the car. "I survived. The hate is gone, and I'm grateful she's someone else's problem."

"Yeah, that's really good." Elliott didn't consider herself very intuitive. To make up for her lack of perception, she was guarded and careful, but she had an ounce of insight now. "There's more to this story."

His eyes found hers and lingered. "Yeah.

But it's not for sharing anytime soon."

Like a lightning bolt illuminating a dark sky, she knew the next part had something to do with her, and she needed to run. He wasn't playing games. He knew her, understood her, was pacing his moves, and she wanted to end everything right now. But they had food to deliver and a teen to visit first.

They sat there for a moment, staring ahead at the garage that was separate from the house. The two-car garage had been converted into a full apartment with amenities, and Jason and his Memaw were using it.

She opened the car door. "We should get the food and go inside."

Without a word they carried the food across a stone path to the garage apartment. Trent knocked.

"Hello?" A shaky voice spoke through the crack, still secured by a chain lock.

"Hello, Mary Lou. It's Elliott. And I have a . . . a friend with me." Why had Trent told her that story? But it wasn't the story that nagged at her. It was the feeling that she was in over her head.

The door shut, but Elliott could hear her unlocking the chain. The door opened wide. "Hello!" She backed up in her wheelchair.

"Jason?"

A moment later he entered. "Need help, Memaw?" He spotted Elliott. "Oh, hi." He looked tired and anxious. She remembered how it felt to be a teen and it seeming as if nothing ever went her way. He needed a break, so she wouldn't ask him about homework tonight. It was a Friday, and they could study or do homework Sunday evening. "Mary Lou and Jason, this is Trent Gledhill."

Within a few seconds Jason was asking Trent if he ever played Rock Band.

"I have." Trent took just a few steps and set the containers on the counter. "Put a plastic guitar in my hand, and I'm fantastic at music."

Jason laughed. "I'd like to see that." He grabbed a control and turned on the system before passing Trent a plastic guitar. "A PlayStation 3 came with this place, along with all the bedding and stuff."

"Cool." Trent took the control.

Elliott lifted the stockpot a bit. "Does soup sound good?"

"Oh, yes, sweetie. Right this way."

"How you are faring, Mary Lou?"

"Well, I'll tell you the truth. I'm so thankful for the family that's letting us stay here and even more grateful for you and Hadley.

I don't know what I'd have done without good people helping me. The Browns took care of me when Jason was in the hospital."

Elliott couldn't keep her eyes off Trent and Jason as they played dueling guitars and laughed.

"Would you join me for some dinner? I like you, Elliott. You and Hadley are two of the few people I can actually stand to talk to."

Elliott chuckled. "Well, thank you, ma'am. But we already ate. I would be honored to serve you a bowl and share conversation though."

She set up the older woman with a bowl of soup, bread, cut fruit, water, and utensils and then took the chair next to her wheel-chair at the table.

Mary Lou took a spoonful of soup. "All these years I've known you, I've never seen you bring a boy around." She gestured with her head to where Trent was playing video games with Jason. "Must be something special, judging by the way you look at him."

Elliott's cheeks felt hot, and she looked down at her lap. "Oh, we're just friends."

"Does he know that?"

"Definitely."

"That's too bad. I do worry about you sometimes, Elliott." She broke off a piece of bread and dipped it in the soup.

"Me?"

She nodded. "You remind me too much of my younger self. I thought I didn't need friends or support. But these days my advice always is not to be like me. I've lived too closed off. Always afraid to live. And here I am, old and wishing I'd dared to live and love when I was your age. Life is going to hurt, so let it be because you dared to love and trust with all you are. It's like that old saying, 'It's better to have loved and lost than never to have loved at all.' "

For the second time today, Elliott's intuition kicked in, and she was absolutely positive God wanted her to hear Mary Lou and open her heart to Trent.

They visited for more than an hour and could stay longer, but she needed a little time with Trent to find out the rest of the story she'd run from. "Hey, guys, I think Trent and I should go."

"Sure." Trent took off the guitar strap and pointed the plastic neck of the toy instrument at Jason. "Next time, man, I'll show you how fantastic I am."

"You had it on beginner mode, and you still missed notes! I had mine on expert." Jason was laughing, though, visibly more relaxed than when they had arrived.

They told them good night and left. It was dark outside, and the stars shone brightly. The breeze carried the smells of fall as they walked to the car. Elliott slipped her hand in Trent's, and he stopped cold, staring at her.

She squeezed. "I want to hear the rest of that story."

He nodded, and they got into the car. "Let's get some ice cream and take it somewhere that we can talk."

"This might sound weird, but let's go to Cold Stone Creamery downtown and then stop by to see how the apartment construction is going. We won't be able to see much with it being dark, but maybe they'll have the new roof on."

"Not weird at all."

They chatted about little things — her watch preferences, his love of Hondas, his allergy to cats, and her favorite flavors of ice cream. Thirty minutes later with ice cream in cups sitting in the car's cup holders, Trent pulled into the apartment parking lot, found a good spot, and turned off his car. The construction was on hold for the night, but with the streetlights they could see that the roof was partially installed on Elliott's section of the building. That was good progress at least.

"So . . . what's the rest of the story?" Elliott dipped her spoon into the coffee-flavored ice cream.

He drew a deep breath, sounding a little nervous. "About eighteen months after the breakup, I was to the point of having only a few bad days here and there. But I was having one the first time I saw you, and I can't explain exactly what happened. You were at the nurse's station on the cardiac floor, and this voice inside me said, *Someone like her.* When you went into a patient's room, I stood in the hall next to that door and listened as you worked with an obese woman. You were kind and yet simultaneously honest. The remaining shackles of caring about Ansley fell off. I was free. Ansley hadn't shattered my dreams. She'd broken the illusion I was after. She'd made me wake from a nightmare I hadn't known I was in."

Elliott no longer wanted to run from this man. "That's when you started observing me whenever I was around."

"You're pretty fascinating."

"I guess so." She relaxed against the seat. "I like the part where you saw me. It feels as if you actually saw *me.*"

"A tiny glimpse. I didn't want to read too much into it, so when I asked you out and you turned me down, I accepted it."

"But you must've stayed open to the idea of us."

"Apparently so." He smiled.

She returned his smile. "Would you go on a date with me?"

He angled his head, grinning. "I'm really not all that interested . . ."

She laughed. "This is going to be fun, isn't it?"

"Definitely." He eased her hand to his lips and kissed it. "Thank you, and I say the following with all earnestness even though I know you aren't the biggest fan of Monroe, but —"

"Seriously?"

"See, I have an invite to a Mt. Pisgah Medical Group employee and patient appreciation and charity dinner at the Biltmore. It takes place two weeks from today, and I can bring a plus one."

"Black-tie event with Monroe in attendance? I'll pass on that one."

"No, it's not black tie, although you can wear a nice dress if you feel like it. It's an outdoor masquerade/costume party with a live jazz band and good food. I want to go because some of my patients from the clinic will be there, and it will give me a chance to get to know them and their families outside of the facility. It could be helpful if I can observe and ask questions in that setting. Also, several other doctors I know from different rotation sites will be there."

"Oh. I can see where that's sort of a big deal."

He got out of the car, went around it, and opened her door. "Is that a yes?"

"Sure, why not?"

"Yes." He fisted both hands before holding out one to her.

She took it and got out. They leaned against the side of the car, looking skyward. The night was gorgeous, certainly one to remember. He held her hand. "I won't be able to sleep a wink tonight." He moved in front of her and put his warm hands on her face. "Here's to us, to faithfulness to God and each other." He leaned in, and Elliott received the first kiss of her life.

A few moments later he took a step back. "Better than every imagination."

She nodded. "It was."

He moved beside her, holding her hand and staring at the sky. "One of my friends and former roommates, Sam, who I promise is a good guy, needs a date too. Any chance Hadley would go with him?"

"Yeah, she'll go."

"You're that sure?"

"I am. She's seeing too much of Monroe,

and she needs to date someone worthy of her."

16

Walking up the asphalt path and partial stone stairs that led to a high hill on part of the Biltmore Estate, Monroe tried not to zone out as Vickie talked. She was still thrilled about the art gallery tour she had taken with his mother last week. On the positive side, his parents had given up taking him to things like art gallery tours, so he hadn't been invited. Tonight's event at the Biltmore was different, though, and he had to be here for the sake of business.

The cool, damp air smelled of mountain laurel mingled with a hint of cinnamon apples, apparently coming from food that would be served at tonight's dinner. The late-afternoon light filtered through the golden-fading-to-red leaves of a maple tree fully decked in its autumn hues. Soon they were on the brick walkway, and he could see the Biltmore mansion, resembling a magnificent castle, on a grassy plateau below them. The mountains rising behind the mansion looked as if they had been tucked in a beautiful Technicolor blanket of scarlet, amber, and earthy tones. The statue of Diana stood before Monroe and Vickie, surrounded by six columns and a pergola. This place was so far removed from the campground a young woman was living in that it was impossible to grasp.

A large white event tent came into view.

Vickie splayed her hands, gesturing as she talked. "And she said we are invited next week to an exclusive watercolor workshop with one of the artists. Do you enjoy painting?"

"Uh, sometimes." *With my pediatric patients.*

He was here because his patients would be here, along with donors and employees. All of them were important to Children's Therapy and other area clinics of the Mt. Pisgah Medical Group. Trent got an invite. Monroe wondered if he would bring Elliott as his plus one. Watching Trent attempt to break through the thick emotional armor that Elliott had worn all these years could make things at least a little interesting. But that thought also made his chest ache with regret. What would it be like to let down his own guard for a bit and enjoy who Hadley was? Did her temper still get the best of her, or were those days behind her? That was a pointless question. It didn't matter. They were over for a lot of other reasons. If he doubted that, all he had to do was ask Hadley . . . or his parents.

"Look." Vickie chuckled.

Two children in costumes were running toward the tent.

He laughed. "Maybe we should've worn costumes."

Since it was the end of October, everyone invited to the event had the option of wearing a costume. Vickie had opted not to dress in costume, and he had followed her lead, but maybe he should've worn one. It might have amused his kids.

They walked under the enormous tent. Were they late? There were about seventy people already here, some standing around talking and a few special-needs adults dancing to the jazz band's music. He checked his phone for the time. It was five fifteen, so they were fifteen minutes late.

His parents were at the main entrance of the tent, shaking hands as people arrived, and he knew about a hundred and thirty more guests would join them between now and when dinner began at six. He escorted his date to a chair at one of the many round tables covered with white tablecloths. "Would you care for a drink?"

"Sprite, please."

"Sure thing."

"No hurry, though. I think I see an artist I met during the tour, and I'd like to speak with her. I'll meet you back at our table."

He gave her a polite smile and meandered toward the bar, speaking to people as he went. Then he heard *her* voice.

"It goes buh, buh, buh." Hadley sang along with the bass line.

His heart raced. Had he been hoping she'd be here? Where was she? He tried to look more composed than he felt. Then he spotted her kneeling next to Chloe and wearing a lacy black eye mask.

Chloe had on a gray cat costume with little ears on her headband. Hadley was pointing to the upright stringed bass. Monroe started walking toward them.

"Buh, buh, buh." Hadley held Chloe's hand, grinning.

"Buh, buh, buh." Chloe mimicked the sound.

The musician playing the large instrument winked and tipped his head at them.

Hadley stood. Her black tea-length dress and loose curls blew slightly in the autumn breeze.

He needed to get Vickie's Sprite and return to his table, but at this moment his determined, practical side didn't seem to be in control. He edged next to her. "You know, that's not a very good disguise. I could recognize you from across the venue." Of course, he could recognize her anywhere, no matter how many years had passed with no contact between them.

Hadley's smile faded. "If you're politely asking if I've sneaked into the event, I didn't."

What? "No, that's not what I meant at all. I . . . You look nice." *Smooth one.* He considered just leaving things at that, but Hadley deserved to be here as much as any of the other attendees, if not more. She had done good work at Children's Therapy during the past several weeks and for free. "I'm glad you're here. Thank you for all the work you've done at the clinic. I should go. Have fun."

Because of the eye mask, he couldn't quite discern the look on her face, so he walked away to save her the trouble of coming up with a good reply. He should have been the one to invite her, even knowing his parents wouldn't be happy about it.

He walked over to where his mom and dad were standing.

"Monroe, I noticed you talking to Hadley." She had a strained smile on her face, and she'd whispered, probably so that only he and Dad could hear her. "I thought you agreed with us that she shouldn't be working at your center."

"She's a volunteer. I've clarified that already. And she's a good one, as skilled as any fully licensed therapist I've worked with, maybe more so. I didn't invite her, though." Monroe looked at Trent and a man with short, nearly shaved blond hair escorting Elliott and Hadley to a table. "But I should have."

Mom started to say something, but a guest spoke to her, and she turned to chat with him.

Monroe talked with several patients and donors as he got Vickie's drink and wound his way back to the table where his date was waiting.

"Hungry?" Vickie held out a plate. "These starters are pretty good."

The small plate had shrimp covered in a crunchy spring-roll wrapping. "Thank you. Wherever it's held, this event is always nice. Last year it was in a barn."

"A *barn*?"

Monroe shrugged. "It's a fancy barn. They

have weddings there." He took a bite of the shrimp.

"Oh, right, like country chic."

"Sure."

He looked straight ahead and spotted Hadley sitting a few tables over. The guy she was with had his arm draped loosely across the back of her chair. Based on the laughs and animated conversation, the two couples appeared to be having a really good time. Elliott seemed a lot different — happier and less guarded — from who she was in high school. Maybe time had healed a lot and she hadn't carried her former distrust into adulthood. He hoped so for her sake.

Hadley glanced Monroe's way and caught him staring at her. He quickly shifted his attention to Vickie. He told himself it was good that Hadley was having fun with someone. But how amazing would it feel to slip into that man's shoes? To be here with Hadley, just for an evening, without any baggage between them, going to a magical place where he had no memory of her setting a fire and she had no resentment over his leaving her broken and alone.

"Monroe, did you hear what I said?" Vickie arched a perfectly manicured eyebrow at him.

"Um." He tried to make a noncommittal

248

sound so he didn't have to admit the answer. It apparently worked, because she continued talking. They should be mingling. That's what the hors d'oeuvre hour was all about, but he stayed put, too distracted to engage in idle chitchat right now. He forced himself to focus on what Vickie was saying, and they managed a few chuckles as the minutes dragged by.

"Welcome." His mom's voice came through the speaker system. As chairman of the board for Mt. Pisgah Medical Group, she would emcee tonight's event. "If you'll please make your way to a table, dinner will be served shortly. I'd like to thank everyone for coming out . . ." While people settled at various tables, she went through her annual speech, praising the work accomplished, telling a few jokes, and mentioning the need for donations in a warm and jovial way.

Three couples Monroe vaguely knew sat at their table.

Mom blessed the meal, put the microphone in its stand, and she and Dad joined Monroe and Vickie at the circular table. Everyone chatted, and soon plates of delicious-looking salad were set before them. Throughout the various courses, Monroe kept stealing glimpses of Hadley. He couldn't stop himself.

As they were finishing dessert, his parents left the table so his mom could once again thank the attendees from the microphone and invite everyone to dance.

"Ghouls just wanna have fun." Vickie was leaning on an elbow, drawing circles on the tablecloth with her finger.

"Hm?" Did he mishear her?

She touched his arm. "It's a lovely evening. Think you could manage to join me at some point?"

"I'm sorry. I don't mean to be like this." He rubbed his eyes and tried to get in the moment. She deserved his focus.

"I think I get it. I caught a vibe of unease the day we met at your clinic, and I asked your mom about it. She said you and Hadley were an item years ago. So now she's reappeared, like a magic trick gone wrong — at least for me." Vickie shrugged. "And based on some of the looks I've seen on her face, for her too. But it would be sad if years from now you're looking at me across a room, and Hadley is long gone — because she will be — and you think, 'Vickie is great. I should've been present for one of our dates.' " She smiled. "Just a thought."

"You're right." He stood and offered his hand to Vickie. "Care to dance?"

"Why thank you." She gracefully took his

hand and stood.

He tried to shake off the negativity and escorted his date to the dance floor. The band was playing "Fly Me to the Moon," and several of his pediatric patients were dancing.

Despite seven-year-old Braden having juvenile arthritis, he was dancing his heart out to the swing number. Monroe high-fived Braden when he danced past Vickie and him. Braden's parents were nearby, watching their son and talking to each other. Monroe waved. "So glad you guys could make it."

"In other words, please be true . . ." The female singer belted the high note as Monroe spun Vickie, making her long, full skirt spin into a circle.

He looked down to see Chloe standing next to the dance floor but not dancing. Where was Hadley?

Contrary to the song lyrics, he wasn't being true. Not to himself or anyone else. Even though the sight of Hadley lighting the fire was forever seared into his memories, he was still drawn to her. But it was in both of their best interests not to be together. Why wasn't knowing that enough?

The band played the final chord of the song. Monroe caught Vickie's hands as she finished spinning, and she smiled at him. "That was fun."

"Yes, it was. You're a lovely dancer. You'll have to excuse me for this number, though, because I see a little patient of mine that might need some help. Maybe check out the desserts, and I'll meet you back at the table soon?"

Her smile faded a little. "Okay."

Monroe walked to Chloe at the edge of the dance floor. "I wonder if Chloe-kitty would like to dance with me."

Chloe held her hands up and Monroe grabbed them, but she didn't budge. She pulled one hand away from him and reached out. He looked up to see Hadley walking toward her.

Hadley took her small hand. "I'll dance with you, sweetie."

"Da-ance?" Chloe's sweet voice rose in pitch at the end of the syllable.

She spoke!

Hadley looked at Monroe and smiled, a huge, beautiful smile that made his heart leap.

"Monroe, do you think Chloe is asking both of us to dance with her?"

"I do." He held her gaze. "And we have to. It was a huge milestone for her to say the word."

Hadley peered at Chloe, looking pleased with her. "It was." She leaned down and kissed Chloe's head between the kitty ears. "Come on, let's swing dance. Not that I know how." She held Chloe by one hand and reached out to Monroe.

His breath about caught as he took her hand. Her skin was as warm and soft as he remembered. The three of them moved to the center of the floor, a sea of other young patients and adults flowing around them.

"This song is called 'Begin the Beguine,' " Monroe said. "But it's usually done as a swing tune, not a beguine, which is a Latin dance close to a slow rumba. It's ironic, really." Just as ironic as his wanting to see more of Hadley but not being able to do so without involving a patient.

"Yeah?" Hadley's face reflected amusement, as if he was entertaining in ways he hadn't intended to be. It seemed her guard was down over the joy of Chloe speaking.

He shrugged. "Music appreciation in college."

She grinned. "You always knew all sorts of random things."

"But not the important stuff, I'm afraid." *Like how to navigate contract deals without bending to my parents' whims.*

The singer's voice flowed across the

crowd. She had on a forties-style dress and gestured to the area around her.

Fading sunlight cast a golden wash on the mountain. Monroe wished he could whisk Hadley away somewhere private, if only for a few minutes. What would happen if he was honest with her after all these years — about the deal, why he had to walk away, and how he gave her the only gift a powerless teenager could give? Was it possible for both of them to let go of the past and start again?

Chloe jumped, and Hadley lost her balance. She stepped on his foot and ran into him. He let go of her hand and steadied her shoulder with his arm.

"I'm sorry." She sounded breathless. "I didn't mean to."

"It's okay. I probably deserve that." He turned to their third party in this dance. "What does Chloe think?"

Chloe smiled and stepped on his other foot, most definitely on purpose.

"You too?" He grinned and touched her nose.

"You oo?" Chloe smiled and poked his belly.

Hadley's eyes were wide as saucers when Monroe looked up. Beyond Hadley, he saw Alan and Kate at the edge of the floor, watching their attempts at dancing. "Care if

I pick your girl up?"

Alan chuckled. "Be my guest."

Monroe lifted Chloe off her feet, swinging her in a circle, and the little girl squealed with laughter. He danced across the floor with her in his arms, moving to the swing beat, and then put her in her father's arms, encouraging Chloe's parents to dance.

Hadley started to leave the dance floor, but he caught her by the hand. *Now what, genius?* He wasn't supposed to dance with her, but Chloe had given them the perfect reason to share a moment. "We haven't finished the dance we started." That was an understatement the size of the Biltmore castle. They'd begun a dance in his soul almost thirteen years ago.

She narrowed her eyes at him, but she went along with it. He wrapped an arm around her waist. For numerous reasons — his parents watching, Vickie waiting at the table, Hadley's request to keep their relationship focused only on Chloe's therapy — he shouldn't be doing this. And yet he couldn't let the chance sneak by.

The vocalist was singing about longing to relive memories, even though the previous goodbye was painful. "To live it again . . ."

"I've missed you, Hads."

"I . . ." Her eyes held confusion.

255

"It's okay. I understand why you'll never trust me. But I'm glad we've had this time, you know, at the clinic."

She said nothing, and they finished the dance in silence. When the music ended, he released her. She backed away, seeming to fade into the crowd. Would they ever get this chance again? How could it possibly be enough for a lifetime if, after Chloe was talking, he never saw Hadley again?

17

One . . . two . . . three . . . one . . . two . . . three . . . Hadley continued the repetitive count while walking away. But her go-to trick to calm herself wasn't working. She pulled off the mask and wove through the crowd, eyes on the brick herringbone-pattern floor, trying to put as many bodies as she could between Monroe and herself. What had she been thinking to agree to finish the dance with him, just the two of them?

Her shoulder lightly touched someone. "Excuse me." She didn't bother to glance up.

"Hadley, honey," Mrs. Birch said, her voice soft, but firm.

Hadley looked up.

"Mind if we speak with you for a moment?" The way Mrs. Birch spoke and carried herself screamed of wealth and power. That hadn't changed in ten years.

"I'm sorry. Maybe another time." Hadley

was desperate to leave the tent and hide for a few minutes, just until her overworked emotions weren't written all over her face. She pasted on a smile and tried to move toward an exit in the tent.

"Please." Mr. Birch stepped in front of her. "We just need a minute."

"Okay . . ." Hadley looked from one to the other.

"We only wish to confirm . . . Well, our concern is that your volunteer work at the clinic may be too much strain on your schedule."

What? Confusion spun from her heart to her mind, mixing and swirling, but coming up with nothing that made sense. Were they beating around the bush of a subject? "You seem to need something from me."

"Yes," Mr. Birch said. "My wife is being too tactful. We liked you, Hadley. We were pulling for you to overcome your background, to rise above it, but you didn't. After that unfortunate event with the Reeds' home, we felt a need to step in and help. So we created a special scholarship just for you."

"You . . . did what?" Hadley felt caught in a dream that made no sense.

Monroe's mother smiled, showing her overly white teeth. "So we're invested in your education, and we think your volunteer work is taking up too much of your study time."

Hadley's cheeks were on fire, and there wasn't enough air to breathe, despite the fact that she was near the exit of the tent. The gentle words Monroe's parents were speaking belied their actual meaning, and her stomach turned. They wanted her out of the clinic. Period. Everything else was just a polite way of accomplishing their goal.

"I'm sure you can understand, honey."

Thoughts churned, like muddy water in a flooded river. "You . . . you mean the whole time I've been in college? Undergrad and all?"

Monroe's father nodded. "We're so glad you've made it this far, even though you've obviously hit some roadblocks, or you wouldn't still be in school at twenty-seven."

Hadley had believed she'd earned the scholarship through hard work. If they were paying all the while . . .

Mrs. Birch ran a manicured nail down the side of her neck. "The problem is we really can't, in good faith, continue to fund your schooling if you are going to pursue a relationship with our son."

"What? I'm not —"

"We saw you two dancing." Mrs. Birch

gave a half smile that didn't reach her eyes, while he continued to nod.

The conversation finally made sense. This was a thinly veiled threat to remove her scholarship. The whole family seemed to run on assumption and manipulation. "I assure you I have no interest in Monroe." She should have walked away as soon as Chloe was with her parents.

"Then no harm's been done as long as your visits to the clinic are done. Completely done." Mr. Birch wrapped an arm around his wife's waist. "They have very capable therapists there, and you have to focus on that schooling." They walked away.

Hadley stood there, dazed and watching them go to the dance floor. She was a fraud without realizing it. She hadn't earned the scholarship. It had been based on her past connections to a wealthy family. But why would they do that for her? It was clear they believed the worst and had no respect for her.

Elliott spotted her and made a beeline. "What's wrong?" Elliott glanced behind her. "I saw you dancing. Did Monroe say something to you?"

Hadley fought to speak. "No . . . he was perfectly nice. I . . . I can't talk about it now. It's . . . beyond belief. His parents . . ."

Hadley closed her eyes, her chest threatening to explode with anger. "I need to get out of here for a few minutes and go . . . somewhere and think." She turned to look at their table. "But Sam."

"I'll cover for you. No problem."

"Thanks." Hadley immediately headed out of the tent. Once free of it, she took longer strides, but her dress and heels didn't allow her a lot of freedom. It was a big mistake to come here, and she'd spent thirty dollars on the dress, mask, and bag from Goodwill. Money she and Elliott could have spent on therapy toys or on something to better their lives.

As thoughts of money tumbled through her, she felt determination rise strong inside her. She had to come up with a way to repay the money to the Birches. Not that she had any clue how to do that since thirty dollars seemed like a large amount. It would be easier to come up with more money if she could get her license, but to get her license, she had to have a master's degree. And to get that, she had to attend school. What a mess.

She walked as fast as she could, but she couldn't outrun the tears. She was such a fool to think she was good enough to earn a scholarship like that.

"Hadley, wait!" Monroe's voice. She wasn't stopping. Not going to happen.

"Please, just leave me alone," she called over her shoulder as she kept walking down the grassy hill, away from the crowded event tent. But she could tell by the sound of footfalls that he was quickly catching up with her. It was unfair that men's dress shoes didn't impede walking in grass.

"What did my parents say?" He was beside her now.

She shook her head, not looking at him. "I always wondered if you felt guilty for leaving me minutes before I was handcuffed. I wondered how you slept all those years. But your parents washed the guilt away with a load of money, didn't they? And now? I feel filthy."

"They told you about the scholarship and the lawyer."

She stopped and faced him. "Lawyer?" She was drowning now, just as surely as if the Birches had tossed her into a swift, deep river. It was unnerving to realize how much they knew about her life, how much control they'd had while she rocked along in ignorance. "How could you do that to me?"

"Hadley, I *loved* you. I wanted a better life for you. I couldn't make the arson charges go away, but I could see that you had two things you desperately needed: a good lawyer and a scholarship. I was a kid, and the only leverage I had to help you was to agree to end our relationship. I wanted to give you your dream of working in speech therapy."

She wanted to clench her fist and deck him. "My career wasn't my only dream. I wanted a life with you. We would have found a way to get through school without your parents' backing."

"You needed a good lawyer, the kind that required money, or you'd have been found guilty of arson, and I couldn't let you go to jail. A felony sentence, regardless how light, would've stopped you from ever being allowed to work somewhere decent, much less with children."

"So what was I to you, a charity case?" She paused, and new thoughts streamed into her brain. "Seems like you were a teen rebelling against your parents, and I was the perfect solution. It's really worked out for you in the long run. It sounds as if they've given you money, living quarters, and a business in order to get you back on the straight and narrow, which means without me. And then you talked them into paying for my lawyer and my education so you'd feel less guilty for using me, is that it?"

"No! It's not like that." He rubbed his temples. "Hadley, you're forgetting. I *saw* you that day."

"Oh, that again. What exactly do you think you saw — since I didn't do it!"

"It's what I said ten years ago. I was driving past the Reed place with my parents. I . . . I saw you pour a liquid into a ditch of leaves and tree limbs and light it. My first thought was you were helping them because Mr. Reed had been in the hospital and unable to tend to his yard. Later I realized what you were doing. But I loved you enough never to put myself in a position where I had to say that in court."

"When did you stop believing in me, Monroe?"

He studied her. "I . . . I . . ."

"Oh, come on. Spill the truth. If you believed in me that day, there was a specific moment when you stopped."

"The facts came out."

"The facts came out before I was even arrested?" She leaned in, challenging his statement. "Because that's when you broke up with me — before I was handcuffed."

"Yeah. My mom used her inside information from the police and years of experience as a lawyer and walked me through everything step-by-step."

Hadley's heart broke all over again. He had truly thought she was guilty all this time. She determined to speak softly and keep as much emotion out of her words as possible. The sooner she washed her life of the Birches, the better. "Feelings of remorse had washed over me as I walked past the Reed place, and I made a rash decision to try to make up for the bad blood with them. So I was doing yard work, and I started the fire to burn the leaves, just as Mr. Reed always did. It wasn't wise, but that's all I'm guilty of — being a teen who didn't dream an act of kindness could be seen as a criminal act."

Monroe blinked and shook his head. "It couldn't be that simple . . ." He studied her before turning his head and looking at the tent or maybe at his parents. "My folks would've . . ." He returned his attention to her, and his confusion seemed to fade, as if something was dawning on him.

But Hadley didn't care, not right now while she grappled with her own overload of new information. "You know what. You're right, Monroe. I've been lying all these years. I set their house on fire." She walked off.

"Hadley, wait." He stepped in front of her and lifted her chin with his hand, making her look in his eyes. "It was that simple, wasn't it?"

She could see something new reflecting in their blue depths. Was it realization? If so, it was too late. "It doesn't matter anymore."

"I thought . . . I was told . . ." He shook his head. "I'm sorry. I can't blame anyone else, as much as I'd like to. I believed you at first, and then I let myself believe the easy thing about you, that you were guilty. I'm so sorry, Hads."

She pushed his hand away and took a step back from him. "I've been working with you for Chloe's sake and hopefully also to help Jason, who could really use a break in this hard world. But now that I've been effectively banned from your clinic, you and I can part ways for good."

"I don't want that."

"There's nothing left to say. At least everything is in the open now. But there is no solution to the pain we've caused each other." She took off her shoes and walked down the grass hill, confident he wouldn't try to stop her again.

18

Monroe lowered himself in the green plush armchair across the desk from April Parker, J.D, as printed on her brass desk plate. Any doubt he had about Hadley's innocence was gone — one hundred percent — but he needed to hear all the facts from her lawyer before he confronted his mother.

"Thank you for meeting with me so quickly."

"Of course. Anything for Lisa's family." April had gone to law school with Monroe's mother and was in the same sorority. They apparently had taken some kind of lifetime oath to be as loyal to each other as sisters, even after school was over. He needed to tread lightly, because he was already in hot water with another one of his mom's sorority sisters after his dates with Vickie.

"Could you look up some details concerning a client you represented in 2003?"

"Two thousand and three? The one involving your high school girlfriend?"

"Yes, please."

"I doubt I'd need to look up anything." The woman with pixie-cut red hair nodded. "I took the case for your mom, and Hadley Granger, whether one agrees with her or not, isn't one to fade from memory. What do you need to know?"

Monroe took a deep breath. How could he frame these questions in the most inoffensive way possible? He had rehearsed them in his head on the way here, but none of those versions were coming to him. "Could we keep everything we say off the record?"

She laughed. "That case was closed long ago. Everything is public record, so that's not a problem."

"Yeah, I know what the papers said. Hadley was accused of arson, and the whole time she declared herself innocent."

April fidgeted with a pen. "She was adamant. But the thing is, every kid her age takes a plea deal if one's offered. They're scared of jail and just want to settle matters — guilty or not. But she would not budge."

"The day of the fire I was driving by, and I . . . saw her start it."

"You and two other witnesses. It's safe to assume you kept that quiet so you didn't have to testify against her."

He nodded.

She folded her hands on her cherrywood desk. "She never denied starting the fire. But she said Mr. and Mrs. Reed pulled into the driveway and got out of their car, and Mr. Reed tried to kick her off the property as Mrs. Reed went inside. Hadley picked up the hose to douse the fire, and he snatched it from her and told her he'd call the police if she didn't leave. I hired a team of investigators, and they spent weeks canvassing the neighborhood, looking for a witness who saw more than her starting the fire. The investigators finally caught a break." She leaned back, smiling.

"I read that the case was dismissed on a technicality."

"Yes, I don't know why the journalists worded it that way. But discs with video footage were found, and one clip showed Mr. Reed jerking the hose from her hand, turning it off, and making her leave his property."

"A video clip?"

"I know. It was as if God was busy being a father to the fatherless. A group of middle schoolers from a different neighborhood had been in the vicinity of the Reed place every afternoon for a week, filming for a school project. They had no idea what they had on those discs. But once we viewed the discs, we saw everything unfold as Hadley had described. The judge dismissed the case and warned Hadley to stay out of trouble."

Monroe's world slowed as he tried to process the information. He felt *so* stupid. How could he have doubted Hadley? He stared at his folded hands, remembering months of misery when he was unable to think, eat, or sleep for missing Hadley. "It was all for nothing."

"For nothing?"

He looked up, realizing he'd mumbled his thoughts. "Just thinking out loud, I guess."

"Monroe, I've answered your questions, at least the ones you've asked so far. What's nagging at you about this?"

He hesitated. "I made a deal with my parents to stay away from Hadley in exchange for a good lawyer for her. They agreed to other things, but the only reason I gave in to what they wanted was to be sure Hadley had proper counsel, and now I realize she didn't need you."

"She did, actually. There was her confession that she started the fire, corroborated by two witnesses, and she'd been before a judge once before due to vandalism of the Reed property. She needed me, and my expensive team, or the evidence that set her free wouldn't have been found, or at least not for years. A court-appointed lawyer wouldn't have had investigators searching for evidence for weeks on end."

So he'd done one thing right. That helped. A lot.

"I appreciate knowing that." His heart felt a little lighter, and his head cleared a bit. "Why did Mr. Reed kick her off the property and then act as if he didn't?"

"His behavior that day seemed to have been linked to the fact that he'd had a medical event a few days prior. He was on powerful medicines. Long story short, I talked to the lawyer who watched Mr. Reed's face when he saw the video clip the first time. That lawyer firmly believed Mr. Reed had no recollection at all of the exchange between him and Hadley. He said that all he remembered was her hurrying away from his property, and then his house burned down about an hour later."

How often were foster kids falsely accused, falsely imprisoned because they had no one to fight for them? He thanked God that his sacrifice to get her a good lawyer had made a positive difference for Hadley, but how much better would their lives be if he'd defied his parents and been honest with Hadley about why he had to end things? Then she would've known he was on her side and by her side, even if he couldn't be there physically.

"That answers all I needed to know." He couldn't stay here any longer. He stood and offered his hand. "Thank you."

She shook it. "I'm puzzled why you didn't come by here a decade ago and ask questions, but I'm glad to be of help."

Why hadn't he asked earlier? Was it to keep the deal with his parents or because, after she left with Kyle, Monroe started guarding his heart? After she ran off, he found it comforting to believe she was guilty and he'd done his fair share by ensuring she had a good lawyer.

"I do have one more question. Did my parents know all this?"

She seemed hesitant, but after a few moments she nodded. "Not in time to stop Hadley from running off. But, yes, a few hours after the case was dismissed, I spoke to your mom and filled her in."

He thanked her and left the downtown Asheville law office, with the guilt of how he'd hurt Hadley because of his doubts weighing heavily with his every step. When he reached his car, he pulled out his iPhone and touched the number he had gleaned from Hadley's volunteer intake form.

"Hello?" The voice was definitely not Hadley's.

"Elliott? This is Monroe. May I speak with Hadley?"

"Go away." Her voice was calm, but he heard no give to it. "You walked away from her before. Do her a favor and walk away now. Doesn't she deserve to be free of you?"

"You may be right, but she and I need the one thing we never got — closure."

"Now? You mutilated her heart ten years ago, and *now* you want a heartwarming resolution?"

"I made mistakes. Huge ones. But I . . . I was also lied to. There were things, important things, I didn't know, Elliott."

She said nothing.

"Elliott, think back. I was desperately trying to get to her the night she was picked up. We tried to find where they'd taken her, remember?"

"Yeah. But evidently you were just good at pretending that you were looking for her so it made you appear to care."

It dawned on him that there was a third victim in this mess. Elliott. She'd turned her life upside down to help Hadley regain her footing after the trial. "I wasn't pretending, Elliott. Could I talk to Hadley?"

She sighed. "Hang on."

He heard footsteps and maybe a door opening and then garbled talk between two people. While listening and waiting, a plan came to him.

"She says no."

"Tell her I have ideas of ways to help Chloe. Ask if she can meet me at our spot."

"Is that actually true?" Elliott asked. "You know what. Never mind. Hold on."

He heard garbled voices again.

"She's agreed to meet you there in an hour, and, Monroe, if she returns hurt and upset, I'm going to —"

"She won't." He hoped he could keep his word. He was going to give it all he had.

A little less than an hour later he was standing at the overlook to the French Broad River, his car a few feet away on the asphalt-and-gravel parking area sticking out from the road. He looked at the black BMW he'd kept all these years. If he was honest with himself, he supposed it was a way of holding on to his memories of driving and riding with Hadley.

Hadley's Civic pulled into a spot a few spaces away from his BMW. It was the only other space available. Apparently many people liked the idea of driving on the Blue Ridge Parkway and stopping at this overlook, despite that it was a cold, late-October afternoon. Monroe walked toward her car. Hadley stepped out, a white crocheted hat covering her curls, and she wrapped a worn wool peacoat around her body. Her eyes caught his, and he could feel the profound hurt behind them.

He took a deep breath and got down on a knee. Hadley's eyes quickly widened, reflecting confusion.

"Hadley, I'm so, so sorry."

She crossed her arms, leaning down to him. "What are you doing? Get up. You look like you are trying to propose to me or something."

He shook his head and gestured to the people around them, who were pretending not to look. "I don't care what others think. I don't care if I look like a fool. I was wrong. When I came to the group home, I didn't tell you the truth of what was going on, of why I needed to break up with you. Worse, I doubted you. I trusted my eyes and my mom's advice more than my faith in you."

She leaned down again. "It means a lot that you don't care what people think, and I get that you need forgiveness, but putting me on the spot isn't working for me." She looked at the gawkers. "Please get up."

Monroe stood. "I'm not asking to be your

boyfriend. But I need you to know that I'm truly sorry for hurting you, for not believing in you or standing by you. We've both paid a high price, and if we could forgive each other and become friends, even ones who only send Christmas cards, I think it would really help us . . . or at least me."

Hadley rubbed her arms, looking cold. "*You* didn't pay."

"But I did. In every sense of the word. I kept my agreement with my parents, thinking it was the only way to get you a good lawyer, but all I wanted was to be standing nearby whenever and wherever you were released. *I* wanted to be the one to run away with you."

"Monroe . . . I didn't run off with Kyle. He picked up Elliott and me from the courthouse, drove us to Gainesville, Georgia, and left the next day. There was nothing romantic between us. I told Tara to tell you I left with Kyle because I wanted to let you know I didn't need you. I wanted to hurt you like you'd hurt me. I'm sorry."

He had reeled in pain from that. "I forgive you, Hadley."

After a few moments of silence, Hadley leaned against her car. "How are we so bad for each other that we continue to cause this much heartache even all these years later?"

"We're not bad for each other. Everything else just gets in the way."

"Everything being in the way is the evidence that we're not good for each other. But I forgive you. You can let go of your guilt. You were a child trying to make adult decisions. We both were. But we're adults now, both of us free to decide what's in our own best interest, and for me I need to be free of the Birches, all of you."

The relief at receiving her forgiveness quickly chilled to an icy barb. "I understand. But our work with Chloe isn't complete. She seems to respond particularly well when we work with her together, don't you think?" Was he grasping at straws to be near Hadley, or was he seeing Chloe's situation correctly? "She said three words for us only a few days ago."

Hadley's eyes rested on the river in the valley below. "I'm aware, and I feel I'm letting her down by not continuing with you and Rebecca at Children's."

"As embarrassing as that situation is, I can't do anything to get you in the door of Children's Therapy. I went into business with my parents. It's my license, but it's their money and rules. I had no idea they were living a lie in order to control me. But if they find you at the clinic again, they could release me and put someone else in charge or even shut it down."

Hadley looked resigned to the situation. "That doesn't surprise me at this point."

He was furious with his parents, and he wasn't yet sure how to handle the situation and move forward. They felt entitled to mislead him as long as they poured money into something for him. Apparently where the faithful believed in washing their sins in the blood of Jesus, his parents believed in washing theirs in their money.

Hadley shivered, and Monroe wanted to take off his thick coat and wrap it around her worn one. He took a deep breath, trying to ignore the volume of emotions churning inside him. "I think we should come up with a new plan, but it can't include Rebecca. It would be unethical to put her between my parents' wishes and mine. I think we need to have the sessions with Chloe somewhere else. She did so well at the nature center and again at the gala event. I bet we could find good settings that would help her make headway."

Hadley's brows narrowed, and she seemed to be pondering his suggestion. About a minute later she nodded. "I love Chloe enough that I'll agree to do that." She turned, and her eyes met his. "I spoke to financial aid at school this morning. I removed the scholarship your parents created from my account, and I'm in the process of applying for student loans. In case you don't know, repayment of student loans won't kick in until after I graduate. I'll finish my degree, but I've removed your parents' right to lord that over me."

Monroe nodded. She clearly intended to leave no ties to him intact.

Hadley walked to her car and opened the door. "Send a text of when and where you'd like me to meet with Chloe." She got in and drove away.

Monroe got in his own car and leaned his forehead on the worn leather steering wheel cover. Her forgiveness helped. Knowing the whole story helped. But he ached for the future they should have had together. He had given it all up for what amounted to so little.

Hadley dried her tears as she pulled into the driveway. Why did he still get to her like this? She should be unemotional at this point and able to do what she needed to do and move on from Monroe for good.

She parked the car. After taking a moment

to get control of her emotions, she got out and walked to the apartment door.

Elliott looked up from her spot on the couch. "Hey, Hadley, everything go okay?"

"Sure, just wrapping up loose ends." Hadley took a seat next to her, unwilling to talk about it just yet. "What's in your hand?"

Elliott wobbled a letter. "I just received it. Apparently the landlords couldn't find us when we were camping, but once we started living here and turned in a change of address, they sent us this. I don't know why they didn't just call, but our apartment is actually reopening soon. According to the letter, we get to move back, and it doesn't even mention the eviction notice."

"That's good." Hadley rubbed her eyes. Between lack of sleep and crying, they ached and felt as if they were full of sand. "Think there's some kind of forgiveness-on-back-rent-due-to-fire plan?" She chuckled at her nonsense.

"Probably more of an oversight on their part, but it could buy us some time before the back rent is due." Elliott's eyes moved from the letter to Hadley's face. "Ready to talk yet?"

Elliott knew her well. "Monroe apologized. It was a real apology, like literally on a knee. I forgave him, and all the missing, angering pieces fit now. But, Ellie, I thought growing up without parents was bad. It seems that having two-faced, manipulative, rich ones might actually be worse."

Elliott blinked. "Does this mean he's not at all the jerk we thought?"

Hadley explained everything.

"Wow, Hads. How confusing for you. I mean, how are you supposed to feel about Monroe now?"

"I know. I feel less hostile but still not interested. He proved then that he has the ability to leave. It doesn't matter his reasons. When he had a chance at the group home to tell me the truth of what was going on, he didn't. He left me broken when I was at the legal system's mercy and terrified of the future. A man like that can't be trusted."

"Except he wasn't a man. He was a confused teen being manipulated by his family."

"He was old enough, but that brings me to another point. His family is a worse mess to deal with than having no family, and I *will* choose someone who has good, loving parents so that my future children have a support system, grandparents, and beautiful memories growing up. That's the kind of man I want, and I won't settle for anyone whose family is a train wreck like Monroe's.

And clearly Lisa and Greg Birch are a train wreck. They just don't know it."

Elliott wrapped an arm around Hadley's shoulders. Hadley laid her head against her, and they sat in silence for several moments.

Elliott squeezed her shoulders. "We need a treat. I have twenty dollars in my pocket. Let's go for hot chocolate. We need a good chat and a couple of good books to curl up with and escape into before we fall asleep."

Hadley agreed, and about half an hour later they were sitting next to the tall windows of a downtown bookshop and café, hot chocolate in hand.

As she sipped her hot chocolate, Hadley looked out the window at the crowds walking by. "What if we can't get Chloe to talk? In addition to the heartbreaking reality of watching her not be able to speak, we haven't been able to find an alternate job prospect for Jason."

"Didn't she say three words at the dance? That has to be significant progress."

Hadley nodded. She broke a shortbread cookie in two and dipped a piece in the sweet liquid. "As much as I wanted to completely shut Monroe out of my life after finding out what his parents did —"

"Which was absolutely outrageous and is still hard to fathom." Elliott lifted her cup to her lips. "Sorry, continue."

"Chloe does the best when Monroe and I are working with her together. I'm going to meet him outside of the clinic, and we'll continue working with Chloe."

Elliott reached forward and placed her hand on Hadley's. "That has to be hard, but you are doing the right thing by sticking with that sweet girl. I'm proud of you, Hads."

"Thanks."

19

Monroe paced the hall of his flat, his soft-soled shoes squeaking against the glossy hardwood floors. He caught glimpses of rooms as he walked, each with impeccably selected decorations that he hadn't chosen or paid for. His heart raced, and he was pretty sure if he held out his hands, he'd see they were shaking. His parents would arrive any moment. His entire life he'd operated under the assumption that they knew best.

They didn't.

A light knock let him know they were here. He crossed the spacious apartment living room and opened the door.

"Hey, sweetie." His mom gave him a hug before entering.

"Your text was rather cryptic." Dad walked in. "Asking us to come by after work but not saying why."

"Yeah, too much to cover via text or a

call." Monroe gestured to the two chairs by the gas fireplace. "Have a seat." He closed the door.

"Already cold out this year." Dad flipped the switch next to the hearth, and the fire instantly came to life. His parents settled into the chairs.

Monroe sat on the edge of the oak coffee table at the center of the room. He leaned forward and put his elbows on his knees, making eye contact with one and then the other. "Okay. I need to tell you several things without interruption. Can you allow me that?"

Dad furrowed his brows. "I suppose so."

Mom nodded, concern etched on her face. "What's this about?"

Monroe's heart pounded. Why was it so difficult to confront a parent? He swallowed hard. "I spoke with April Parker. Hadley was innocent. You knew that, but you didn't tell me."

Dad adjusted his glasses. "Now, Son —"

Monroe held up a hand. "Let me finish. You *knew* she was truly innocent, but you let me believe for all these years that the fire I saw her start was the cause of the Reed house burning to the ground. You let me believe her temper and spite got the best of her, but the truth was she was doing yard work for them. Contrition for the arguments they'd had. You knew all that, which means you've lied to me by omission. And even now, a decade later, you've been manipulating me — and Hadley — based on my misconceptions." He pulled out the worn set of keys that went to the BMW they'd given him on his sixteenth birthday. "I'm done." He held them out to his father. "These are to the car and the condo. I'll be out in a week, and then I'll mail you the other set. Sell, rent, do whatever you want. I didn't buy it, and I don't want it or anything else from either of you."

His parents stared at him, neither one taking the keys, so he set them on the coffee table.

His mom's eyes were wide, but she leaned forward to put a hand on his. "Monroe, no."

Monroe pulled back.

"Honey, we're not the way you're depicting us." Mom glanced at Dad, as if she was unsure of her own words. "We've always tried to help you become the successful professional we knew you could be. The car and condo were gifts. You don't need to return our gifts just because you are upset about something that doesn't even affect you anymore."

Monroe stood. "It affects me every day.

Did you ever care about what *I* wanted out of life? I did everything your way because I genuinely thought you were good and honest people who gave wise advice. I ignored what I wanted because I kept thinking, *Trust your parents, not yourself. Look at the person you fell in love with. You don't know what's best, Monroe. Mom and Dad do.* So I've followed your counsel, but I've never been happy, and that's because the life I actually wanted, aside from my degree in speech therapy, was nothing like this." He gestured at the luxury condo.

"And what life would that be?" His father tapped his fingers together. "Let's say we hadn't intervened and you two had eloped as teenagers." Dad made a running motion with his fingers. "Best-case scenario you'd be living paycheck to paycheck with someone whose background is totally unknown. You don't know her family or genetics. All you know is that she came from a household dysfunctional enough that *both* parents lost custody of her. Excuse my clumsy metaphor, but she's like a mutt that comes with no guarantees. She could carry the gene for bipolar or worse. If she were to leave you after you fathered a baby or two or three with her, your dream would become an instant nightmare. You would end up paying child support your entire life, and she'd have the most influence over who those children became, which could prove really embarrassing for you. Someone of your quality and heritage doesn't make a family with someone like that."

Monroe's blood boiled at his father's callous words. How could he think something that dehumanizing about anyone, but especially Hadley? "The absolute best thing I can imagine is having a whole litter of 'mutts' and us all enjoying each other."

His mom stood and put her hands up as if to stem the flow of anger. "You're upset, and I get it. But we did what we thought was best for you, and we went out of our way to keep our end of the bargain, so that should show you our hearts are in the right place." She took the keys off the coffee table and tried to hand them back to Monroe.

He shook his head. "This isn't something I'm going to change my mind about."

"That's absurd, Monroe. You're talking as if this situation is a reality. Hadley isn't even in your life anymore. She told us she wasn't interested in you. I'm sure she has someone. She's never been without a boyfriend for long, including the one she left the courthouse with after *we* paid to keep her out of jail." Despite her gentle demeanor, his mom was using her lawyer tactics, making and embellishing points at all costs, spinning half-truths to her advantage.

He raked his hands through his hair. "Nice, Mom. Real nice."

"Your mother is right." Dad folded his hands. "You'll meet a woman who's right for you. I'm sure of it. In fact, I may even know —"

"No." Monroe backed away from both of them. "I don't want to be with the type of person you think I need. Just how many couples that are well bred, wealthy, educated, and pushed into a relationship by their parents are actually happy?"

"You're talking nonsense, Son. The people you refer to sacrificed a lot to build a life worth having, and because of that, they have it all."

"Yeah, they have everything except gratefulness, thankfulness, and a willingness to live modestly. Take away the money, and almost every one of those families would fall apart in a matter of months. The only thing they have is money and what money can buy. That's not me. Not anymore."

"Oh no, no, no." Dad stood, determination reflecting in his face. "We are not doing this, Monroe. We have an agreement, and we've paid good money to keep up our end of it. The legal fees alone were staggering, and then we followed through to the tune of almost twenty-five thousand dollars a year for her undergrad years. Don't make us out to be the bad guys because you've suddenly decided you don't like the deal." He pointed. "If you can't follow our agreement, we *will* remove you from the clinic and appoint someone more stable that will reflect the type of leadership that Mt. Pisgah Medical Group wants."

Monroe couldn't believe their lack of give and their inability to see that they were wrong. "Now *that* is absurd. It was bizarre and unprofessional for you to put that provision in the partnership agreement. I have patients who rely on the care they get from me — children from all walks of life."

"That is where we stand." His father looked over to his mother, and she nodded.

Monroe remembered Jesus's words in Matthew to the rich young man seeking true happiness. *Sell what you have, give it to the poor, and come follow me.* Monroe didn't believe everyone needed to do that, but those words spoke to him. They had spoken to him most of his life . . . when he was listening. He hadn't earned the clinic or any of the riches in his life. He would just have to trust that the board would see potential for the business and would appoint an adequate director at Children's Therapy. He nodded at his parents, and his mom smiled slightly, probably thinking the matter was settled.

Their smugness got under his skin, and he wanted them to understand he was serious about not giving in to any more of their manipulation. He loved them. He was grateful to them for so many things in life, including paying for Hadley's legal fees, but being thankful was different from being molded by their vision of his future.

Monroe took a deep breath. "Why don't you just assume we're a couple, Hadley and I." He cringed at the hint of a lie, but they'd manipulated every part of his life with their lies.

"Is that true?" Mom studied him.

"I'll serve as director of the clinic until the end of the year to tie up loose ends with patients. I'll even resign to save you the embarrassment of firing me."

His mother looked as if he'd confessed to murder. His father's hands were clenched so tightly that his knuckles were white. Without another word his dad wrapped an arm around his mom's shoulders and escorted her out of the apartment.

After the door closed, Monroe collapsed

on the couch, dragging his hand down his face. He stared at the smooth, vaulted ceiling. He had no idea where he was going to live or where he would work, but he felt lighter than he had in years.

He had about ten thousand dollars in his bank account, left from the comparatively small salary he'd drawn during the two years he worked as director of Children's Therapy. Since it was set up as a junior partnership and he didn't complete it, he had relatively little to show for his work. Should he donate it all since it came from the clinic, which his parents had purchased? That wouldn't be very responsible because then he would need to rely on others until he found a job and worked enough weeks to get a paycheck. He also had a large trust fund in his name set up by his maternal grandparents. He hadn't checked to see how much money was in that account. He would have to pray about where to put that capital.

But as sure as the setting sun, he wasn't using it on himself. The money in and of itself wasn't bad, but he hadn't earned it.

He pulled his iPhone from his pocket. He might need to mail it back too, but without any doubt he needed to get off his parents' plan and get his own plan. Everything he had was tied to what his parents had given him, and he hadn't thought much about it — until now.

He touched the contact for Trent.

"Hey, boss." Trent's monotone voice rang clear.

"Not your boss for much longer."

"Yeah, yeah. What are you going to do without me after I'm done with my research at your clinic?"

Monroe laughed hard, and it surprised him.

"Didn't think it was that funny."

"You might not now, but I bet you will soon. Can you give me a ride to work tomorrow?" His parents had taken the keys, and Monroe wondered if they had driven the car home.

"Something wrong with your car? And if so, aren't you going to rent some fantastic machine?"

"No and no. I gave the car back to my parents. And anything else I could. I'll, uh, tell you later. You still have that room available in your house vacated by Sam?"

"Yes . . ." Trent drew out the word.

"Could I sublease it from you?"

"Are you trying to punk me? I mean, the room is yours if you need it, but I'm waiting for the punch line here."

"Thanks, man. I'll tell you the whole thing

tomorrow."

"Okay, see you then."

Monroe pushed the red circle to end the call and tossed the device gently on the coffee table.

Hadley would never take him back, but he could still live his life the way he had always intended. And that was to live it with purpose, to do as much good as he could. He didn't need the prestige or expensive possessions. He never had.

20

Hadley smelled the fragrant steam coming off the quiche she carried, and her stomach growled. She followed Elliott from the car to Trent's small porch, the front of a gray ranch-style residence with a red door.

Hadley peeled back the tinfoil that covered the top of the pie dish to take a peek. Browned to perfection. Elliott had gotten up early to make this and had put a lot of care into it. "You better watch out, or I may take this dish and run. Then it wouldn't be much of a surprise breakfast date." The aromas of egg, cheese, bacon, and veggies were even more tempting up close.

Elliott looked over her shoulder and narrowed her eyes. "There's plenty to go around." She pressed the small glowing doorbell. "Besides, I'm carrying arguably the more important part to Trent: the coffee." She held up a thermal carafe.

The door opened, and Trent's large frame

came into view. "Oh." His face lit up as his eyes rested on Elliott. "Well hello."

"Good morning," Elliott's cheery voice returned.

"Could there be a more amazing sight on this Sunday morning? A beautiful girl surprising me with coffee."

Hadley couldn't see Elliott's face, but she bet that her friend was blushing at being called beautiful. It had been out of Elliott's comfort zone to let Trent into her life, but Hadley was so glad for her.

He pretended to look around. "I assume you brought a carafe for you too?"

Elliott laughed. "No, but we have quiche."

"Quiche too? Awesome. Um, come on in, but I need to tell you both something."

They followed him into the small house. A loud steam whistle went off, interrupting whatever Trent was trying to say.

"Oops." He stepped off to the side into the narrow kitchen and removed the whistling teakettle from the burner. "I was going to make pour-over coffee, but it looks like you have it covered."

The kitchen, which was visible from the front door, needed at least twenty minutes of straightening, with obvious remnants of dinner from the night before. A few dress shirts and pants hung over the backs of the dining room chairs, and the sliding wooden doors to the adjoining laundry closet had been left ajar. Boxes — some opened, some taped shut — sat on the floor.

"Hey, Trent," — Monroe's voice made Hadley jump — "you weren't kidding when you said I could run out of hot water."

His voice seemed to come from the hall. A moment later he appeared, walking toward them, a beige towel draped over his head. He had on a white T-shirt and gray sweatpants printed with the light blue UNC logo.

Trent chuckled. "Dude, I warned you not to take a long shower. It's only a twenty-five gallon tank."

"Huh. I thought that was some kind of sitcom joke." His face was hidden as he scrubbed his head with the towel, drying that thick mop of brown hair. "I didn't think it actually happened in real life." He dropped the towel over his shoulders. "Oh . . ." His eyes met Hadley's, and he stopped in his tracks.

"By the way, Hadley and Elliott are here." Trent turned toward them. "By the way, Monroe is here. Sorry."

Hadley averted her eyes, but not because he lacked clothing. His gaze made her uncomfortable, as if he searched to see more of her thoughts than she was willing to reveal. What was he doing taking a shower at Trent's?

"Hadley." He nodded at her and then Elliott. "Uh, hi. Trent didn't say you were coming — not that it's a problem. I mean, I'm glad to see you."

Was he? He didn't look glad, just rattled. It'd been two weeks since he'd asked her to forgive him, and they'd met at an appointed spot to work with Chloe four times since then. But that was easier than this meeting. When helping Chloe, they were professional in their work and parted ways afterward. But the recollection of his kneeling at their old spot had startled her awake numerous times and forced its way into her mind throughout the day.

"Elliott made breakfast for Trent, and I tagged along."

"Ah, well, that's good." He walked to the kitchen table and picked up a dress shirt and pair of slacks that were hanging on the back of a dining chair. "Excuse me." He walked back through the narrow hallway to what Hadley assumed was a bedroom.

Elliott pointed at Trent with the carafe she was still holding. "You didn't tell us Monroe was rooming with you. How long has this been going on and why?"

"About two weeks. He gave up his apartment. I didn't say anything because it's his news to tell, not mine."

"Fair enough." Elliott shrugged at Hadley and then set the thermos on the kitchen counter.

Hadley set the dish she was carrying next to it. "I should go," she said softly.

Elliott angled her head, looking unsure whether to question Hadley or support her decision.

Trent set a few dirty dishes in the sink. "You don't know, do you?"

"Know what?" Hadley asked.

"I hope you'll excuse my intrusion in the matter." Trent gestured in the direction where Monroe had exited. "But I've been the listening ear while Monroe adjusts to all the new information, and he's not going to tell you something I think you need to know."

"Tell me what?"

"The deal he made with his parents to get a lawyer for you is what kept you from going to jail for a crime you didn't commit."

Unease settled over Hadley. She shouldn't have come. It should've dawned on her that Trent and Monroe were close friends. But Trent couldn't be blamed for this conversation. She would stick up for Elliott in the same way. "Well, maybe."

"Not maybe. The lawyer he bartered your relationship for hired a very expensive investigative team, and that team uncovered the evidence that proved you were innocent. The chance that a court-appointed lawyer would have had the resources or determination to uncover that evidence is slim to none."

Hadley's appetite instantly disappeared. Was that true? If so, why hadn't Monroe mentioned what he'd done for her? Had his character stopped him, or did he think she wouldn't believe him, so he didn't even try?

"I . . . I don't know what to say to that. Or what to think."

She caught Elliott's eye and nodded toward the door. Trent could drive Elliott home later.

Elliott put a hand on her arm. "Don't go, Hads. You were looking forward to our eating breakfast with Trent."

"I needed to get that off my chest. What you do with it is up to you, but let's change the subject. Come on, you girls have a seat." Trent's voice was cheerful. He looked at the table covered in laundry. "Hold on." He picked up all the articles of clothing and dumped them in a nearby basket and then walked the few steps back to the kitchen.

"I'll pour the coffee and put breakfast on plates."

Hadley and Elliott sat next to each other at the small, round table. With Trent in the kitchen, Elliott leaned in. "Hadley, I saw Monroe at school the day after you were caught and picked up, after he tried to meet up with you but couldn't. He was distraught. We did everything we could in order to find where you were taken. Later, after he broke up with you, I convinced myself that he'd been acting. I was so angry with him for you and with you. Now I think he was sincere. I don't know if it helps to hear that part all these years later."

Hadley drew a deep breath and slowly released it, asking herself the same question time and again. Who was Monroe? She offered Elliott a smile and a nod before looking out the window. The view was of a small part of town, a busy street, and beyond that, mountains on fire with fall colors.

Who was Monroe? She wished the question would go away.

He had the ability to walk away, which had repelled her. But she had also seen him stick around to help Chloe even outside of paid sessions, when it would have been much easier to drop Hadley's involvement. When they were volunteers in high school, he used to give of himself if his actions could help a child's situation. And patience? He had it in spades, both with her when they were in a relationship and with his young patients at the clinic.

Trent returned to the table with three plates of quiche on one arm and three cups of coffee in the other hand.

"Whoa, do you need help?" Elliott started to stand up.

"Nope." Trent expertly spread the plates and cups across the table to their three places. "Waiter skills. Got me through undergrad."

They said grace and began eating. Hadley took a bite and discovered it was as delicious as she'd predicted. Trent and Elliott chatted about hospital happenings.

As the two talked, Hadley's eyes wandered over the living space. An opened cardboard box sat on the floor near the table. She leaned over slightly to see its contents. A framed picture was stacked on top of several other frames. In the photograph Monroe was sitting with about thirty children. She picked it up. Elementary school–age kids, who looked to be from a South or Central American country, were climbing on his head and shoulders, a brilliant smile lit up his unshaven face, and an opened storybook rested in his lap.

Monroe entered the room, dressed more like she was used to seeing him — in gray slacks and a blue, collared shirt. He gestured at the picture. "Find something interesting?"

She jolted, realizing she still had the picture in her hand. She couldn't shove it back in its box and ask, "What picture?" So she held it up. "Where are you?"

"El Salvador." He turned to Trent. "We still going to church this morning?"

She couldn't take her eyes off the man standing in front of her. She had been so blinded by her past hurts that she was ignoring the blaringly obvious. He was the wonderful and kind person she had fallen in love with all those years ago. And he couldn't help who his parents were any more than she could. Just because she wasn't interested in being tied romantically to that family, she saw no reason not to enjoy having him as a friend. Would he still be willing for them to be friends? She'd been really difficult and aloof since showing up at his clinic almost two months ago.

Trent nodded. "I was planning on it. How about it, Elliott? Do you and Hadley want to come with us? We could ride together."

"Yeah." Hadley answered, still eyeing

Monroe.

He looked at her, his head tilted slightly, the corner of one lip turned up. She knew her response was puzzling. She smiled and shrugged a shoulder.

"Fix a plate and come eat with us," Elliott said. "You do know how to dish prepared food onto a plate, right?"

"Maybe." Monroe smiled, fixed a plate, and sat with them. Hadley's mind jumped to Chloe. "Oh, Monroe, I stood Chloe on the bathroom countertop this morning and faced her toward the mirror. Then I held up different items, and she watched her mouth while saying each one."

His eyes grew wide. "That's great."

During their last session Chloe had mimicked every word they asked her to and had done so clearly enough anyone could have understood her. But parroting a word and being able to say it without being coaxed were two very different skill sets.

Hadley nodded. "It is. And it's a huge leap from what she was doing just last week. But she only managed to say the word that matched the toy one time clearly. When she tried to repeat the word, it wasn't recognizable without knowing what she was trying to say."

"But still, that's a huge improvement. It

means she's improving by leaps and bounds."

"It does." Hadley shrugged.

"But?" Monroe asked.

"Why doesn't she mimic words back to her mom and dad?"

"One step at a time, Hads. First she has to be capable of forming words on her own. Then, if selective mutism is a part of this, we'll break through that too."

"Yeah. You're right. I'll put the cart back behind the horse." She took a bite of food and changed the topic to one that included all four of them.

After finishing breakfast they walked out to the driveway to Trent's gold Honda. Where was Monroe's car? Come to think of it, she didn't remember seeing it when they met with Chloe.

Hadley looked over the top of Trent's car to catch Monroe's eyes. "Okay, I have to ask. What's wrong with the Batmobile?" Before she thought about it, she had used the name she called it in high school to tease Monroe regarding his black BMW. Maybe she shouldn't have been that familiar.

He laughed as he opened one of the back-seat passenger doors. "Nothing. Still running just fine. I imagine it's parked at stately Wayne Manor."

They rode together in the back seat in pleasant silence, the radio playing softly and Elliott and Trent chatting up front.

She sneaked a few more glances at Monroe before she finally gained the courage to say what was on her mind. "It's good hiking weather. Want to change clothes after church and go?"

"Like, go get Chloe?"

She shook her head. "No, just you and me." Could she possibly ask for friendship from him after the way she'd been acting?

"Yeah. That sounds fun."

"Good." She breathed a sigh of relief. "I was worried that I'd pushed you away too many times to ask and that you might not want —"

"It's okay." He slid his hand to touch hers for a brief moment. "But I do, and I'm not going anywhere. Before we dated, we were friends. I've missed that friendship."

21

Row after neat row of verdant Fraser fir Christmas trees cascaded down the rolling hills of the valley, with the seemingly boundless mountain range rising nearby. A light dusting of snow was on the ground and the evergreens, with the peaks around them getting progressively whiter as the elevation increased. Most people waited until after Thanksgiving to get a Christmas tree, but at the last speech session, Chloe had pointed at a tree and said the word "tree" very clearly, so they'd planned today's outing. And one of these freshly cut trees would absolutely last to Christmas and beyond.

Monroe watched as Chloe dashed in and out of the rows of the Christmas tree farm. Hadley peeked around the trees, playing a preschool version of tag that was mixed with hide and seek. Hadley wore a red crocheted cap, making her easy to spot, and Chloe's all pink jacket stood out well in the field of green and white.

Monroe walked toward them, filming with the handheld video camera owned by the clinic. Hadley wanted Chloe to be able to give an account of what Jason had done the day of the fire, but Monroe wasn't sure that would happen in time for Jason to step into the job opportunity at All-in-One Auto. Chloe was making great progress, and maybe Hadley could talk Alan into extending the cutoff. She was persuasive when she put her mind to it. But whether Alan lengthened the job's hiring window or not, Monroe would gladly continue the extra sessions as long as Hadley wanted. It seemed rather miraculous that in the last eight weeks since Hadley had reentered his life, the two of them had learned how to communicate remarkably well.

"Tag! Tag!" Hadley jumped out from behind a large round tree, and Chloe giggled in response.

"Tag!" Chloe yelled back. She could mimic anything these days, which was great. But that wouldn't help clear up what'd taken place the night of the fire. It was paramount that they didn't coax her or ask leading questions.

Chloe's parents were back at the log house that served as the tree farm's shop and hot chocolate concession stand. Before Hadley and the small family arrived, Monroe had handed the owner fifty dollars and asked the shop to tell Alan and Kate that Chloe could pick out a tree because someone anonymous had paid it forward.

Hadley and Chloe ran down several rows, and Monroe hustled to catch up, trying to keep the camera from jostling too much.

The three of them walked on, the trees getting smaller as they continued through the large farm.

"Oh, look at these baby trees." Hadley patted a knee-high tree as if it were a puppy. "I remember your little garden, Chloe. It was on the side of the apartment building. The maintenance people marked off a small square just for you. Imagine having a garden this size!" She spread her arms wide, gesturing to the sloping valley of trees.

"Chloe garden . . ." Chloe stopped walking.

Hadley's face held a dozen emotions, and he imagined her heart was threatening to stop. If she longed to yell *yes!* and twirl Chloe through the air, she repressed it well. Hadley knew from her training that in treating selective mutism, which might be part of Chloe's issue, the therapist wasn't supposed to get overly excited when a child spoke on her own. She crouched next to Chloe and smiled at her, cupping the little girl's face with her hands. "Very good." Hadley's voice held complete pleasure. "Very, very good, Chloe." Gentle, loving encouragement.

Monroe held his breath as he moved closer, but he remained far enough back that he hoped he wouldn't disturb the moment.

"You loved that garden."

Chloe nodded. "Mama be mad."

"Mad?" Hadley smiled, shaking her head. "No, sweetie. Mama's promised not to be mad. Dadda too. Did you do something you shouldn't have?"

Chloe nodded.

"Well, that happens to all of us. But you won't get in trouble. I promise."

"Mama said . . ." Chloe's voice was nearly a whisper.

Monroe moved closer and knelt beside Hadley. Her eyes met his for the briefest moment before returning to Chloe, and he saw hope.

"Mama said no." Chloe pointed her little finger at Hadley. "No!"

"She did say that. But it's okay now."

"Water. Seeds. Chloe garden." She pointed to herself.

Hadley nodded. "When?"

Chloe stroked the tree, looking at it with awe. Cold water from the melted snow seeped through the thick fabric covering Monroe's knees as he remained kneeling while one long minute after another ticked by.

Hadley waited patiently, giving Chloe time. Tears welled in Chloe's eyes. Hadley removed her gloves and took Chloe's hands. "You watered the seeds in your garden?"

Chloe nodded.

"When?"

"Fire. Big fire."

"The fire was scary, wasn't it?"

Tears fell down Chloe's face. "I yell, 'Mama, run! Run!' " She shook her little head. "I try go in."

"You tried to go inside?"

She nodded. "Big fire."

"Where were you when you saw the big fire?"

"Chloe garden."

"That's a long way from your room."

"Out window."

"Did someone go with you?"

She shook her head. "Do by self. Then big fire. Tried to get Mama out."

"You tried to get your Mama out?"

Chloe nodded. "Jase grabbed me. Ran.

Big boom." She folded her arms, frowned, and stomped feet. "Mama! Run, Mama!"

"Mama got out, sweetie. She's safe. Dadda's safe. Everyone is safe."

"Dadda mad at Jase. Chased him." The little girl broke into sobs. "Dadda be mad at me too."

"Hugs?" Hadley held out her arms.

Chloe nodded, and Hadley wrapped her arms around the girl's small body. She rubbed Chloe's back. "You're not in trouble. Mama and Dadda won't be mad." Hadley released Chloe and cupped her sweet face. "We all love you, and love forgives so big" — Hadley stretched her arms as wide as they could go — "that no one minds one bit." She looked at Monroe, and he saw exhilaration in her beautiful, wide-open eyes. This was the breakthrough they had been hoping for Chloe, and Monroe's heart soared for her. It should also make the necessary difference for Jason's future. They had done it, and it was all on film.

Chloe wiped tears and Hadley kept holding her, lifting her up and letting Chloe rest her head on Hadley's shoulder. Monroe stood, leaving the camera on just in case she said more.

"Can we go talk to Mama and Dadda now?" Hadley asked. "They aren't going to be mad. They are going to be very, very happy you told me that."

Chloe nodded, not letting go of Hadley's neck. " 'Kay."

When they arrived back at the shop's porch, Monroe explained the situation to Chloe's parents, and Kate started crying.

"Mama mad." Chloe was looking down at the rough wood floor.

Kate knelt down on Chloe's level. "No, honey, I'm not." She cooed softly. "I'm crying because I'm so happy. So very happy." She laughed and cried even more. "I've missed your voice so, so much. Oh, my girl." She hugged her daughter, and Monroe noticed Hadley's eyes were wet too. This was the goal she had worked toward for months.

Alan knelt down and kissed his wife and daughter, wrapping his arms around his family. After several moments the parents got to their feet.

"I'd like to show you . . ." Monroe tapped the camera. "Good footage."

The code was to keep Chloe from feeling self-conscious or realizing she was in the eye of a storm.

Kate tried to pass Chloe to Hadley, but the girl held on tightly to her mom. "No mad?"

Kate rubbed her back. "I promise." But clearly it would take days, maybe weeks before Chloe relaxed. "Hey, how about if we shop for one special ornament to hang on our tree?"

"We, a tree?"

"A live, beautiful tree." Kate looked at Monroe. "Because apparently *someone* nearby thinks it's important, and your dad and I agree . . . maybe just for this year, though."

It wouldn't be for just this year, not if Monroe could figure out how to get the family some extra income. Maybe Kate could help clean the clinic and take Chloe with . . . Oh, he no longer had control of the clinic or managed the hiring. It was an odd feeling to realize he didn't have power at his fingertips, and yet he was an adult with a good education. How must Hadley and Elliott have felt so often in life?

Chloe grinned and pointed into the store. Hadley and Kate took Chloe inside the shop. Monroe showed Alan the video.

Alan was silent for several minutes. "Jason seemed to be trying to rescue her. Do you think that's true?"

"It seems like it to me." Monroe made sure to speak very evenly. He wasn't here to lead or guide Alan's thinking, only present facts.

Alan nodded. "Emotions were so high that day, and my trust level for Jason was already at zero. And I . . . I thought . . . but now . . ." Alan watched again the clip of Chloe telling Hadley what had happened the day of the fire. "Wait." Alan motioned. "Back that up."

Monroe did so.

"Listen." Alan pointed. "Right there." They listened as Chloe explained things. "If Jason hadn't grabbed her up and run from the building, she would've been seriously injured by the blast that put Jason in the hospital." He choked up. "It might have killed her."

"When all the pieces are put together — what happened to Jason and what Chloe said — it does sound that way."

Alan offered his hand to Monroe, who took it. "Thank you for all you've done. Do you have some sort of boss you answer to that I could send a positive review to? I know it helps me at work when someone does that."

Maybe give that positive review to the curly-haired woman showing Christmas decorations to your daughter? But he didn't dare say it out loud. Not that one good thing, or even a slew of good things, could bring him back to datable in Hadley's eyes. He'd have to be content that he was able to help in this situation that meant so much to her.

"That's not necessary. Just enjoy your family."

Alan drew a shaky breath. "It's a horrible thing to live with — to accuse some poor kid of wrongdoing and then find out he's the one who rescued my daughter when she needed it most. I'm not sure how I'll live with that."

"It's not easy. I know from personal experience. My advice is don't withdraw. Dare to step forward and be present in Jason's life. The rest will work itself out."

"Good input. I'll do that." He smiled and nodded before pulling a cell phone from his pocket. He touched a button and held the device to his ear. "Hi, Mary Lou? This is Alan Powell. Is Jason where I could speak to him? I have some good news."

22

Elliott surveyed the small apartment, her arms full of clear plastic garment bags. "That was a lot of buildup to get back to this little, rough-and-tumble place, and yet I'm oddly grateful to be here."

Hadley laughed. "Exactly." She walked inside and set the small box containing their paltry set of pots and pans in the kitchen.

The place looked about as they'd left it, save for the freshly steam-cleaned furniture and painted walls. The apartment management had hired professionals to clean. She laid the wrapped clothes on top of the sofa.

Hadley lifted a stack of cleaned bedding off the table, probably put there by the cleaners. Their sheets had a series of small holes in them, ones they'd had for several years. "Some things change. Some things stay the same."

Elliott laughed. "Home, sweet home."

"I'm tempted for us to go out and bargain

hunt for new bedding, but there's no time before the party."

The apartment management was throwing a "Welcome Back/Christmas/Tenant Appreciation" party at the small clubhouse next to the rarely used pool. Although Elliott wasn't as outgoing and social as Hadley, they were both excited to see the neighbors together again. It was such a relief to be home, but she would miss seeing the Powells daily, especially Chloe. They weren't moving back to the complex, but they would be at the party. At least their new place wasn't far. Jason and Memaw were moving back into their old building. Elliott was excited to see Jason working with Alan at the All-in-One Auto.

"Trent is picking me up in" — Elliott looked at her watch — "half an hour."

Hadley wrapped an arm around her shoulders. "I'm glad for you. Let's go see our neighbors."

They left their apartment and soon stepped into the clubhouse. The managers had set out about twenty folding chairs around a long table with a few refreshments. It looked like instant hot cider, meatballs, and store-bought red and green frosted cookies. A somewhat meager party if compared to the one she'd attended at the

318

Biltmore, but this one welcomed them and had good friends. There was a string of lights on the wall and a prelit miniature Christmas tree with tiny ornaments sitting on a table. Chloe was touching the small, probably breakable ornaments, and her mom was watching her closely. When Hadley walked toward them, Elliott went to the table and got a cookie. She saw the new apartment manager, the one who'd taken over a week, more or less, before the fire. He was a short man, about her height, with black hair except for the bald spots. He had on a sweater with a cartoon reindeer that had blinking lights on its antlers.

"Elliott Carmichael. Glad you could make it."

"Doug." She covered her mouth with a napkin as she continued chewing. "Thank you." She remembered his name well because he'd been rather short with her when she went to him and asked for a delay in being evicted. But he had agreed to give her the names of his superiors.

"The management team is very glad to get to reopen your building."

"We're glad of it too."

He leaned in a little closer. "About your back-rent situation . . ."

She stopped chewing the cookie. Had the

apartment management made a mistake in sending Hadley and Elliott the letter? Maybe it was a form letter sent to every tenant at the time of the fire.

He smiled. "We'd like to officially forgive you of the back-rent debt and give you the next two months rent-free. Your actions at the fire were impressive and admirable. We love that a nurse of your caliber chooses to reside here, and we want to keep it that way. We also heard about how Hadley worked with the Powells' little girl after the fire. We'd hate to lose tenants like you two. Starting March first, just make sure the rent is on time." He offered his hand.

"That's great," Elliott mumbled and swallowed the confection. She shook his hand. "Of course. Thank you, sir." She made a beeline to Hadley to tell her, and after they celebrated, grinning and giggling like school girls and thanking God, Elliott excused herself. She grabbed her coat and walked to the parking lot, where Trent's car was waiting. When he saw her approaching, he jumped out with a gift about the size of a thin book in his hand. He hurried to get the passenger door for her.

Elliott narrowed her eyes at him. "What have you done, Trent Gledhill?"

"Me?" He hid the gold-wrapped gift

behind his back. "I wouldn't dream of doing anything, my lady." He bowed low as she got in the car. He held the door open.

"Mixed messages." She gazed up at him. "Is that the plan? Gift, hiding the gift, but you bowed low. I'm confused."

"Yeah, and I'm a bit nervous." He held the gift out to her.

She eyed him. "You're also cute." She took the gift. "Thank you."

He closed the door carefully, walked to the driver's side, and got in.

She ran her fingers over the glossy paper. "So where are we going? I know the live music at the Orange Peel isn't until later."

"There's a table at the Chocolate Lounge with our names on it. Well, our names aren't actually on it because they don't take reservations. But, yeah, you can tease me about how much sugar I put in my coffee."

"Sounds like a lovely date. And this?" She barely waved the gift box back and forth.

"Before you open it, I should probably explain a bit . . . since it may be emotionally charged."

Suspicion mixed with intrigue. "Yes . . ." She drew out the word.

"The picture from your childhood — I couldn't get it off my mind. I did some research, and I found a clue."

Her heart lurched. "You did? How? Because I've googled 'wood train trestle' and 'Gainesville, Georgia' a bazillion times and never found anything. When we lived in Gainesville, I showed the picture to several people, and no one had any idea what it was. We could have been on a trip anywhere in the Southeast when that picture was taken. We moved around a lot."

"You're right, but I went a step further. I snapped a picture on my phone and blurred out the two faces. Without mentioning your name or anything about the picture, I posted a question on a private Google group of my study buddies from college, asking if anyone knew where this trestle was located. You don't mind that I did that, do you?"

"No." Her voice faltered her, and she cleared it. "Not at all." The timbre of her voice changed at the end of the word. He was so sweet and tender.

"I heard back from a professor who is teaching at the University of Georgia, in Athens. Turns out *that* trestle is a local landmark."

"What?" She felt dizzy, but she leaned in. "Really?"

His smile was warm and filled with understanding. "I think you're ready to open the gift now."

Elliott couldn't manage another word, so with trembling fingers she removed the ribbon and the wrapping paper. She couldn't believe her eyes. "A record?" She ran her fingers over the smooth cover.

"When I learned the history of the trestle in your picture, I searched through record stores until I found this."

"R.E.M." was printed in big letters, and the record's title, *Murmur,* was underneath in smaller print. A faded image of kudzu blanketed the landscape on the front of the album. It appeared to be a decade or two old.

"Turn it over, Ellie."

She knew that's what she needed to do before he said it, but her body wasn't co-operating. Every part of her was screaming that she was on the brink of understanding something about herself, something about where she'd been when that lone picture was taken.

Trent eased his fingers over the album and helped her turn it over. Her breath caught as she recognized the wooden train trestle on the back. The image was more faded than the front cover, but she was clearly looking at the same trestle as the one in the picture of her and the other girl. "Oh, Trent." Her eyes welled with tears, and she couldn't say more. This was the kind of clue she'd been looking for her whole life.

"Merry Christmas, Ellie."

She nodded, wiping tears. "This is . . . amazing. I can't believe it."

"It's the Trail Creek Trestle, also known as the Murmur Trestle, in Athens, Georgia. I know you asked about your family in and around Gainesville, but maybe Athens is where you needed to look. My former professor said it's a tight community among the nonstudent permanent residents, and many of the elders' memories go back a long time. If you reach out and ask the right questions, you might be able to find some sort of clue."

"Wouldn't it be amazing to learn a little something about my roots?"

"Yeah, it would." He smiled, looking a bit unsure but hopeful for her. "I'd like to make that trip with you, if you will let me."

She loved the idea, but . . . "Seems a little soon for that kind of trip."

Trent shook his head. "If you prefer I not go, that's fine. But we could go together and stay in separate motel rooms. Maybe by the end of the trip you'll know more about your family and me."

It surprised her how much she liked the sound of that.

"You know what? Yeah. Let's do it." She reached over the console and hugged him. His gentle embrace warmed her. She had no words to express what this meant, but she imagined he didn't mind a bit.

23

Flurries of snow swirled, tickling Hadley's nose and melting in her hair. She remained on the wooden bench in Biltmore Village. When she was a kid, it'd taken her a while to understand that Biltmore Village was simply a part of Asheville and not part of the estate.

Waiting for someone often assaulted her need to stay busy but not this evening. The aroma of roasting nuts filled the air, making her mouth water and her stomach growl. From this spot she could catch glimpses of the small booth that sold the roasted nuts in the middle of the square. Judging by the length of the line to the vendor, maybe she should splurge and purchase some. The "Old Fashioned Dickens of a Christmas Festival" was in full swing. When she'd read about it online or in a newspaper, it'd seemed like an excuse to encourage people to shop, but even if that was true, tonight she didn't mind.

December first, and Asheville had already had two small sprinklings of snow. She shook out her hair and removed the red crocheted cap from a jacket pocket and pulled it over her head. She had purchased it on a whim a few years back from a downtown thrift store, and it had become her favorite go-to in the fall and winter.

A small group of female carolers, approximately age fifty and up and wearing Victorian period costumes, were harmonizing on a rendition of "Carol of the Bells." The singers weren't the only people dressed in costumes that could be from *A Christmas Carol*. Several performers — ladies in full skirts with winter bonnets and men in top hats and long-tailed suits carrying canes — were mixed among the shoppers in modern clothes. Despite the dusk of early evening and the snow flurries, the lanes were illuminated with old-fashioned lampposts and glowing decorations, and each shop was lined with white twinkling lights. A large Christmas tree stood in the center of the square, lit by countless multicolored radiant bulbs.

A quite-familiar, modern-looking man walked toward her along the sidewalk under the streetlamps, a wool scarf wrapped around his neck, hands tucked into the pockets of his leather jacket. Monroe spotted her, and a smile spread across his face. When she had seen the picture of him in El Salvador with a group of children, his grin had been genuine, and this one was just as brilliant and real. But it made her feel a bit sad and empty. If his parents weren't so very set against her or so blind to how dysfunctional they were . . .

Perhaps if she and Monroe had lived in another time period, maybe the one people were pretending to be from tonight, they would have been able to make a life together.

She stood, sticking her hands in her coat pockets. "Thanks for meeting me."

"Sure. Anytime." He glanced around at the costumed people. "You know, I've heard about this event but never attended."

"Me neither. And Elliott and I practically live within walking distance." She wanted to ask him why he was living with Trent. When she had gently brought up the topic during one of the two hikes they'd taken together outside of Chloe's sessions, he politely changed the subject. Was he lonely? Or if his home needed repairs or something, surely he could easily afford another place.

He glanced as a horse and carriage passed

by. "It may be a little cliché, but would you want to get a carriage ride? Also something smells really good." He inhaled deeply, looking around as if trying to find the source of the fragrance.

She liked the idea. It would be memorable and a good time to share her heart before they said a peaceful goodbye. "That would be nice."

While they stood in one line to get roasted chestnuts and in another line to get tickets for the carriage ride, they chatted about little things — Hadley's move back to the apartment, the surprise of Elliott being so taken with Trent, what some of their high school friends were doing these days. Soon they were sitting in a horse-drawn carriage, sharing roasted chestnuts out of brown, cone-shaped paper. Hadley found herself leaning against his shoulder for warmth, but Monroe didn't seem to mind. Some familiarity apparently never left, even all these years later.

"You cold?" He unwrapped his scarf from around his neck and tucked it around hers — a gesture that was also familiar from their dating days, when her winter gear was sorely lacking compared to his.

"It's not so bad." She fidgeted with the soft material wrapped around her neck. It smelled like him. "Especially now. Thanks. What a beautiful night with all the Christmas lights on the buildings."

"It is." But he didn't seem to be looking around at the snow and lights.

She willed herself to remain calm and her breathing to stay even. She had so much she wanted to tell him, but where to begin?

Monroe cleared his throat. "I, uh, have something I need to tell you." He looked up at the cloudy dark sky. "I've resigned from Children's Therapy, effective at the end of this month. I knew you'd learn about it soon, not that I was trying to keep it from you. Well, I've been reluctant to tell you."

Neither her mouth nor brain seemed able to manage a response. Was it because of the trouble she'd caused by insisting on working with Chloe? "Wait, because of me? I . . . I didn't mean to trigger issues for you." His parents were fundamentally opposed to her. Had she ruined his dream of running Children's Therapy?

"No. I chose to resign, and I did it for me. It's also why I've been living at Trent's. I gave my parents back all the lavish gifts that I could: the condo, the car, even the clinic. They weren't really gifts as much as bribery, and I don't want live under their thumb. They lied, Hadley, for the last decade. They manipulated me so I'd be who they wanted as a son. But no more. I've decided to follow my dreams, and as crazy as most people would think I am, I've applied for several public school speech therapist jobs."

Her head spun. Guilt pressed in. She wanted to be vindicated, but she didn't want this. "That's . . . wow." She tried to take in all that information. As sad as the news was, she saw the man she'd always thought he'd become — caring and independent. "I'm sorry for my part in this."

"No. Don't be, and please don't worry about me, Hads. I'm a very fortunate man. I have two master's degrees with no debt and some good experience under my belt. I wouldn't bring this up except you were bound to find out, and I thought it should come from me."

Fresh guilt pressed in. "Monroe, I've been unfair to you."

"How so?" He looked adorably puzzled, which was funny to her, considering everything.

She set the package of chestnuts on the seat and took his hands into hers. She held his gaze. "For years I thought you'd pulled the wool over my eyes and were this fake person. I believed the worst of you, and maybe it was part of the survival method I clung to. But whatever the reasons, I was wrong. That's not you at all. You are beautifully true, a person who bartered your life on my behalf, even when you believed I could be guilty."

Was she about to make a fool of herself? She paused for a moment. "When Elliott and I were young, we used to love this old book that was set during the Great Depression. In order to provide, the dad left the family for months, sometimes years, at a time. His absence was unbearably tough on the mom and children. The mom and kids dealt with multiple sicknesses and crushing loneliness on a defunct farm in the middle of nowhere. But the choice was they could either all die together, or the dad could leave and send money back to the family. Elliott and I used to pretend that our parents were off doing something noble like that and they would one day return. But I completely missed it when it actually happened in my life. You left, yes, but it was to provide for me in the only way you knew how."

"Hadley . . . thank you." His blue eyes reflected gratitude, as if her words were a precious gift.

"Um, there's more." She drew a deep breath. "And it's why I asked you to meet me here." She shuddered. "I'm a little nervous."

He laughed, squeezing her hand. "*You* are nervous? That's a first. I've known you to stare down police officers and force your way into a respectable clinic against the will of the boss."

"Hush." She playfully punched his arm with her free hand, thankful that he broke the tension. "Monroe, I know I've been sending mixed messages, and I'm sorry."

"You don't have to apologize."

Hadley looked at the swirling snow flurries, taking a moment to center herself. "But I do. I told you at the overlook that I needed to be free of you, and yet I keep asking to see you. And now that Chloe is speaking again, the only thing constantly running through my mind from the time I wake up until I close my eyes at night is that I can't stand the thought of never seeing you again. Never getting to laugh at our inside jokes. Never watching you work with the children you love so much." She turned to meet his eyes. "Never looking into your eyes and having you just know what I'm thinking and feeling. I can never be free of you because I'm in love with you." The words felt so odd to her mouth. She hadn't said them in a decade. "Emotions aside, I know there are way too many obstacles and differences for us to be a couple again. But I had to tell you."

"Obstacles?" He turned his head slightly.

How could she begin to articulate the cultural divide that had always separated them? But if he was no longer working under his parents . . . No more obstacles? Could it really be this easy? Nothing in their path as a couple had been easy.

The driver slowed the horse down as they approached the area where their ride began. The carriage jaunt was drawing to a close. With the way Monroe and she were communicating, she wished it could continue a hundred more blocks.

He handed the driver a few dollars as a tip and stepped off the carriage onto the curb. He offered her a hand down. "You mentioned obstacles to our being together, but I don't think I see any."

She stared at him, taken aback by his declaration. She stood and reached for his hand. Instead, he gently lifted her by the waist to move her from the carriage step to the pavement. He took her hand and pulled her away from the thick of the crowds to the snow-dusted lawn in front of the Cathedral of All Souls. Her breath came fast, as if they had been hiking up a mountain.

"Monroe, wait." She tugged at his hand. He stopped and turned around.

Her heart thudded wildly. "What do you mean?"

Moving in close, he squeezed her hand gently. "I mean if you want me, I'm yours."

Tears threatened, and she blinked them back. What was happening?

He gave a lopsided smile. "For friendship, for dating, for anything, forever. I love you, Hadley. I never stopped, and I never will."

Tears broke free, and the chilly air stung her eyes and cheeks. Was this real? Standing in front of the beautiful stone-and-brick-faced cathedral in the snow, it seemed to be a scene out of a dream. A dream she had long suppressed while feeding her cynical side that told her the relationship she and Monroe had couldn't have been as profound as she thought. He had loved her this whole time and still did?

"I love you too."

He smiled, and the warmth of it thawed her all the way down to her toes. He tipped her face up toward his and kissed her. She had never felt such a sense of belonging as she did in this moment.

24

Monroe lifted Hadley from the ground and set her on her feet on a large, flat rock a little ways from the base of the waterfall. Looking Glass Falls had a veneer of ice around its edges and on some surrounding rocks, but the water still rushed freely, creating a cold mist around them. It was refreshing, but he also found himself looking forward to making a fire with her in the fireplace at his and Trent's place. It had been Hadley's idea to take a winter picnic, away from the shopping crowds in Asheville, and he was glad to oblige, despite the chill.

"I am perfectly capable of climbing down myself, you know." Despite her admonishing words, she was smiling.

He took hold of a curl that was falling in her face and tucked it under her hat. "Sorry. I know you are. I just wanted to help."

The happiness he'd felt these past three

weeks had been almost overwhelming. He took off his backpack and pulled out two heavy blankets: one to sit on and one to wrap around them as they had their picnic.

Hadley looked at the water, rocks, and forest. "It's extra pretty with no other people here." Hadley noticed him pulling the blanket from the backpack, and she stepped out of the way.

Monroe covered the flat rock with the picnic blanket. "Not a big surprise that it's empty. We are the only ones crazy enough to brave the cold on Christmas Eve."

"We'll be plenty warm." She pulled two large insulated food canisters out of her knapsack and held them up. He knew one was full of hot chocolate and one had homemade vegetable beef soup. He'd helped Hadley and Elliott prepare the stew by chopping the vegetables earlier in the day and was amazed at how talented and resourceful they were to create something so delicious out of inexpensive ingredients.

He smiled at her. "Yeah, we'll stay warm." She was just too lovable. How did he get so lucky to be here with her this Christmas Eve?

They sat on the blanket and pulled a heavy quilt over their legs. He poured hot chocolate into two blue enamel camp mugs while Hadley filled two additional mugs with hot soup. They used the rock as a table and slowly ate and drank. Was she the only woman in the world who he could share such engaging conversations with? He knew if they had a lifetime, they'd never run out of things to talk about. What he didn't know was how such an incredible connection with another person was possible.

Daylight was fading fast, and their late-afternoon winter picnic would have to wrap up before either of them was ready.

After he finished his soup and the last sips of hot chocolate, he stacked the mugs and reached in his backpack. He pulled out a small green gift bag stuffed with tissue paper. He hoped she liked her Christmas present, and he prayed it didn't stir bad memories. With Christmas fast approaching, it'd taken him weeks to find someone who could make what he was looking for.

"Merry Christmas." He handed her the bag. "Want to open it here?" He could have given her the gift when they went back to the house to join Trent and Elliott, but he wanted privacy. Would she find these items as powerful and moving as he did? When Hadley asked if he wanted to hike to the waterfall for a picnic, he decided it was the perfect time to give it to her.

"Okay. Thank you." She pulled the white tissue paper from the bag, reached in, and lifted out the gift: two clear, blown-glass lovebirds with a vibrant array of rainbow glass fragments inside their centers. They fit together, their necks in an embrace.

He touched the side of her face with his hand. "Is that okay?"

"They're beautiful." Her gorgeous brown eyes were brimming with tears. She kissed him, and they slowly parted.

He wiped a tear tenderly with his thumb. "When I gave you the glass rainbow for Christmas all those years ago, I promised that I would take care of you, but our dream of being together ended up smashed and shattered. I've carried the pieces of that dream in my heart all this time, and you did as well. And somehow God brought us back together and made us whole again. I saved the broken glass you handed me at the overlook the night we planned to run away. No matter where I've lived since then, I've thrown them in with knickknacks and taken them with me, acting as if it was no big deal, but knowing those pieces mattered. And always would. I got an artist to put those rainbow pieces into these birds, along with some additional bits of colored glass left over from pieces he's worked on throughout the years we've been apart."

She held up the glass birds to the fading light of the sky. "Monroe . . . that's amazing." She set them gently in their tissue paper and wiped away more tears with her thick coat sleeve, laughing a little. "And I thought I was going to surprise you. Just, wow. Thank you."

"Surprise me?" What was that about?

She grinned. "I have a gift for you, but you may not want to use them right away." She pulled a small velvet pouch out of her coat pocket and then cupped his hand and carefully shook two silver rings into it. One was slightly larger than the other, and both had lines carved into the metal to make them textured like bark on a birch tree. Inside each ring the letters M+H were carved, as one would carve them on a tree.

She grabbed his other hand. "Monroe, will you marry me? There has been no one else, even throughout all the years I was angry with you. It doesn't have to be now. I know we just rekindled our relationship, and I can wait as long as you want to."

She wanted to marry him? The world seemed to stop in that moment in front of the frost-rimmed waterfall with the woman he loved more than anything else sitting in front of him holding a set of wedding rings.

In a daze he squeezed her hand before letting it go and pulling out his newly acquired flip phone. He didn't know the number off the top of his head and would need to call information since he didn't have an Internet browser anymore. The person at the cell phone store thought he was crazy for downgrading from an iPhone.

She chuckled. "What are you doing?"

"I'm calling the courthouse. Just maybe they will stay open for us."

She covered her mouth, laughing hard before hitting him on the shoulder. "Right now? It's Christmas Eve! They aren't going to be open."

"It's a Monday. They might be."

"You didn't officially give me an answer." She looked completely amused despite narrowing her eyes.

"Hmm . . ." He couldn't resist teasing her. "Going to go with 'maybe.' "

"Monroe!" She playfully hit him again on the shoulder through his thick winter coat.

He put the phone in his coat pocket and closed his fingers around the wedding bands. He took Hadley's hand. "The answer for you is always yes." They leaned forward and shared another kiss in the cold, clear air.

After tucking the gifts safely away, they

cleaned up their picnic, walked up the ramp, and loaded everything in Hadley's car. They drove slowly on the way back to Monroe and Trent's rental house, excitement high. There was so much they would have to figure out.

"You know" — Hadley turned on the blinker — "Elliott would be pretty mad if we actually went to the courthouse tonight and she wasn't invited."

"I figure it'll take years to get back in Elliott's good graces. Not that I ever really was. But I'm up for the challenge."

Hadley chuckled. "She helped me pick out the rings."

That was surprising, but Elliott seemed to have changed a lot over the years. He saw no hints that she still harbored deep-seated anger against men, which was good for Trent.

As Hadley pulled the car into the driveway, Monroe saw a tan Lexus SUV parked to the side of Trent's car. His mom and dad were here? Was his sister okay? He hadn't answered their calls over the past several weeks, figuring if it was important, they would leave a message.

Hadley pulled into her usual place in the driveway and put her car in Park. "Is that —"

"My parents' car." Worry mingled with anxiety, but he tried to keep his voice upbeat for Hadley. He touched her hand as it rested on the parking brake. "Could you give me a minute?"

She nodded. He got out, closed the door behind him, and walked toward their car. His mom and dad got out of the SUV and joined him in the cold. How long had they been sitting there?

Over the past few weeks, Monroe had felt a sense of peace about how he had severed ties with them. They weren't bad parents, and he truly loved them. But that didn't mean he could condone their actions or was willing to be manipulated by them ever again.

"Are Nicole and everyone else okay?" He broke the silence with his most pressing concern. He had talked with his sister a few days ago and was planning to get together with her, her husband, and their two children later in the week. True to her nature, Nicole remained neutral in what was happening between Monroe and their parents. She wanted to stay out of the fray, mind her own business, and get along with everyone. He was fine with that.

His dad took a few steps toward him and then stopped about six feet away. "Yes, she and her family flew in for Christmas and are at our house. Sorry to surprise you like this, but we couldn't reach you on the phone. When we knocked on your, or rather, Trent's door, he answered and invited us in. But we wanted a moment of privacy with you. There's . . . something important we need to say."

To come to any sort of peace, he'd had to compartmentalize their behavior in a logical way. In his view they had a type of disrupted brain structure when it came to seeing the value of those who had less than they did, similar to the way a child with apraxia has a disrupted brain structure. But unlike children with speech issues, his parents were culpable. They'd chosen to manipulate him so he would line up with their desires.

Mom got out of the car and joined Dad in the driveway. "Monroe, we're here to say we're so sorry."

What? His cynical side said this was a trick. But he didn't want to give in to that kind of thinking. Could they really be here to try to mend things? If so, they needed to apologize to Hadley more than to him.

"We are sorry." Dad nodded. "It's been a hard few weeks. We've talked with our therapist and our pastor several times. It's not easy to admit, but I think we are finally getting it. We were wrong."

Mom studied the car he'd gotten out of. "Is that Hadley?" Did she sound hopeful? "Could . . . we speak with her too?"

Monroe glanced over his shoulder. Hadley was still in the car, waiting as he'd asked. He motioned for her to join them. A few moments later she was by his side. He reached out and took her hand.

Mom walked forward and put a hand on Hadley's shoulder. "Hadley, we have judged you and treated you badly. We're sorry."

Dad walked forward to stand in front of Monroe. "For so long we believed we were superior because we used our money to help others. But without love it's worthless."

"I've already forgiven you." Hadley offered a hug to his mom, who took it.

Monroe admired Hadley's strength, her ability to let go of injustice and keep moving forward. But right now he was most thankful that she was able to let this bit of healing take place between them and his parents. He would have to keep firm boundaries in place with his parents. He wouldn't allow money or extravagant gifts from them, ever.

"I've forgiven too." He embraced his father, who returned the hug warmly.

EPILOGUE

Four Christmases later . . .

The familiar warmth of gratefulness radiated in Hadley as she stepped over a pile of discarded, colorful wrapping paper. She watched her footing carefully as she carried a tray to the dining room table. Being a little more than seven months pregnant, she was losing some agility. But that didn't stop her from holding the now-annual gathering of friends and family on the evening of Christmas Day.

Kate and Alan were on the couch with their five-week-old baby asleep in Kate's arms. Jason and his fiancée were sitting nearby, all four talking fast and furiously about a dozen things while sipping on the decaf coffee Hadley had served them a few minutes ago.

With a bit of hovering and pushing by Hadley and Monroe, Jason had graduated from high school. Before that wonderful event, he began working part-time at the garage Alan managed. He'd learned the trade and now was a well-paid mechanic. Alan and Kate were growing closer each year to having enough money to open their own garage.

Two little girls dashed in front of Hadley, almost causing her to drop the tray of miniature mugs of hot cocoa she was carrying.

"Whoa, girls." Hadley raised a brow, suppressing a smile. "Chloe and May, did the rules change while I wasn't looking?"

Eight-year-old Chloe twirled around to face her, long blond hair flying. "Sorry, Hads. We'll slow down."

"Are those for us, Mama?" Six-year-old May looked up, her sandy-brown hair falling slightly over her sweet dark eyes. The words *mama* and *daddy* felt beautifully right every time May or Isla used them, but they'd only used those terms during the last year. Before that they called Hadley and Monroe by their first names.

Four-year-old Isla paused from drawing pictures with her new crayons, and from her spot on the couch, she studied the two older girls and Hadley.

"Yep, sweetie," Hadley said. "And I made

those homemade chocolate minimarshmallows you and your sister like so much. But all three of you need to hop over to the dining room table to drink and eat, okay?" The floor plan was open, and one room flowed into another.

"Yummy!" May squealed.

Monroe stepped from the kitchen island, wearing a chef's apron, an ironic wedding gift from Trent. He caught her eye and grinned. "Everything going okay?"

When she saw him like this and their home was like this, she felt as if she was living the most amazing of dreams — chaos and humor included. She chuckled and nodded. "We're quite good. Thanks."

He retreated to the kitchen.

The older girls skipped to the table, and Isla tiptoed across the room. Hadley followed them with the tray and set it down in the center of the table. The hot chocolate was more like warmed chocolate since kids were involved.

She would not have guessed that after just three and a half years of marriage, they would be parents to a six-year-old, a four-year-old, and soon a newborn. Within a year of being married, Hadley and Monroe had gone through the training and licensing to become foster parents. Not long after that,

the girls — three-year-old May and one-
year-old Isla — were removed from their
parents by social services. Because May was
nonverbal, social services asked Hadley and
Monroe to accept them into their home.
Despite going into the arrangement with
realistic expectations of the girls returning
to their parents within a few months, Monroe and Hadley were instantly in love with
them.

Life always brought surprises, but with
Monroe and her as a team, the surprises
were gifts and challenges they relished. She
looked at her favorite wedding picture,
framed on the wall above the dining room
table. It was one of many pictures throughout their small house; the walls and mantel
overflowed with them after four years of
their being a couple. In the photo she and
Monroe were wet from the gentle rain that
had started in the middle of their outdoor
ceremony on the Blue Ridge Parkway. There
was no pavilion to run to, so they asked for
the small ceremony to continue. In the
photograph, the pastor, holding an um-
brella, had just declared them man and wife,
and after their kiss, Monroe and Hadley had
their foreheads together, stealing one more
moment before facing the world for the first
time as a married couple. She could recall

the moment as if it were yesterday. The photographer had managed to capture the elation on both of their faces, with the cloud-covered mountains behind them.

"Sweetheart." Monroe called from the kitchen island. "As a heads-up, I . . . um . . . may need some assistance in a few minutes."

"Okay. No prob. I'm here for you," she teased.

He laughed. "Thanks."

Her husband had insisted on doing the baking for the upcoming gathering. The results, based on the mixture of good and odd aromas, were to be determined.

Before they married, Monroe had accepted a job as a speech therapist in the Asheville City School district. They were able to purchase a modest house with a basement that was perfect for their quickly growing family.

Hadley had graduated eighteen months ago with a master's in speech-language pathology, and she worked at a private clinic near the hospital. On the day of her graduation, seemingly out of the blue, Monroe knew what they should do with the trust fund his grandparents had set up for him. They were using it to open a not-for-profit speech and occupational therapy clinic.

She pulled her attention from the wedding photograph and walked into the kitchen adjacent to the living area. Two dozen tiny brown cakes covered the narrow countertop. To Hadley's knowledge, chocolate wasn't involved.

"Cupcakes are *supposed* to be chewy, right?"

She picked one up and bit into it. "Chewy" was a good description. She tried to swallow quickly. "Well . . . maybe the frosting will help."

He pointed to the neon-green store-bought frosting. "I didn't mess that up."

She suppressed a giggle. "You sure about that?"

He shook his head, laughing. "On the upside I didn't burn them."

"This is . . . technically true." She opened the round container and dipped a clean spoon into the frosting to steal a taste and maybe get rid of the bitterness of the overdone flour and sugar she had just sampled.

Monroe moved in behind her. He wrapped an arm around her waist and pulled her close. He gently moved her hair to the side and kissed her neck. "I keep asking," he whispered, "just where is the chef and maid service in this place?"

She stuck the spoon in her mouth and

pulled it back out. "You don't know?" She pointed. "Go down this hall and turn right."

"They're in the bathroom?"

"Yeah, if you look in the mirror, you'll see them."

He chuckled. "I love you, Hads, from dawn to dusk, from dusk to dawn, sleeping, awake, dazed, or alert. I am crazy in love."

She turned. "I know." She cupped his face in her hands. "For richer or poorer, edible cupcakes or not, until death do us part, possibly from your lack of culinary skills, I love you too."

He kissed her lightly, and it quickly deepened.

The doorbell rang, and they ended the kiss, smiling. He released her.

Hadley went to answer the door, which was only a few steps from the kitchen, and sure enough, her best friend was waiting with Trent standing behind her carrying a red tray of what looked like brownies. She hugged Elliott tight. "You know you can just come on in."

"And miss making you come to the door? No way." Elliott chuckled and entered.

"It's about time." Monroe joined them at the front door, pointing at Trent with a rubber spatula covered in green frosting. "If you'd come earlier, I could've used the distraction as my excuse for the way the food turned out."

"How's it going, man? Need a hand?" Trent walked inside, carrying a tray of brownies covered with clear wrap.

Monroe looked at the chocolate confection. "Yes, let me pretend those are what I made for dessert."

"No way," Trent gasped. "And rob Betty Crocker of all the credit?"

The men talked as they went toward the kitchen island. Elliott shook her head, chuckling. "We live dangerously leaving those two alone in a kitchen."

Elliott and Trent had married a little more than two years ago at their church. Elliott had finished her RN and was in school to become a nurse practitioner. Trent often joked that she would make more money than he would when she was done. That would be true except Elliott and Trent had recently learned they were expecting their first little one, and they had hopes of having another in a few years. So Elliott intended to work only part-time for the next decade.

Just as Hadley started to talk to Elliott, someone knocked on the door. Hadley opened it.

"Merry Christmas," Monroe's parents chimed. They gave Hadley a quick hug and spoke to everyone in the room as they entered the house.

"Where are those grand girls?" Lisa bent as if sneaking in.

"Where are they?" Greg looked around as if he couldn't see them sitting at the table. "There they are!"

The girls squealed and ran to Lisa and Greg, giving hugs with messy hands. Chloe watched, grinning, but she continued eating her cookies.

In less than a minute after speaking to Monroe and Trent, Lisa and Greg were on the floor between the beige IKEA couches, playing pretend with May and Isla.

Gregory Birch, for all his prestige as an influential doctor, soon had a fluffy pink princess crown on his head as the petite four-year-old with strawberry-blond hair directed him and his wife in their make-believe game. The prejudices that the Birches held for so long had started to thaw before they came to Hadley and Monroe to apologize. But whatever icy attitudes still clung to them after that had melted completely when they fell in love with May and Isla.

Elliott leaned in. "Do they know yet, Hads?"

Hadley shook her head and motioned for

Elliott to follow her. They went to the tree, and Hadley pulled out a simple red bag and pushed aside the tissue paper to reveal a box of Kleenex.

Elliott chuckled. "So tonight they'll learn the adoption went through last Thursday?"

"Yeah. We went to court December 22, and that date will mean something very special in this family every year moving forward. I couldn't stop myself from calling Tara and telling her the news as we were leaving the courthouse. She's so excited and is coming to visit tomorrow. But we wanted that news to be a lovely surprise Christmas gift for Lisa and Gregory. And you know they'll need those tissues." Hadley covered the box of Kleenex with the tissue paper again. "We're going to tell everyone tonight after dinner and lighting candles on the Christmas cake."

Elliott reached in the bag and snagged one of the Kleenexes to dab her eyes. "What an emotional journey this has been for you and Monroe."

"Very true. But it was worth far more than the price paid."

When Trent and Elliott took a trip to Athens, Georgia, four years ago, what they learned had also been an emotional journey. The girl in the picture with Elliott at Trail

Creek Trestle turned out to be Heather, her half sister on her dad's side. But not long after that picture was made, Elliott's parents left the state with her, and that was the last Heather or her mom ever heard from any of them. Elliott found a few relatives and pieced together more of what had taken place, but most of their lives were a train wreck. So she could see why no one had searched for her or been willing to take her in . . . if the state had found them and asked. Still, Heather and Elliott visited each other a couple of times each year, and they were slowly growing closer.

Elliott placed a hand on Hadley's round stomach. "How's this guy doing?"

Hadley looked down at the spot where Elliott's hand was. "I can't tell if he's kicking his feet out or showing us his backside."

Elliott laughed. "I'm still so excited that our babies will grow up together."

Monroe and Trent came out of the kitchen.

Monroe winked at her. "The rolls and sweet potato pie need about ten minutes."

The four of them settled on chairs or couches with their other guests in front of the fire. Hadley leaned back into Monroe's arms on the loveseat. They were still reeling with excitement that the adoptions for their girls had gone through, but there had been plenty of times of angst and tears along the way. Despite loving the girls as if they were their own, they'd pulled for the birth parents to get off drugs and get their girls back. When that failed time and again, they prayed the girls wouldn't spend a lifetime in foster care, waiting and hoping their parents cared enough to keep trying to win them back from the state. A year ago their parents had signed over their parental rights.

Hadley knew that life would never be completely easy. There would always be hard decisions and challenges, like deciding whether she'd accept the job offer at a different private clinic only a few months after the baby was born. But as she sat in the cozy warmth of her living room, the multicolored Christmas lights glittering on the evergreen tree, the love and tenderness felt almost palpable around her.

She knew she would always have what was most important.

ACKNOWLEDGMENTS

From Cindy and Erin

Thank you to Shweta and Justin Woodsmall, Kaden's mom and dad, for answering our many questions about apraxia of speech, for sharing your ideas and much, much more. Like all parents, you had hopes and dreams of what the first years with Kaden would be like, but when his needs proved to be different, you looked at him with love and acceptance and asked God and each other, What does Kaden need from us? What do we need to do, and whom do we need to become to be the parents *this* child needs? You rearranged every plan and continue to do so, and our entire family is blessed by who you are.

To the people of Asheville, North Carolina, thank you! You made the time and trips there for research fun and productive! A very special thank-you to Superior Court

Judicial Assistant Cindy Crawford for taking time out of your busy schedule to answer questions about Hadley's journey. Thank you to all the friendly and helpful people at the Buncombe County Courthouse. That face-to-face time at Buncombe County Courthouse was invaluable in shaping the story. Thank you to Mission Health Hospital for uncovering the protocols for 2012. Thank you to the kind downtown policemen who let us accost them with questions and to others whom we crossed paths with that were so kind. You helped us walk in the shoes of the characters that reside in *Gift of Christmas Past.* Your city was special to us before writing this story, and now it's even more so.

We enjoyed our time at the French Broad Chocolate Lounge, Biltmore Estate, Western North Carolina Nature Center, and the many other wonderful places in Asheville.

Thank you to Adam Woodsmall for your help in making Monroe sound the way a true young health-care professional and business owner would.

To Lucy Woodsmall for modeling for Chloe and inspiring her cute personality. You danced on the Biltmore tent floor that Chloe danced on, and you inspired us.

To Tyler Woodsmall for doing many small

odd jobs and for sharing the book with people on social media.

To Cindy's longtime editor, Shannon Marchese, for your experience, honesty, and talent for turning our raw rough draft into a polished work that we're so excited to share.

To our favorite copy and line editor, Carol Bartley, for your attention to detail, precision, and quick turn-around times.

To our incredible group of proofreaders, Catherine King, Janet Rainwater, Norma Rainwater, and Jessica Yaun for your sharp eyes and precious time.

To our cover designer and text formatter, Ken Raney, for making the book look fabulous.

To Tracy Higley and StoneWater Books for getting the books on store shelves in this new indie venture.

From Cindy

To my sweet husband, Tommy. Thank you for doing all you can to make time for me to write. To my daughter-in-law, Erin. Thank you for your gracious, sweet spirit. Thank you for your encouragement and belief that I can indeed meet my deadlines, for the drop-off lunches and coffee you provide, and for helping me uncover new ways of staying organized. What a wonderful journey writing this book with you was! You said researching the places would be fun, and you were so very right. What wonderful memories! Thank you to my daughter-in-law Shweta for the times you fixed extra food when preparing dinner for your family and brought it to us. Thank you for making time to talk shop about the story while driving to and from work. And thank you for allowing me the privilege of being in the inner circle of your lives and all that means.

From Erin

I would like to thank Cindy for drawing me into her world of fiction more than a decade ago. You have an amazing gift, and the world is infinitely brighter because you are in it. You've cheered countless readers' hearts through your dynamic characters, who feel as real as if I knew them personally. I'm blessed beyond measure to have you in my life and to get to create with you. You are the very best teacher, mentor, example, confidante, partner, mother-in-love (law), and friend. I want to write hundreds of stories with you.

To my husband, Adam, my high school sweetheart turned love of my life. Our romance is one I get to live every day. Life together is better than I could have imagined.

To my children, Lucy, Caleb, and Silas. Thanks for your patience as I put on a different hat than "Mommy."

To Iris, my baby in heaven too soon. I didn't get to raise you, but you changed me forever. I channeled my grief into learning new skills, and this book wouldn't be here without your brief life.

To all of Cindy's readers for being so kind and encouraging and giving me this chance to cowrite. You are wonderful, and I hope you fall in love with these characters and this setting as much as Cindy and I did.

Chorizo and Sweet Potato Enchiladas

Adapted from Budget Bytes (www.budgetbytes.com).

1 large sweet potato, cut into 1/4 inch cubes

1 poblano pepper, or green bell pepper, diced

2 cloves of garlic, minced

3 links chorizo sausage (found in Mexican Food section of store)

2 tablespoons coarsely chopped fresh cilantro

homemade enchilada sauce, recommended (see recipe on page 367). Or 1 1/2 ten-ounce cans of enchilada sauce

2 cups shredded cheese (cheddar or Mexican blend)

8 seven-inch tortillas

2 tablespoons vegetable oil

Preheat the oven to 375. Heat a large skillet over medium heat. Swirl 1 tablespoon of the oil around the pan to coat. Add cubed sweet potato, pepper, and garlic. Cook 7 minutes or until the ingredients begin to soften. Squeeze the chorizo out of its casing and into the skillet. Sauté until the sausage is fully cooked. Use remaining oil to grease a large casserole dish. Scoop 1/2 cup of the filling in the skillet into each tortilla, roll, and place in dish. Pour enchilada sauce over rolled tortillas and top with shredded cheese. Bake in preheated oven 20 minutes or until sauce is bubbling on the edges. Top with fresh cilantro.

Enchilada Sauce

2 tablespoons vegetable oil
2 tablespoons all-purpose flour
2 tablespoons chili powder
2 cups water
3 oz. can tomato paste
1/2 teaspoon cumin
1/2 teaspoon garlic powder
1/4 teaspoon cayenne pepper (or to taste)
1/2 teaspoon salt (or to taste)

Heat vegetable oil in a pot over medium-high heat. Whisk in flour and chili powder. Cook for one minute or until it starts bubbling. Whisk in water, tomato paste, cumin, garlic powder, cayenne pepper (if you are using it), and salt until the sauce is smooth. Bring the sauce to a simmer, allowing to thicken slightly, and taste the spices. Add more salt if needed. Use as needed in the recipe above, and freeze the remainder for later use.

Elliott's Chicken Noodle Soup
Serves six

6 cups chicken broth (preferably home-made)

2 lbs. cooked, shredded chicken

2 large carrots, sliced or diced

1 small onion, diced

2 ribs celery, sliced or diced

1 package frozen home-style egg noodles (such as Reames), or use homemade

1 bay leaf

1 tablespoon fresh thyme or 1/2 teaspoon powered dried thyme

2 teaspoons chopped fresh oregano or 1/2 teaspoon dried oregano

1 tablespoon butter or oil

Salt and freshly ground pepper to taste

In large stockpot, sauté the vegetables and spices in butter or oil over medium heat. When the onions are translucent, add the stock and chicken. Bring to a simmer. Add the noodles and cook to the time the package indicates (or ten minutes if using home-made). Stir and taste, adding salt and pepper as desired.

DISCUSSION QUESTIONS FOR THE GIFT OF CHRISTMAS PAST

1. When Hadley was young, she had a fierce temper, which landed her in trouble for keying the Reeds' car. Consider Proverbs 15:18, which says, "A hot-tempered man stirs up strife, but he who is slow to anger quiets contention." What is an example of a mistake in your own life, whether in youth or adulthood, that could have been more easily navigated if you hadn't lost your temper?

2. Monroe's parents judge Hadley based on her past, deciding she is guilty of the arson before her trial. But when they find out she is innocent, they don't tell Monroe. When have you unfairly judged someone? How did you make it up to him or her once you realized you were in the wrong?

3. Discuss what "affluenza" means: the materialism and consumerism from extreme

wealth that makes people unsatisfied with life and prone to dysfunctional relationships. If you were Monroe, what steps would you take to avoid this?

4. When Dianna expelled Hadley from her home in response to Hadley's repeated offenses, was she justified? Why or why not? If she had reacted with forgiveness and let Hadley stay in the foster home, would it have made a difference in Hadley's life?

5. As adults Hadley and Elliott are used to making do and being thankful for what they have. What are some things you do to minimize your economical or environmental expenses, such as reusing items, recycling, or generating less waste? In what ways could you do more?

6. When they end up facing eviction, Hadley and Elliott are afraid to go to their church for help because they haven't been regular attenders. If they went to your church or were your friends, how would you offer to help them, either in advice or deeds?

7. Monroe works hard at Children's Therapy because he genuinely wants to help kids with speech disorders, but he stays in his comfort zone of relative wealth until Hadley

arrives. In what ways have you helped in your community while remaining in your comfort zone? In what ways have you been called out of it?

8. Alan struggles to forgive Jason for previously stealing his property and nearly misses a chance to help a young man who saved his daughter's life. If you caught someone stealing something expensive from you, what would it take for you to forgive him or her?

9. Hadley finds comfort in the beauty of the mountains, specifically at the French Broad Overlook. Are there any special places in nature where you find God's peace in an especially powerful way?

10. Elliott treats all men with suspicion, including Trent. But when she lets him in, she finds a beautiful friendship. Have you been in a situation where you kept your guard up? Were you right or wrong to do so? What was the outcome?

11. Monroe remembers the story of the rich young man from Mark 10. Verse 21 and 22 say, "And Jesus, looking at him, loved him, and said to him, 'You lack one thing: go, sell all that you have and give to the poor,

and you will have treasure in heaven; and come, follow me.' Disheartened by the saying, he went away sorrowful, for he had great possessions." How do you think this applies to people today? Does it apply in your own life?

12. When Monroe gives up his parents' gifts, including his business, he lets his parents assume that he and Hadley are in a relationship. Was it wrong of him to let them think something that was untrue, even if he was trying to do the right thing?

13. Hadley and Monroe decide to forgive the Birches after they apologize. If someone who had brought you pain from the past came back into your life, what would you say?

ABOUT THE AUTHORS

Cindy Woodsmall is a *New York Times* and CBA bestselling author of twenty works of fiction. She's been featured in national media outlets such as ABC's *Nightline* and the *Wall Street Journal*. Cindy has won numerous awards and has also been a finalist for the prestigious Christy, Rita, and Carol Awards. Cindy and her husband reside near the foothills of the North Georgia Mountains.

Erin Woodsmall is a writer, musician, wife, and mom of the three. She has edited, brainstormed, and researched books with Cindy for almost a decade. She's very excited about their first coauthored book. How could a Southern gal not enjoy research time in Asheville, North Carolina, as part of the job?

The employees of Thorndike Press hope you have enjoyed this Large Print book. All our Thorndike, Wheeler, and Kennebec Large Print titles are designed for easy reading, and all our books are made to last. Other Thorndike Press Large Print books are available at your library, through selected bookstores, or directly from us.

For information about titles, please call:
(800) 223-1244

or visit our website at:
gale.com/thorndike

To share your comments, please write:
Publisher
Thorndike Press
10 Water St., Suite 310
Waterville, ME 04901